Treading Water

Yvonne Leslie

To Renate

Heaven seems a little closer when you are near the ocean. Enjoy!

Y Leslie

©2013 by Yvonne Leslie

First edition

ISBN-13: 978-1490543413
ISBN-10: 1490543414

Book design: Y42K Book Production Services
http://www.y42k.com/bookproduction.html

*For Trevor, Paige and Hayden –
I could not have done this without you*

For whatever we lose (like a you or a me)
It's always ourselves we find in the sea.
                                e. e. cummings

PROLOGUE

July 1978

Maggie woke up early. The sun was just coming up and streamed through the windows of the cottage. She lay back on the pillow, enjoying the gentle rocking movement of the baby inside her. She had started to wear a man's dress shirt to bed to accommodate her growing breasts and stomach, and now she unbuttoned the bottom to examine her tummy more closely. Every so often a small fist would create a soft bump on her stomach. Maggie would gently push back and it would disappear only to appear in a different spot, silently playing a game of hand-to-hand. Maggie was mesmerized. She could hardly wait to meet this little person inside her.

She gazed at the movements passing over the smooth surface like gentle waves. There wasn't much room left in there and she was excited that the baby would be coming soon. She had to admit she was scared, too. What mother wouldn't be? She spent a lot of time imagining what the baby would look like, wondering if it would be a boy or a girl, what kind of personality he or she would have, but she spent just as much time worrying about whether she would be a good mother, whether they could make their plans work, and whether she'd be able to actually give birth to this watermelon.

She lay there dreamily rubbing her tummy and humming. He wasn't coming until lunchtime, so she should probably get up and do something with her time. She made herself a cup of tea, rubbing her back while she waited for the water to boil. She picked up the one blueberry muffin still left from her mother's visit and went to sit outside on the porch.

She was really going to miss this place. She had gotten so used to the sound of the waves, they were like a constant lullaby in the background, calling her to wake in the morning and soothing her to sleep at night. She walked along the beach every day with her faithful companion Stinker, and felt healthy and refreshed. Why would anyone want to ever leave this ocean playground?

She sipped her tea and went back inside to put the finishing touches on the quilt she was working on. She had been so creative; she had even surprised herself. It really was quite a stretch when she thought back to the home economics class last year. She and Val had been hopeless. In cooking class they had worked in pairs, and of course she and Val were always together. Their muffins had turned out completely flat. They had argued that they still tasted the same, but the teacher had just shaken her head. In sewing class they had been learning how to knit and the requirement had been to knit a square. Somehow they both managed to create a triangle, which they felt was a much tougher feat than making a square, and broke into squeals of laughter trying to find uses for their triangles.

She looked at her watch for what seemed like the hundredth time, and then the door opened and he breezed in with a burst of wind. His blond hair was a mess as always, but it was what she loved most about his looks. His bangs hung in his eyes and the rest was blown haphazardly in every direction. He shifted his head to one side to flick the hair off his face. Maggie smiled happily and put her stitching supplies back into the basket before attempting to get up. She put out her hand, looking for some assistance, but he moved past her to the kitchen and started unpacking bags.

"Hi," she said. "I'm glad you're here. How are you?"

He barely looked up, but continued packing the knapsack, pulling drinks and water from the fridge. "You look like you're ready for a nap. Are you ready for our picnic?"

"Of course. The baby was moving a lot this morning, so we've been up since sunrise. We're both ready to go. All these little stitches are hard on the eyes after a while, but I think I'm done," Maggie said, holding the quilt up proudly

"Why don't we take it along on the picnic with us? The knapsack is all packed up — I even brought along a bottle of red grape juice for you. You can't have a picnic without wine. Let's go."

They made their way along the beach, Stinker playing in the waves along the way and every so often catching up to give them a spray bath. The sky was a brilliant blue, with the sun out full and a nice breeze coming off the water. Along the way they navigated a pile of boulders as stepping stones that took them to the beach on the other side. No one else ever seemed to bother going any farther. In all the times they had gone there, they had never run into anyone and so they had christened the little cove as theirs. Pieces of driftwood deposited by the incoming tide lay scattered all around the beach, so Driftwood Cove seemed an appropriate name. He waited as she carefully made her way across.

The cove jutted in and away from the beach and provided a warm spot out of the wind. She spread out the quilt and sat down to catch her breath. He busied himself with arranging the picnic. He had barely said two words to her on the way but then walking and talking at the same time was nearly impossible for her these days. The waves crashed and receded behind them, their sound muffled by the dunes. She moved in closer to him, snuggling into the front of his chest so her stomach wouldn't be in the way and wrapping his arms around her.

She sighed. "This is perfect. I'm going to miss this place when the baby comes."

He didn't respond right away, and when she tried to look back at him, he gently pushed her aside. When she looked at his face she knew instantly that something was wrong. His deep grey eyes, usually so full of life and excitement, were clouded over, as if a shadow had passed over him.

"What is it? Has something happened?"

"No, nothing like that," he said. He avoided her eyes and appeared to be very interested in the stitching on the quilt. She started to get a sinking feeling in the pit of her stomach. Something wasn't right and she wished he would just hurry up and tell her.

"Maggie ... I'm not really sure where to start." He started picking up handfuls of sand, letting the grains sift through his fingers as if he were an hourglass. She waited anxiously for him to continue. "Maggie ... this is the hardest thing I have ever had to do."

"What are you talking about? Just tell me," she practically yelled at him.

"I need to tell you ..." He looked out at the water, not meeting her eyes. He took a deep breath and the words followed all at once. "I need to tell you ... that I don't love you anymore."

The words hung in the air like daggers ready to pierce her heart. Her head felt dizzy, and she couldn't focus. What was he saying? She couldn't have heard him right. The surf must be confusing his words.

"What did you say?" she whispered.

"I said, I don't love you." He sounded more convincing as he continued. "I thought I did, but I don't. I think I was in love with the idea of us. The idea of having a baby and having a family — I loved the idea of all of it. But every day I come out to this cottage I feel trapped, like I'm doing something I don't want to do."

"It's not true — I don't believe you. After all the time we've spent this summer — after all the plans that we've made! This is not happening!"

She beat on his chest with her fists, willing him to take back his words.

"But it is, Maggie. My dad applied for a transfer to Ottawa and he got it, so I'm going to school at Carleton for engineering. I need to do something more with my life."

He said it so matter-of-factly that Maggie barely

recognized his voice.

"This is all your parents' fault. You never had any plans to go to school for engineering. You never even mentioned it. After all of our talks, I know everything about you. You need to stand up for yourself, stand up to them. Tell them how much you love this baby. How much you love me!"

He shook his head, "It's not true, Maggie. I'm really sorry, but that's what it has to be. I can't do this."

"I know this isn't you ... Just let me talk to them. They'll see how good we are together." Maggie was on her knees, begging now. She just couldn't let this happen. "What about the baby? What about us?"

Tears streamed down Maggie's face. She tried to wipe them away but they kept coming. She kept shaking her head no, no.

"The baby will be fine — we could give it up for adoption and then we can both get on with our lives," he said. "At least your mom would be happy."

"How can you even say that? Mom was starting to come around, especially when she saw that you were looking for a job and ready to look after us," she pleaded.

"Maybe, but this is not what I want."

"It's not true. I don't believe you!" Maggie continued to hammer on his chest, as though that might change something.

"Sorry, Maggie. We leave tomorrow." He turned and started to walk away.

Maggie picked the closest thing to her and heaved it at him. She took each item off the blanket one by one and hurled it at him — the salt shaker, an apple, cookies, even chicken legs. Pretty soon the entire picnic had been tossed in his direction. He didn't say a word. When Maggie had calmed down a little, he walked over to take her hand.

"C'mon. We should go."

Maggie pulled her hand away. "Don't touch me! Just go!"

"I get that, Maggie, but I'd feel a whole lot better if you would just let me take you across the rocks. Then you can go the rest of the beach on your own if you want."

He sounded sincere but Maggie couldn't stand to be near him anymore. She was seething. If it was over, then it was over.

"I don't need your help. I walk this beach every day. Leave me alone and just go."

He put the empty bottle into the backpack and left the remnants of lunch for the seagulls that were already squawking closer and closer to the blanket. Maggie watched him go. Every so often he would turn and look in her direction. She pulled the quilt around her shoulders and kept staring out at the horizon. She saw his shape grow smaller and disappear into the distance, the afternoon fog already starting to move in. She waited until she could no longer see him before starting her own trek back to the cottage.

"C'mon, Stinker, let's go, buddy." Maggie heaved herself up heavily from the ground.

She reached the patch of boulders and paused to catch her breath. Stinker splashed through the pools of water created between the rocks. As the tide came in, the rocks were disappearing, looking like black icebergs with just the tips peeking out of the water. The fog was rolling in and Maggie felt the mist on her face. She could barely make out the yellow cottage in the distance, but she knew exactly where she was going. Once she got past these rocks she just needed to follow along the beach a little farther. Stinker eagerly clipped his way across the stones to the beach on the other side. She said a silent prayer as she began to navigate her way. She felt her foot slide away from her, but caught herself in time. Her heart hammering in her throat, she continued working her way across slowly, when an incoming wave suddenly caught her off guard. Arms flailing, she attempted to stretch to the next rock, but lost her balance. She instinctively wrapped her arms across her belly as she braced for the inevitable. She screamed and went down hard. She lay awkwardly between the rocks as her hair ebbed and flowed around her face like seaweed.

Chapter 1

July 1994

Maggie sat on the edge of her daughter's bed, surrounded by stuffed teddy bears, cats and elephants of various sizes and colours. Just looking around the room you would never guess that it belonged to a 16-year-old, except, of course, for the piles of dirty clothes and stray socks scattered everywhere. Organized was probably something Abby would never be, but a mother could always hope, couldn't she? Abby and Penny were leaving for their annual summer trip Down East tomorrow.

Maggie pulled her strawberry-blonde hair off her neck and grabbed one of Abby's stuffed toys. Fuzzy Bear had been a gift from her best friend Val right before they left Nova Scotia. He wasn't particularly fuzzy anymore, as a result of many hugs over the years. Maggie ran her fingers lovingly over the worn fur. So much had changed since then. Maggie had decided right after they moved that they would try to visit Nova Scotia every summer. Things hadn't worked out exactly as planned, what with a lack of money and an excess of work commitments, and a few more years had passed.

Once Penny was born, they decided that they had waited long enough. It had been five years since they had gone back and it was important that Maggie and Glen share the ocean with their girls, since it was so much a part of who they were. Maggie herself couldn't seem to get enough of the salt air, especially now that they were living in Ontario. Every summer she went home and tried to fill herself up with everything she had left behind, and hoped that it would be enough to keep her going until the next summer. If only she could find some way to bottle it. She suffered symptoms of withdrawal every time they came back to Ontario, feeling sad and out of sorts for weeks.

At one point they had talked about Gil moving up to Ontario to join them, but her mom just couldn't see leaving the ocean behind. Maggie could certainly appreciate that. Deep down, Maggie was glad that her mother had decided to stay put, not that she couldn't have used the help by having her close. With the crazy life they were leading these days, Gil would certainly have been an asset to help lighten their load once in a while. But the flipside of that was that they wouldn't have had a good reason to go back to Nova Scotia every summer, and that would have broken Maggie's heart, and probably Abby's and Penny's too.

Both Abby and Penny adored their grandmother, but Abby had a close connection with Gil that Maggie had to admire. She had to admit she was even a bit jealous of her own mother. It was the type of relationship she had always hoped she would have with her daughter. Abby meant the world to her and yet here she was a teenager already and it seemed that every word that passed between them had barbs attached. Recently they had spent an afternoon shopping together, and afterwards had gone for a coffee. Abby had chosen her favourite mocha latte and had gushed about how yummy it was. Later on they

Treading Water

had wandered through the stacks of books at Coles, excitedly picking out some choices for summer vacation. Maggie had been feeling good about the lovely afternoon they had shared. But when they got home, Maggie had off-handedly reminded Abby to take out the garbage and Abby had bitten her head off. It was like releasing a firecracker and not knowing exactly when it might go off. Maggie remembered herself as a teenager: mouthy, arrogant, self-centered and feeling she had a right to be that way. Perhaps that gene got passed on from mothers to daughters. Maggie's friends kept telling her that it would pass. It was just a phase. She sure hoped so. It was exhausting.

Maggie picked her way through the miscellaneous clothing items, bending down every few steps to throw something else into the laundry basket. There always seemed to be a never-ending pile, especially since the kids' clothing often went in the wash whether it was dirty or not. After an outfit change, the discarded clothing choice usually ended up on the floor, rather than back in the drawer. Maybe this summer would be a good time to teach the girls how to do their own laundry, so they might appreciate the task a little more. Maggie started to exit the room to start on yet another load when she noticed several more items shoved under the bed. She sighed as she set down the basket and leaned over to pick up the stray items. As she did so, she felt something hard tucked underneath and fumbled through the clothes to find a book. Abby's journal. She paused before picking it up.

In her hands she held her 16-year-old's most

sacred possession. Imagine what it contained. Maggie rubbed her hand lovingly over the cover. Abby had doodled all over it, obliterating any evidence of the original background design. Flowers and hearts competed with stars and swirls, as well as stylized versions of Abby's name. The book bulged with ticket stubs, wrappers and pressed flowers. Maggie remembered her own diary, faithfully putting her thoughts on its pages every night before bed, and how she had used it often as therapy. Her diary too had been filled with stuff, extra pages stapled in to allow room for all the thoughts of a particular day. No journal or diary was fully up to the task of holding a teenager's secrets and dreams.

The sound of footsteps bounding up the stairs interrupted her daydreaming. Abby burst into the room, hair dishevelled and eyes filled with tears. She quickly wiped them away when she saw her mother sitting on her bed.

"What are you doing in my room?" she screamed.

Maggie stood slowly, hugging the pile of clothes that had been on her lap. "Is everything all right?" she asked.

"Fine!" Abby retorted in a tone that indicated that she was anything but fine. "Now could you please get out?"

Maggie backed her way out of Abby's room and was no sooner in the hallway than the door was promptly shut in her face. Maggie looked at the clothes she was still holding in her arms. She bit her lip and turned away from the closed door. She could hear

Treading Water

Abby sniffling in her room but knew better than to ask her about it at that moment.

It was the end of the school year so Abby had been up to her eyeballs studying for exams. She also planned to add to her life-guarding certification over the summer so she had continued on with the swim team to stay in shape. And of course there was "the boyfriend," Tyson, who seemed to Maggie to be more aggravation than he was worth. One minute he was calling to set something up with Abby and the next he was changing the plans. Abby felt the need to either see him or chat with him every day and that too cut into her study time, leaving her no choice but to stay up late some nights to finish. It seemed like it was starting to take its toll.

Unfortunately Maggie hadn't been much help to Abby lately. She'd had her own deadlines for summer articles thrown on top of the usual day-to-day assignments. Why did these things seem to happen all at once? She had been at the *Brickton Herald* for almost 12 years now and was still waiting for a real break. She had taken the position at the Life Desk straight out of school in hopes that she could work her way up to a journalist position. She looked forward to having the opportunity to cover some stories with a little more meat to them, but spent more time covering graduations and lives-lived obituaries than anything really interesting. She had submitted articles on topics that she thought would grab her boss's interest but he always brought her back to focusing on the local small-town stuff. After all, that was her job.

It was driving her crazy. She had continued taking journalism courses after graduating and had never turned down a project that was offered to her. She had been recognized for her photographic contributions to the paper, so at least that counted for something, but for all the work she was doing, she wasn't getting anywhere in a hurry.

For the past week she had been trying to hire an assistant to help with the advertisement phone calls and follow-ups. She had interviewed so many people they were all starting to run together in her mind and she had no idea which one to hire. It was giving her headaches. It felt like when you were dating, and each time you ticked off the qualities that you liked in a guy, there always seemed to be something missing.

Sometimes she felt like she was back working on the high school newspaper. She realized she had enjoyed it a lot more back then, and now, not so much. She hated the deadlines. She hated the black inky smears that darkened her hands for the better part of the day. She hated the phones that seemed to be ringing constantly. It was incessant bustle and noise. There was a time when she would have enjoyed the excitement of all that activity but lately it had just stressed her out.

Thank goodness Glen was able to help Abby with her homework. They would sit down at the dining room table, heads together, and work out a reasonable study schedule. Abby always breathed a little easier after she and her dad had mapped out a plan leading up to exams. They had found a large whiteboard and had sectioned it off with painter's tape; the top half included every assignment and exam and its due date; the bottom divided up the workload to meet those deadlines. Abby would study her heart out on a particular subject, and when she felt prepared her dad would test her on it. He didn't seem to mind at all.

Maggie would sometimes find them hanging out in the garage, Abby with Glen's bulky vest on over her pyjamas to keep warm, his tools clinking as he worked on a motorcycle while she described the relationship between Romeo and Juliet, or outlined the themes in a particular novel. At some point Abby would come in to make a pot of tea to warm her cold hands, bringing a cup out to her dad as well. The cold never seemed to bother him but he always happily accepted the cup of tea she had made for him.

Maggie pulled herself back to the task of finishing the laundry and realized the basket was still in Abby's room. She'd have to get it later. She bent over to pick up the socks she had dropped and felt something digging into her back. Her stomach did a flip as she discovered she still had Abby's journal tucked into the back of her jeans.

Chapter 2

Abby slammed her bedroom door shut and fell onto the bed. She shoved her face into her pillow's marshmallowy softness and sobbed, hoping her mother wouldn't hear. She certainly hadn't expected to find her mother in her room when she came home and she wasn't in the mood for explaining. Her mother was always questioning her about something; always wondering what was going on. Come to think of it, what was going on with her mother? The way she had backed out of her room, you would think she had seen a ghost or something. She never really knew what to think where her mother was concerned. One minute she was normal and the next, well, she just wasn't.

She rolled over onto her back, wisps of her long brown hair sticking to her cheeks. She grabbed the blue stuffed elephant sitting on the pillow next to her, the one that Tyson had won for her at the Brickton Fair. Tyson had announced that he could win the biggest prize for his girl. He had hit the bull's eye after only three tries, and announced it to anyone within hearing distance, parading the overstuffed toy around like his best buddy for anyone to see. Abby had been secretly glad that he had won it for her, but had wanted to crawl under the pavement from all of his antics. People had started to stare. He hadn't even noticed, or cared.

That was one of the things that really bothered Abby about Tyson. Almost everything Tyson did seemed to be an act. He needed to always be the centre of attention. What Abby didn't understand was why he had to be that way when he was with her. When they were with his group of friends she always worried about whether or not she would fit in, whether they would like her or not. She figured she must worry about it more than they ever did. Often when they went to a movie together she would be drawing up the rear, as though she had just tagged along with the group. Then she would run up to Tyson and grab his hand just to show that she really did belong there. She wondered if it might be because she was a couple of years younger than the rest of the group and they didn't really think she belonged. She and Tyson had been going out for several months now so you'd think they would make some effort to include her.

She had nicknamed the elephant Bullseye. He was about half her size so he was perfect for hugging. Sometimes she would pretend it was Tyson. But not today; he had really pissed her off today. The whole group they usually hung around with had gone to the mall to get triple ice creams to celebrate the end of school. That's where she would be right now if Tyson hadn't ditched her. She just didn't get it. Why would he do this to her right before she was leaving for summer vacation? He would probably drop by tomorrow and say he was sorry all over again. Abby hoped he remembered that her flight left at noon and that he'd come early enough to catch her.

She wiped her eyes and took a deep breath. It wouldn't do any good to have to explain her puffy red eyes at the dinner table. Her mom would get all upset and worried about nothing and she felt badly enough about everything already without having to deal with her too. Besides, they wouldn't understand. Journaling always made her feel better and strangely enough she seemed to be doing a lot more of it lately. She threw Bullseye to the floor and grabbed a pen from the mess of wrappers and spare change on her night table. She looked under her bed, rummaging around for her journal. Where the heck had she put it?

Chapter 3

Maggie plunked herself on the edge of her bed and took a deep breath. She glanced nervously at the closed door before focusing her attention back on the journal.

What on earth was she doing? Here she was, sitting in her bedroom holding her teenage daughter's journal in her hands, and that same daughter was 10 feet away across the hall from her. She hadn't meant to take it, but Abby had come upstairs so quickly she'd had to hide it or risk Abby finding her with it. She had intended to put it on top of Abby's suitcase so she wouldn't forget when she left tomorrow. If Abby should walk in at this very moment it would most certainly be the end of their relationship. The logical thing to do would be to somehow put the journal back as soon as possible and no one would be the wiser. But now that she had it, how could she not read it?

She wondered whether she could even trust Abby anymore. When she thought about it, little things were starting to add up. Like the time she had looked through Abby's purse for the missing house key, and instead had come across a pack of Player's Light and a lighter. Naturally it had come as a shock, but even more so because Abby was totally grossed out by anyone who even smelled of stale cigarette smoke. And yet when Maggie questioned her about it, she totally denied it, saying they belonged to her friend at school whose parents would totally freak out if they knew that *she* smoked. After that incident, she had resolved to keep her eyes open for telltale signs like popping breath mints and singed hair. It made her chuckle to herself. She remembered going out to the woods behind her girlfriend Val's house, when she and Val had been about 15 years old. They had confiscated one whole cigarette from one of the older guys at school, and had snuck a handful of matches from her dad's fireplace box. They tried to shelter themselves from the wind as they attempted to light the match, but each time the wind snuffed it out before they could light the cigarette. They leaned in closer, Maggie with the cigarette firmly planted between her lips and Val attempting to light another match. As Val raised another match — whoosh — Maggie's hair had gone up in a flurry of sparks, the cigarette falling out of her mouth as she screamed. Both girls slapped frantically at Maggie's hair and face. The pungent smell of burned hair lingered in the air as Maggie examined the black and curly ends near her eyebrows. "Oh man, I'm going to be in deep trouble now." Val had tied her hair back and slicked a little of her dad's Brylcreem on the burned ends. Happily no one had noticed, but Maggie still remembered the sick worry she carried around, fearing she might be found out.

    She turned her attention back to the journal. Abby didn't have any dates or headings, writing free-form whenever she was in the mood, for as many pages as were necessary. The book opened tentatively in her hands to a page dog-eared and worn from rereading. Abby's loopy script filled the page, the i's dotted with circles just like Maggie had done at her age. Maggie wondered if things like that could possibly be hereditary, or whether they were perhaps inherent to the sex much in the same way that shoes and shopping were. She chuckled to herself at the similarities.

Then her eyes fell on the page...

Ten Things to Do the Year I Turn 16
  1. *get my driver's license* (this was crossed off)
  2. *have a beer or a real drink with alcohol*
  3. *go to an NSync concert*
  4. *try smoking — maybe grass* (this was crossed off)
  5. *get a tattoo or piercing*
  6. *stay out all night — just once*
  7. *get a part-time job*
  8. *win the school photography contest*
  9. *have the most outrageous cake for my sweet 16!*
  10. *have sex*

After the purse incident she wasn't surprised to see smoking stroked off. But when she hit the last item, she felt as though she had been kicked in the stomach. The good news was that it wasn't crossed off, so she could be fairly certain that Abby hadn't had sex — yet. Or could she? And after all the "sex talks" they had had together, how could Abby be even thinking about it at her age? Who was she kidding? In fact, as a mother she had done a random survey of her friends, asking them whether they had been prepared the first time they had sex — and *all* of them had said no. Even she had to admit to the same. She had made up her mind to "wait" for the right time and yet somehow she had gotten pregnant at 16. She knew all too well about getting caught up in the moment.

And now here she was, sending her daughters off to Nova Scotia with only their grandmother for a chaperone. Penny wouldn't be a problem at age 12, but how was Gil going to keep an eye on Abby? Abby who had a plan? A list? How was Maggie even going to be able to tell her mother what she was worried about without giving Abby away? She and her mother didn't always see eye to eye on things. She put her head in her hands and rubbed her temples as she contemplated her options. She could hardly confront Abby about it because then she would know that her mom had been reading her journal and yet she couldn't just let it go, could she? And how on earth was she going to get the journal back into Abby's room before she left without her noticing? Abby had gone straight back to her room after supper, without any explanation.

Maggie heard car doors slamming in the driveway. Glen and Penny were back from running errands. She quickly slipped the journal under her pillow, took a deep breath and opened the door.

Chapter 4

"So kiddo, are you all packed and ready to go?" Abby asked her sister.

"Of course, I've been throwing stuff into my suitcase for weeks, so by the time we go, it's pretty much packed," Penny grinned. She wore a Red Sox baseball cap that barely succeeded in restraining her wiry curls.

"I guess that is a good system," Abby agreed. "I wish I'd had time to do that too, but exams have been so hard this time. My brain is fried." She stretched her arms dramatically over her head and yawned loudly.

Abby and Penny were curled up on opposite ends of the couch, sporadically watching reruns of *Jeopardy*. Every so often Penny would interrupt their conversation and blurt out an answer like "What is the Liberty Bell?" or "Who was Napoleon?" and Abby would just shake her head. It was hard to believe that Penny was only 12.

"How the heck do you know all that stuff?" Abby asked.

Penny just giggled. "I read."

"Well, so do I," said Abby. "But I still couldn't answer half of the questions on this show."

Penny was a voracious reader. She read anything she could get her hands on: newspapers, magazines, books. She sucked the information out of all of them like a vacuum cleaner. She would pick up promotional items and brochures everywhere they went, and so she knew information and trivia about everything.

"You're going to have to give up your weekly trips to the library while we are Down East. There isn't a branch of the library anywhere close to Grandma Gil's," Abby said.

Grandma Gil's name had undergone a few transformations over the years. She was born Abigail, but her brother Angus had taken to calling her Gail when he was little, but it had sounded more like Gil and it stuck. When the girls started coming out to visit, Abby had found it too much of a mouthful to keep calling her Grandma Gil so it got shortened again to GG. Penny thought it sounded like the name of a classy actress from an old movie and who was Grandma to argue with that?

"That's okay; I'll be busy helping out Mr. Jack with his jobs. And besides, I'll just get you or GG to drive me into Halifax, so I can stock up."

Abby grinned. No moss growing under this girl's feet, she thought. "Sure, Penny, we can do that. I can hardly wait. I'm just looking forward to hanging out with my friends and spending tons of time at the beach and getting away from Mom for a bit. Today, when I got home, Mom was sitting on the bed in my room!"

"She was probably just doing some laundry or something." Penny didn't have any real issues with her mom, but Abby seemed to be fighting with her all the time. "She hasn't been on my case for anything."

"That's because she's always got *me* under the magnifying glass, so she doesn't have time to question *you*. She's always asking me about something I don't want to talk about. The other night, when I went out to the movies with Tyson, she gave me the third degree when I got home, and I didn't even come home late. She even knew exactly what time the movie was going to end, and was sitting on the couch with the TV off, just waiting for me to get home. It's driving me nuts."

She shook her head, thinking about how her mom was always twisting stuff around to catch her at something. Sometimes her mother would "test" her with curfew. Instead of saying she needed to be home at a certain time, she would raise one eyebrow and ask Abby when she was coming home. That's when it got complicated. If Abby picked a time that her mom thought was too late, she would scoff and say No way, and tell her to be home at some ridiculously early hour like 9 p.m., but if she picked a more reasonable time, her mom was more likely to go along with it, pleased that Abby was being so responsible. What bothered Abby the most was that she never knew whether she might have gotten away with a later time if she had suggested it. The way her mom's eyes flared when you said something ridiculous, it was better not to risk it.

"I guess that's why you can't wait to get to Nova Scotia, then. Sarah is going to be there too, isn't she?" Penny asked.

Sarah was Abby's best friend in the whole world. She and her family lived about 10 minutes away from GG's place and the girls were inseparable when Abby was visiting. Abby wished she had a best friend in Ontario, but she knew she could never replace Sarah. They trusted each other completely and could talk to each other about anything. Even when they were apart they wrote each other long letters, and stayed in touch via email on the computer. They were also allowed to call each other once a month and that had kept them close over the years. Abby couldn't imagine a trip to Nova Scotia without Sarah being there.

"Of course, she'll be there. We've been counting down the days on the calendar since January." They both laughed.

"Yeah, I'm really looking forward to it too," Penny said. "It's always so great there."

"It's totally the best part of the summer. And this summer is going to be especially great," she hinted.

Chapter 5

Maggie sighed as she stared at the piles on the dining room table. Stacks of papers covered almost every inch of space, threatening to fall over if anyone dared touch them. File folders leaned into each other, precariously balanced, some sliding randomly into the centre of the table. Her computer was barely visible between the piles. How the heck was she ever going to get through this?

She had definitely taken on more than she could chew, but wasn't that the only way she could hope to get anywhere? It wasn't that she was particularly enamoured by the newspaper business, especially the day-to-day stuff she dealt with at the office, but she loved the journalism aspect of it. She could never get any real work done with all the interruptions, hence the piles on the table at home. It was the only place with a little peace and quiet. The classified job was supposed to have been a stepping stone to bigger and better things. She secretly hoped that one day she might have her own weekly column, discussing real things in the real world, things that mattered to people and the planet. If she didn't find a way to organize herself enough to tackle the important things as they came up, she would never get out of classifieds. She had been dealing with idiots on the phone for more than five years now. She deserved better than this.

Glen walked in behind her and put his hands on her shoulders. She shrugged them off and sat down in the chair, grabbing a pen and a legal pad.

"I really need to get at this or I'm just never going to get out from under these piles," she snapped.

He lifted his hands away as though he had been burned. "I'd say you were buried already," Glen retorted.

Maggie didn't respond, didn't even offer him a smile. She was so overwhelmed that she just wasn't in the mood for his good humour at the moment. "Glen, I don't even know where to start." She sighed and put her elbows on the table, her face in her hands.

"I'll be right back," he said as he turned to walk into the kitchen.

"Where are you going?"

"I just thought I'd go out to the garage and see if I could find a shovel to help you out."

"That just wasn't even funny," Maggie scoffed. She was starting to think she would be better off without him in the room. He was being more distracting than helpful.

"Just trying to lighten things up a bit," he replied. "If you want me, you know where to find me." He went back out to the garage, softly closing the door behind him. Maggie was suddenly disappointed that he was gone. She certainly didn't need any distractions but she didn't mind his company. Usually Glen was plucking out a tune on his guitar in the living room or tinkering with something that needed fixing, and somehow his presence calmed her. She felt bad about being short to him when he was only trying to cheer her up.

Maggie decided she was going to need a little

Treading Water

motivation if she was going to make any headway on all this paperwork, and a glass of wine sounded really good right now. Her doctor had warned her that with her diabetes, she really shouldn't be drinking at all, but one glass wouldn't hurt. She went over to the liquor cabinet and poured herself a glass of Cabernet Sauvignon that she and Glen had opened last night. She swirled the liquid around and inhaled a deep breath of the fruity scent. She took a sip and closed her eyes as she swallowed, thoroughly enjoying the smooth warm sensation, and immediately felt better. She felt a little of the stress slip away from her shoulders. As she took another sip, something in the cabinet caught her eye and she opened the door again to take a look. Tucked away in the bottom corner was the purse-size flask Val had given her as a joke for her 30th birthday. On the front was a perfectly groomed woman wearing sunglasses and a scarf tied around her head, while driving a pink convertible. The caption read: "It's all downhill from here ... might as well enjoy the ride." You're not kidding, she thought. She laughed to herself, remembering the fun they had had that night. She and Val and a couple of girlfriends had gone into downtown Halifax for drinks to celebrate. They had each decided that it would be fun for each of them to choose a different martini off the menu and after each sip they would pass it to the next person to sample. At the end of each round, they had voted on which tasted the best and ordered another round. After several more rounds, they were all in high spirits, laughing over absolutely anything anyone said. She remembered waking up the next morning with a deadly headache but her stomach had hurt even more. When was the last time she'd had a good laugh like that?

Her thoughts came back to Glen. Things had been more than a little strained between them lately. It wasn't that they were fighting; they were never in the same space long enough to fight. She always seemed to be driving the kids somewhere or working on an assignment, and Glen was either at the construction site or out in the garage. It was like he had given up on her. Maybe he had. The other night on one of those rare occasions when they had gotten to bed at the same time, Glen had been relating a story about something that had happened at the site that day and Maggie had been so exhausted she had fallen asleep in the middle of it. She felt terrible about it the next morning. She was going to have to make some changes.

The wine was definitely helping and she warmed to the thought of spending more time with Glen without the girls around. She glanced back at the papers tottering around her computer and wondered how she was ever going to find time for everything. And then a wave of dread came over her as another thought came rushing back to her: What on earth was she going to do about Abby?

Chapter 6

Abby zipped her suitcase shut and dragged it onto the landing for her dad to take downstairs. She grabbed her knapsack and set it on top. She suddenly ran back into her room to grab her camera off the shelf. She couldn't believe that she had almost forgotten it. I must have used up all of my brain cells studying for exams, she thought. Her school was having a photography contest with submissions due at the end of the summer and Abby had every intention of winning it. The prize was a hot-air balloon ride for two, and a new Nikon F50. She was looking forward to getting some great beach shots.

"It's ready, Dad!" she called down the stairs. "You can load it if you want. I just need to find one more thing."

"Okay, babe, be right up," Glen called back.

Abby rummaged around the clothes on the floor, throwing dirty socks and sweaty T-shirts into a pile in the corner. Her journal just had to be here someplace. She wasn't that much of a slob. Well, maybe she was, but it was usually right here beside the bed. She moved the pile of books and papers she had dumped from school yesterday. Maybe it had gotten mixed in with that stuff somehow? Panic rose in her chest. What if she had left it in her locker at school? What if the custodian came across it while cleaning out the lockers? Abby wondered if he would actually read a book that was clearly very private. She certainly hoped not. She would be mortified to think someone else had read her thoughts. But how on earth was she going to get it back? And she certainly wouldn't be able to get it before leaving for Nova Scotia. She was starting to freak out.

"Abby!" she heard her dad call up.

"Yeah?" she called back, her voice muffled as she dug underneath the bed.

"Tyson is here to see you."

Tyson? She whacked her head on the bed frame as she pulled herself up. She hadn't even heard the doorbell. What was he doing here? She had wondered if he might show up before she left. She checked her hair in the mirror, brushing off the dust bunnies that clung to the ends. She quickly ran a brush through it and hurried down the stairs.

Tyson grinned at her, his hands behind his back. "I guess you're leaving soon?"

"Duh," Penny said, rolling her eyes as she snuck past them with her knapsack.

Abby ignored her sister, and tried to focus on Tyson. They faced each other in the hallway, Abby with both her hands shoved into her back pockets. "Uh, yeah, actually we're just loading up. What's up?"

"Well, I felt kind of bad leaving you like that yesterday and I wanted to see you once more before you left. A month is a long time, you know." He kept looking down at his shoes. Abby glanced around to see who might be listening. She didn't want Penny eavesdropping on their conversation, or worse, her mother. Her dad shuffled by with the suitcases and Abby waited until he got to the car before answering.

Treading Water

"Yeah, but it will go by fast," she said half-heartedly.

It was awkward to be standing in the hallway at the front door with all the commotion going on around them. Abby pulled him outside onto the porch, out of the line of traffic. She wished he would hurry up and get on with it.

"I just wanted to give you this, but you can't open it until you get on the plane." Tyson passed her a little white box and continued staring at his shoes.

"What is it?" Abby took it hesitantly. She had no idea what it was and why he would wait until she was leaving to give it to her. If he had come any later he would have missed them completely. It was tied tightly with a thin white string to keep it from opening. It looked like a parcel you would send in the mail at Christmastime, only small enough to fit in the palm of your hand.

"You'll see — just don't open it until you are on the plane. It's just something to remember me while you're away." He looked up at her shyly and then back to his shoes. Abby couldn't remember ever seeing him this nervous. It was totally unlike him.

"Oh, that's sweet, Ty." She looked at him shyly, not knowing what to say, but a knot was forming in her stomach. It wasn't like Tyson to be romantic, and he certainly had never suggested that the two of them were going steady or anything. Why would he do this now? The trunk slammed as luggage was loaded into the car.

"Okay, Abby, we really have to get going." Glen

locked the front door and headed to the car.

"Yeah, I know!"

Tyson rushed on. "So call me when you get back and we'll do something for sure."

"Of course I will. I'd better get going." She tucked the little box in the pocket of her sweatshirt and they gave each other a quick hug, not wanting to embarrass themselves in front of the family. Everyone was waiting to go, standing around the car, half watching, half busying themselves with the luggage. Tyson had marinated himself in his favourite cologne and the smell clung to her. She would probably still be able to smell it when they got to Halifax. Maybe that was part of his plan.

Tyson leaned in to give Abby a quick peck on the cheek. "I'd like to give you a big kiss right on the lips but ... well, you know ..." His whisper tickled her ear.

Abby couldn't bring herself to look at him. She could feel his eyes on her, staring, waiting. She wasn't sure what he expected from her. At that moment all she wanted to do was get in the car and leave. She had a sick feeling in the pit of her stomach.

"Okay, I'll see you, then." She ran down the driveway and quickly hopped into the back seat. She forced a smile and a wave at Tyson as they backed out of the driveway. He just stood there on the stoop, grinning and waving like crazy.

Chapter 7

The air conditioning was on full-force and Maggie blew her bangs off her forehead to dispel the heat. She moaned when they pulled onto the 401 and were immediately slowed by all the traffic.

"Where are all these people going on a Saturday?" she said.

"Probably to the airport, like us!" Glen laughed.

Maggie took off her sunglasses and glanced back inquiringly at Abby.

"What are you looking at me for?" Abby snapped.

"I just hope we're not running too tight on time," Maggie commented. It bothered her that just looking at Abby could spark a confrontation these days. It was a tradition that everyone in the family went along for the ride whenever someone was leaving or being picked up at the airport. Maggie wondered if she should even have bothered coming along this time, with the rare mood that Abby was in.

"Don't blame me. I didn't know that Tyson was going to drop by." Abby tapped her dad on the shoulder. "Oh, Dad, do you think you can stop by the school for me on Monday?"

Maggie noticed that Abby had quickly changed the subject. It wasn't like her to not want to talk about Tyson. She was always going on about him.

"Why's that?" Glen replied, looking at Abby in the rear-view mirror.

"I have no idea where my journal disappeared to. I think I might have left it in my locker at school. If I leave it there past next week, it will be gone when they clean out the lockers for the summer."

"No problem, babe. I'll take care of it."

"Thanks, Daddy," Abby's voice trembled as she spoke. "I sure hope that's where it is. I'll just die if somebody else finds it. But I really wanted to take it with me on the trip."

"Maybe we can look for a nice journal while we're waiting at the airport," Penny offered.

"Thanks, Penny. That's a really nice idea, but I'm just really worried about where mine could have disappeared to," Abby said.

"Don't worry. It'll turn up. I know it will," Penny added.

Maggie quickly turned to face the front so Abby wouldn't see her cheeks flush. She felt like she was hiding a dirty secret. Well, actually, she was. She couldn't stand this conversation any longer. She didn't trust herself to look Abby in the eye, but she knew she needed to say something.

"Actually, I found your journal underneath some clothes when I went into your room to gather up the dirty laundry. Honestly, you can hardly make a path to your bed without tripping on something. It's no wonder you couldn't find it."

"Thanks, Mom, for harping on me as we're leaving," Abby grunted. "I sure hope you didn't read it. But I looked *everywhere* and it wasn't there. So where is it now?" Her attitude had changed back to arrogance and Maggie bit her tongue to avoid being pulled into the storm of Abby's fury.

Maggie stayed silent. She wondered what kind of mother she was turning into, reading her daughter's diary and then feigning ignorance. A good mother, she thought; one that is looking out for her kid. She took a breath before answering, trying to sound nonchalant.

"I stuck it in the front zipper pocket of your suitcase."

"So why didn't you just tell me? You *know* I've been looking all over for it! I thought I'd lost it!" Abby yelled at Maggie, her face red with anger, the words shooting out of her mouth like rifle fire. Penny shrunk lower and lower in her seat, finally pulling her sweatshirt up over her ears to block out the argument.

"I don't know ... I just didn't really have a chance, and I put it in there so I wouldn't forget." Maggie kept her voice low to avoid antagonizing Abby further. This was not how she had envisioned their drive out to the airport. She was beginning to feel that anything she might say or do would trigger another outburst.

Abby rolled her eyes. "Well, thank goodness it isn't at school," she sighed. "I'm going to want it on the plane, though. I don't want to risk losing it in my luggage. Why would you put it in my suitcase?"

"So I wouldn't forget to give it to you." Maggie sighed. She wasn't very good at this lying thing, but God forbid the truth ever came out.

"Never mind, sweetheart," Glen interrupted, putting his hand on Maggie's knee as he spoke, attempting to calm them both at the same time. "We'll pull it out as soon as we get to the airport. I'm sure you'll remind us." He gave Maggie a reassuring look and turned his eyes back to the road. Maggie just sighed and looked straight ahead.

"Aren't you excited, Abby?" Penny exclaimed breathlessly, as she emerged from the safety of her sweatshirt. "I just can't wait to get there and see the beach again." She closed her eyes and inhaled deeply. "Can't you smell the ocean already? And I can't wait to see Grandma Gil and Mr. Jack. I wonder if he's got some business lined up yet for the Odd Couple?" Last summer Penny and her buddy Simon had started up a venture in Nova Scotia called the Odd Couple. She was the short redhead and he was the tall scrawny kid, and together they had done any job that needed doing, even getting T-shirts made so they could advertise their business. They scraped paint off houses, painted window frames and boarded up barns, weeded and watered gardens. You name it. Mr. Jack would put the word out for them, and they always had an endless list of jobs to do. It certainly kept her out of trouble. "I don't know what Mr. Jack would do without me!" Penny said. The words spilled from her mouth like a waterfall and they couldn't help but laugh at her enthusiasm. If it wasn't for Penny's spirit, we might all sink into the abyss, Maggie thought.

Maggie was proud of Penny's enthusiasm and as far as her business ventures were concerned, Penny was tireless. At home, she had a paper route, delivered flyers, shovelled snow in winter and mowed lawns in summer. She was very wise with her money, usually saving up for something that she really wanted, or donating it to her latest cause. Ever since Penny had been old enough to walk, she had been attempting her own business ventures. When she was five years old, the neighbours had appeared at the door with Penny in tow to ask whether they had any idea what their daughter was doing. Apparently Penny had been going door to door, selling rocks. These weren't painted rocks, or rocks that were unique in any special way; they were just rocks that Penny had found along the sides of the train tracks and apparently she had made money doing it. After the incident they had explained to her that she couldn't just go door to door selling whatever she wanted. She seemed to understand, but they could already see the wheels turning as she considered her next venture. After all, the neighbours hadn't seemed too upset.

"I hope I have enough time to get everything done in a month." Penny sounded genuinely concerned.

"I'm sure you will, Penny. Otherwise, you'll just have to find some more recruits to help you out," Glen said. "What about you, Abby? Got anything planned yet?"

Abby looked out the window, fiercely concentrating on the cars zooming past. She seemed like she didn't even hear her dad's question. Maggie glanced over her shoulder to look at Abby. She thought Abby seemed a little distant but didn't dare say anything for fear of another outburst.

"Hey, Abby?" Glen asked again.

Abby quickly came out of her reverie. "What? Oh, yeah. What did you say?"

"I asked if you had made any plans yet with your

friends in Nova Scotia."

"Nothing definite, other than spending tons of time at the beach. Sarah and I will do lots of stuff for sure."

Maggie was glad that Abby had someone to chum around with when she was visiting with Grandma Gil. Abby and Sarah had known each other since they were five, and they spent as much time together as possible while Abby was in Nova Scotia. It had always been that way and Maggie secretly wished Abby had a close friend like Sarah at home. Abby didn't really have one person that she would call a good friend, someone she could hang out with and tell secrets to. It worried Maggie because she knew how important girlfriends could be. Abby had been spending a lot of time with this Tyson boy. Maggie didn't have a good feeling about him, but then she often didn't. She'd prefer that Abby didn't have a boyfriend at all, especially one who was 18 going on 19. Those older boys were nothing but trouble. Maggie hoped this trip would be good for Abby. She seemed distracted and more withdrawn than usual lately and Maggie hoped some time away might change Abby's view of Tyson.

"You're awfully quiet," Maggie said finally, instantly regretting it, and holding her breath for fear of another onslaught. She tried to sound as sympathetic as possible. "Is everything okay?"

"Oh, I was just thinking about Tyson," Abby offered grudgingly. "He gave me something before we left but told me not to open it until I'm on the plane." She resumed looking out the window. "But I'd rather not talk about it, okay?"

Maggie sighed. At least the arguing had subsided and they had moved on. She settled back into her seat, angling the air conditioning directly onto her face. Thank God people weren't able to read your thoughts, because hers would be written all over her face. She couldn't stop thinking about what she had read in Abby's journal and once Abby was gone, she was going to have to figure out what the hell she was going to do about it.

Chapter 8

Abby and Penny tried to contain their excitement as they shuffled down the aisle scanning for their seats. They came to a halt and waited while a man tried unsuccessfully to cram his oversized bag into the compartment.

"What has he got in that bag?" Penny whispered to Abby over her shoulder as she rolled her eyes in disgust. "There is no way in heck he is getting *that* to fit in *there*. Jeez, if there was a whale that needed to be brought back to Nova Scotia, why didn't he just pull it on a flatbed trailer?" Penny continued.

Abby shook her head and gave Penny a scolding look, worried that he might hear her response. She knew Penny was just excited and impatient to get going, but her comments were drawing stares from other people. Abby just smiled back. She leaned forward to shush Penny, and sighed as they waited for the flight attendant to jump in and take action. She wondered where they found the patience to deal with people like this, and was secretly glad that they wouldn't be sitting anywhere near this guy. Penny would probably have told him exactly what she thought of him. The bag was finally lowered, and the man backed into his spot momentarily to let people pass.

"Good luck with that," Penny commented as she went by, and the guy gave her a dirty look.

"Penny, just keep your thoughts to yourself, will you?" Abby said, once they had passed.

They reached their row and Abby scooted across to grab the window seat. It was important to be able to see the trees and lakes coming into view as they flew into Halifax. She knew then that it wouldn't be much longer after that before they would be at the beach. She could almost smell the ocean already. She had to admit she was as excited as Penny. Abby checked her watch.

"We should be taking off soon, kiddo. I brought along some snacks." She pulled some zip-lock baggies with treats out of her knapsack. "I got this fruit and nut bar yesterday at the coffee shop. It's good but it's a little hard. Want some?"

"You did a great job of selling me on it," Penny said sarcastically, "but no thanks, I'm good."

Penny struck up a conversation with the boy sitting across the aisle, who looked to be about her age. Abby figured they'd know each other intimately by the end of the flight. She wished she could be more like that and often wondered where Penny's confidence came from. She glanced over at Penny chatting away effortlessly. If she wanted to say something, she said it; if she wanted to do something, she did it.

Abby remembered a time when Penny was just four years old and they were at the mall with their mom. At the centre of the mall a large crowd was gathered around a stage where a perfume company was promoting a new product called Summer Rain. People from the crowd were invited to perform their rendition of a commercial for the product to win prizes. Their mom had said they could sit closer to the front if they promised to stay together and hold hands.

Yvonne Leslie

The participants put on themed accessories: a rain bonnet, an umbrella and long white cotton gloves, and paraded across the stage while acting out the slogan for the perfume. The prize was a Sony Walkman. Penny begged Abby to take her over and try, but Abby was worried they wouldn't take her because she was too young. Abby tried to pull her away but Penny had yelled at the top of her lungs: "I want to try out, and you can't stop me!" Abby was embarrassed enough so she took Penny to the front and handed her off to the assistant. The transformation was instantaneous, as Penny danced and spiralled her way across the stage, playing to the crowd and the judges as required. When the music stopped the crowd cheered, and Penny grinned and took a bow. It was no contest.

Abby reached down to slide her knapsack under the seat in front of her and felt a small roll of fat sticking out over the top of her jeans. She poked at it like she was the Pillsbury Doughboy. That would have to go. She hadn't had time to do anything except study these past few weeks, not to mention eating a few more cheesies than normal from study stress. She intended to work it off by the end of vacation, planning to be fit and in shape when she got back. She wondered whether Tyson had ever noticed. She quickly pulled her hoodie into her lap to cover herself up and felt something hard push against her leg. Tyson's present! She had completely forgotten about it. He had told her not to open it until she was on the plane. Well, she was on the plane now! But why the secrecy, she wondered? She glanced over at Penny, who was still engrossed

Treading Water

with her new friend. They had already pulled out a pack of cards, so she was paying no attention whatsoever to Abby.

Butterflies fluttered in Abby's stomach. She had no idea what could be in the box and was half afraid to open it; afraid of what it might mean. It was small enough to hold a ring, but she hoped that he would give her something as special as that in person. She was able to pull away the string easily and carefully opened the flap on the small cardboard box. There was a small tuft of red tissue paper sitting on top. She pulled it off to find a Hershey's Kiss and a necklace with a thick chain knotted in the middle. Underneath lay a note, folded several times into a teeny square.

She turned herself away from Penny and pulled it open carefully. In Tyson's familiar scrawl he had written: *"Enjoy yourself, but I know you'll save yourself for me."* Abby quickly refolded the note and shoved it in her pocket. He had never truly come out and said he loved her, so what was this supposed to mean? He never seemed to know what he really wanted and yet when they were together she was in heaven. He was such an amazing kisser that she got wet just thinking about it. And whenever they had a fight he would always show up with flowers or chocolates to make up for it. Was she supposed to wait for him, even though she was the one who had gone away?

Abby had hinted at some things she intended to do during her birthday year, without actually telling him about what she had written in her journal. He'd just think she was being corny. Being two years older,

Abby figured he would be able to help her with what she had in mind. She was even glad that he wasn't a virgin anymore because she was counting on him to know what to do when the time came. She smiled to herself just thinking about it.

But suddenly she felt angry. How dare he drop this present on her this way? Now she would spend her whole trip worrying about what it really meant. Screw that. She was still upset that he had messed up the one night they had planned before she went away, and now this. How dare he keep tabs on her when they weren't together? She intended to have a good time regardless of what he was insinuating and would deal with it when she got back.

She turned toward the window and carefully pulled out the necklace for a closer look. It was interesting the way it came together in the middle, as though the chain had thickened and pulled itself into a knot. You couldn't tell where the chain ended and the knot began. Did the knot imply something? She stuffed the box back into the pouch of her hoodie, and shoved the necklace into her pants pocket. The whole thing was making her feel really anxious and she felt an overwhelming urge to throw up. She climbed over Penny's knees and made a beeline for the stall at the back of the plane. She pushed the Occupied sign into place and leaned over the small tin toilet. The space was so small she could hardly bend over. The relief was instantaneous. She splashed her face gently with water and checked herself in the mirror. Much better, she thought. She pulled the necklace out of her pocket again and felt its cool chain between her fingers. She carefully clasped the necklace around her neck before edging her way back to her seat.

Chapter 9

Maggie picked at her food, despite the fact that she and Glen were finally enjoying a rare dinner alone. She was deep in thought over what she should do about Abby's diary. After dropping the girls at the airport, Glen had happily prepared a tasty meal of steaks on the barbecue, complete with his favourite mushrooms and peppers on the side. He had ceremoniously opened a bottle of wine to celebrate the fact that they were officially alone. Glen savoured his meal as though he hadn't eaten in weeks, but Maggie's meal remained virtually untouched.

"Something wrong, Mags?" Glen mumbled as he devoured another medium-rare mouthful smothered in mushrooms. "You've hardly touched your dinner — are you missing the girls already?"

Maggie took a sip of wine. "Of course I miss them… It's so much quieter when it's just you and me." She paused, taking another deep swig of wine. "Actually, there's something I need to talk to you about."

Glen's fork stopped in mid-air. "Is everything okay?"

Maggie noted Glen's puzzled expression as he tried to figure out what she was referring to. He probably thinks it's about us, she thought, and he has every right to think that. They had both been so focused on their own projects that they'd all but forgotten about each other. The disconnection was adding to the stress of the household but there always

Treading Water

seemed to be something more urgent to be dealt with first. Like this. Glen looked her in the eyes and placed his hands gently over hers. Maggie relaxed a little, feeling the warmth of his touch.

"I know we've both been running in different directions, Maggie. I was hoping with the girls being away, we could find some time for each other. There won't be as many demands or distractions, and we could arrange some dates with each other. Something we never quite learned to do properly." His deep brown eyes looked at her lovingly, full of warmth and expectation as Maggie realized he was waiting for her response.

Maggie frowned. She was so focused on what she was going to say that she had only half-heard what Glen was saying. She nodded fiercely, trying to cover the fact that she hadn't been paying attention.

"Of course, yes, that would be lovely, but that's not what I wanted to talk to you about. It's actually about Abby ... I read something disturbing in her journal."

"You read her journal?" Glen's eyes, so warm and gentle a moment ago, were fairly popping out of his head. "Do you have any idea how she would react if she knew?" Glen typically deferred to Maggie in decisions involving Abby, as she was the most involved and seemed to know best, but his reaction suggested he felt otherwise in this case. He set his cutlery on the edge of his plate and continued to look at her in disbelief. She knew exactly how Abby would react and she didn't really want to think about it. They were well past worrying about that now.

"Yes, of course I do, but she's not going to find out."

"You said you had found it, but why didn't you just leave it where it was?" Glen asked. He looked so worried Maggie wondered if she had done the right thing.

"Abby was in such a rush to get everything ready, and I was just trying to help with the laundry when I just happened across it. I had just picked it up when she came rushing into her room. She caught me by surprise, so I hid it in the back of my jeans. I know that sounds wrong but I had no choice, or risk her finding out. I left the room so quickly there was nothing else I could have done. I never intended to actually read it, but later, one of the pages caught my eye and next thing I knew, I was hooked."

"So, what was so addictive that you couldn't just leave well enough alone?" He had leaned back in his chair, arms crossed, waiting uncertainly for what she had to say next. Maggie could see that Glen was unhappy with the way she had handled this, but it had all happened by accident, and now that she knew what was written in the journal she couldn't just ignore it. She stopped and looked him in the eyes. She needed him to know how serious she was about all of this; how serious the situation was.

"Glen ... she has a list."

"A list? What kind of list?"

"A to-do list. A Things to Do the Year I Turn 16 list."

Treading Water

"Okay." He paused for a moment, resting his elbows on the table and rubbing his forehead with his fingers. He looked up at her again. "Do I want to know what's on this list?"

"Have my first shooter, smoke a joint." She paused. "Have sex ..."

"Have sex?" Glen raised both eyebrows in surprise. She could tell it was hard for him to picture his little girl in this light; it was hard for her, too. He had probably never even considered the possibility, but he certainly was considering it now.

Maggie could feel her cheeks burning. She had violated her daughter's privacy in a big way. It hadn't seemed such an awful thing to do when she was reading it by herself. At that point nobody knew but her. But now that she was saying it out loud, it seemed like she had crossed a line. But all she was really trying to do was protect Abby. Wasn't that what she had done her whole life? Or was she just worried that history would repeat itself? She wasn't sure she could bear it. And now this journal entry proved it, didn't it? Her worst fears seemed to be coming true.

"So what do you plan to do?" Glen asked.

"Me? It's what *we* have to do. We have to do *something*, Glen. She's off in Nova Scotia on her own, and knowing her, she'll be on a mission to work through that list. And without us there to keep an eye on her ..." She let the sentence hang. "She'll be 17 in August, so her time as a 16-year-old is running out."

"Oh come on, Maggie. She's not on her own. She's with your mom and she's no slouch. Do you really think Abby is the type to just take on the world in four short weeks? I'm more worried about her finding out that you stole her journal."

"I didn't steal it!"

"Whatever. It will seem that way to her if she ever finds out." Glen had pushed his chair back from the table, and was pacing back and forth the length of the dining room.

"She is *not* going to find out!" Maggie put her face in her hands. She had given this a lot of thought, and knew what she had to do. She had made up her mind. Ever since she had read the diary she had been going over all the options and she hoped that Glen would understand. She took a deep breath. "I have to go too," she murmured through her fingers.

Glen stopped pacing and turned to face her. "What? Have to go where?"

"Home. I have to go to Nova Scotia." Maggie couldn't look at him. She knew that she needed to do this, that it was the right decision, but if she looked at him, he might see that bit of doubt and try to talk her out of it. She knew she was the only one who could protect Abby from doing anything she might regret later. And if she didn't go and something happened, she would always blame herself. She had to do this.

Glen poured himself some more wine and leaned against the countertop. Maggie could almost see the wheels turning as he considered what she was suggesting. She also knew deep down that even though he might not agree with her, he would never challenge her as far as Abby was concerned. It had always been that way. It had to be that way. He took a long time to respond.

"I guess if you think it's the best idea. Have you thought about what reason you are going to give the girls for showing up unexpectedly?"

Maggie slouched back in the chair, relieved to have this part of the conversation out of the way. She took another big sip of wine. "No, but I'll think of something."

Chapter 10

"I see the Hallelujah tree!" hollered Penny from the back seat. "Grandma Gil, she needs to be properly dressed for summer. Can I do it?"

Abby had to laugh too. "Yeah, GG — she's half-naked."

And it was true. The old maple tree had been on the property as long as anyone could remember. It stood at the end of the lane just to the left of the house, its two large arms reaching in opposite directions. The tree was dying and even though it no longer produced any leaves, no one had the heart to actually chop it down. As the story went, one day Grandma Gil had hung her wash out to dry in a very stiff breeze and one of her sheets had come loose. The wind had carried it up and it had become entangled in the old maple. When they all came out to have a look, it looked like an angel with her arms stretched to heaven and from then on it became the Hallelujah tree. Once they had put a large caftan on it to look like a witch, and so it became a seasonal tradition to change her outfit.

GG pulled the car into the grassy spot beside the house. The car had barely reached a full stop before the doors flew open and the girls jumped out, running to the bluff to get a view of the ocean.

"Can we go down to the beach, GG?" Penny called back excitedly.

"Just relax a minute, Miss Penny. You're here for a whole month. There will be lots of time to do everything." GG chuckled as she joined them at the

Treading Water

edge of the bluff. "It's not like we have to do everything on the first day."

"But we have to go down to the beach first, GG, before we do anything else!" Abby put in. The anticipation of being able to run along the beach splashing through the waves was almost too much for her. After all, she had been waiting a whole year to do this again.

"I know, I know," GG said. "Your mother is the same way. The first thing she does when she gets here is go down to the beach too. You two sit tight for a minute while I go grab my running shoes." The girls tried to be patient as GG sauntered back to the house.

"You know what?" Penny stood at the edge of the bluff and looked out across the water.

"Yeah?" Abby said dreamily as she closed her eyes and breathed in deeply.

"Everything connected to the beach seems to start with the letter S: salt, sand, seashells, starfish, sandpipers, surf, sea glass, seaweed, stones ..."

"Okay, okay. I get the picture," Abby said. "You are absolutely right. I never thought of that before."

And sailboats too, Abby thought. She watched them tacking back and forth across the water in the stiff breeze. She gazed out over the water, squinting from the brightness of the sun sparkling off the waves like crystals. The sky was a brilliant blue, the shade of blue you would choose from a box of crayons, and the clouds so thick and fluffy that you truly believed you could jump into them without falling through.

This is going to be an awesome summer, she

thought to herself. It was going to be such a relief to not have her mother breathing down her neck and questioning her every move. She held her arms out to the side to catch the breeze and breathed a deep sigh of freedom. Now that she had her license, she and Sarah could go to the beach every day if they wanted. She'd just have to figure out a way to talk GG into letting her have the car. That shouldn't be too difficult, she thought. GG was a real pushover when it came to letting the girls do things. She spoiled the girls rotten.

Suddenly a black and white dog came barrelling around from the side of the house. Jeopardy was in his usual form, bounding across the grass to where they were standing on the bluff. He jumped up on their legs, insistently begging for acknowledgement. Jep was a black border collie, with paws that looked like they had been dipped in white paint. His face was mostly black too, but with a large white patch around one eye that gave him a somewhat lopsided look.

"Hey ol' Jep, You remember me?"

Abby scratched him behind the ears and within seconds he was off to greet Penny. Jeopardy came by his name honestly. Anytime Jep was missing, you could count on him being in a situation that he couldn't get out of by himself. Abby remembered one time they were sitting on the front porch, and they had heard Jep barking from what seemed like a long way off. They had walked to the bluff to see him perched on a large rock that was getting gradually smaller with the incoming tide. He had been scrambling for purchase as the rock got slipperier with each crashing wave. They

Treading Water

had been able to wade out and rescue him from his predicament, but once back on the beach, Jep had taken off like he hadn't a worry in the world. He really should have been a cat for all the lives he had survived already. He was always putting himself in jeopardy. The name suited him perfectly.

"You know, if people were more like Jeopardy, the world would be a happier place," announced Penny, kneeling down to rub his belly as he flipped over in the grass.

"Yeah, how's that, kiddo?" asked Abby.

"Well, it's like this. Jep loves everybody, so everybody loves Jep. Every time he sees you, he greets you like you have been away for years. How can you not love that? Same thing works for people; if you smile and act like you care, people will like you more too. It's pretty simple, actually," Penny replied confidently.

"That's actually pretty smart, Penny. I could learn a lot from you," Abby joked and shook her head in disbelief. Abby was sure she had never come up with deep thoughts like that when she was Penny's age. They turned to see GG making her way across the yard in her blue tennis shoes.

"GG's here! Let's go!" Penny was off like a flash. GG caught up with them but took her time navigating the steep path down to the beach.

"You girls go on. I'll be right behind you," GG said. The grassy path wound its way down to a pile of boulders at the bottom that involved some stepping-stone jumps in order to land on the beach. The girls ran ahead, their feet barely touching the rocks, waiting breathlessly on the beach like they had done hundreds of times before. GG paused to catch her breath, and sat down on a rock to take off her sneakers.

"Hey GG, is Mr. Jack coming over?" Penny asked.

Mr. Jack was GG's gentleman friend and lived only a stone's throw from her house. They had gotten to know each other better after GG's husband, Cliff, had passed away. He often joined them for dinner, regaling them with stories of the high seas. GG would never have admitted to calling him her actual boyfriend, but Abby knew that he was.

"He'll be over directly, dear. I invited him for some sweet tea and fresh-baked scones. He should be here by the time we get back to the house; said something about a project that he needed to talk to you about." GG chuckled as she said this, knowing it would get Penny's attention. Abby couldn't believe that Penny wanted to work all summer when all she wanted to do was hang out at the beach and relax.

"Oh, good! Maybe we should skip the beach and just go up to see him," Penny said. Abby squealed as the cold waves hit her feet.

"Forget that! I'll race you to the first sand dune ..."

And they were off, everything else forgotten for the moment.

Chapter 11

"Yes, yes, Bill. The timing isn't good, I know, but who plans these things, right?"

Maggie sat at the dining room table amidst the piles of folders and articles that needed attention. She gripped the phone tightly in her right hand while she tried to avoid another avalanche with her left. It wasn't easy trying to convince her boss that she needed some time off. She knew the timing wasn't good, but then it never was. Abby was more important than work at the moment, and she was willing to pay the price to be able to take this trip.

"Of course, I'll tell her. Yes, I'm sure she'll be fine ... I just need to spend some time with my mom. Yes, I really do need to go right now." Maggie figured attending to her mother would be the most convincing way to get some time off work, but it was still proving difficult. There was no way she could tell her boss the real reason, so being vague about her mother's medical issues was the best she could do at short notice. Not that there was anything wrong with her mother, but Bill didn't need to know that. Besides, their relationship needed some attention, so she wasn't actually lying. Not really. She held the receiver away from her ear as Bill's voice increased in intensity. She cringed as he continued ranting.

"I know, I know. I'll get right on it as soon as I get back. I've got Andrea doing some background work on it now so I'm hoping ... Well, thank you, but ... yes, I know, I know. I'll get right on it as soon as I ... Sure, if I have to give it up to someone else, then I guess that's what... Sure, whatever you need to do. I'll do some research on the subject while I'm away, and if you could give me that opportunity again when I return I'd be really grateful." Maggie felt like she was on the floor grovelling at her boss's feet. The conversation ended abruptly as she replaced the receiver, leaned back in her chair and sighed deeply. She would have to deal with the fallout later. She dreaded to think what that might mean, but this was what she needed to do right now.

She reached for the phone again and her elbow accidentally bumped the pile leaning dangerously close to the edge of the table. In slow motion the files fell, fanning out in all directions as they hit the floor, papers scattering everywhere. She leaned over in a half-hearted attempt to start organizing the papers, but shook her head and gave up. She dialled the number she knew by heart and waited for it to ring. She heard her mother pick up, her voice clear across the miles. Maggie took a breath, trying to sound casual.

"Hey Mom, it's me, Maggie." She pulled distractedly on the cord, waiting for her mother to reply.

"Oh, hi, dear. Don't worry — the girls got here all right," Gil said.

"Oh good ... Listen, Mom, the reason I'm calling is ... I wanted to let you know that I've decided to come home for a few weeks." Maggie hesitated, knowing her mother would be suspicious about her coming now that the girls had already arrived. It would have been so much easier if she had just gone with them.

"Why on earth would you be deciding to come now?" Gil hardly missed a beat. "Do you think I'm getting too old to look after the girls?"

It was uncanny that within seconds Gil had pretty much summed up her reason for coming. How could she possibly know? It always amazed Maggie how her mother could make her feel like a child again, even when she herself was a mother and an adult.

"I just thought it might be nice to spend a little extra time with the girls ... and you, of course. It's been a few years since I've been home, so I just thought now would be as good time as any," Maggie said.

"Why wouldn't you have decided that before the girls left? You could have come together." Gil obviously knew that something was up, but Maggie couldn't understand why she was giving her the third degree about it. Maggie wished her mother could just be happy that she was coming.

"It was kind of last-minute ... and I'll have to do some work, some research, while I'm home." It was partially true but again, she couldn't tell her mother the real reason.

"Well, whatever you think, dear. When are you coming?"

"I have a flight booked for the day after tomorrow — in the afternoon. I plan to rent a car, so I'll find my own way from the airport," Maggie said.

"Okay, we'll see you when you get here, then."

And the line went dead. Never one to waste words, Maggie thought, as she held the receiver in her hand, the dial tone buzzing in her ear. She leaned back in her chair and rubbed her temples. A conversation with her mother always left her feeling stressed. Maybe it was time to try and diffuse some of the tension between them. She was going to have to find a way to get rid of some of the stress in her life. It seemed to be coming at her from every direction lately. This trip might be a good idea for more reasons than just Abby. Maybe it would give her a chance to gain some perspective on things.

Maggie hoped she hadn't opened a can of worms with this "journal thing," as she had begun to call it. Glen hadn't exactly approved of her idea, but then he knew she would have gone anyway. She would discuss it with Val when she got back to Nova Scotia. They had been friends since grade school and she knew Maggie better than anybody. Maggie felt instantly better. Val would know how to handle it.

She was secretly glad that she now had some idea what her daughter was thinking. It was so hard to know what went on in a teenager's mind these days. Being away together in Nova Scotia would give her an opportunity to talk to Abby about Tyson. Maggie's friends were appalled that she and Glen let Abby date a guy who was two years older. They kept saying things like "Don't you know how an 18-year-old guy thinks?" Of course she knew. She had been there herself at the same age, but she wasn't about to tell Abby that. And what exactly were Maggie and Glen supposed to do about it? They could forbid Abby from seeing him, but that usually backfired. This trip would be a good test for their relationship.

Maggie dragged her suitcase out from under the bed. A puff of dust flew up and she realized it had been awhile since she had used it. She smiled to herself. Now that she had made the decision to go to Nova Scotia, she couldn't wait to get back. Every trip Down East was the same: she would get on the plane, and chant her mantra to herself — take me home, take me home. Over the years they had considered moving back to Nova Scotia to keep an eye on her mom, but Gil wouldn't hear of it. Gil was as happy as a clam in the beach house on the water. She spent her days puttering around in her garden and helping out with the Ladies' Auxiliary, and her evenings were full of card nights and quilting bees. Maggie secretly hoped that her mom would change her mind and give them a real reason to consider moving back. She knew how the kids would feel about it. Penny would initially be upset about losing her "business connections," but would love the idea. Maggie chuckled to herself. That kid was a going concern. As for Abby, she was happier when she was Down East. She's a lot like me, thought Maggie. The ocean rejuvenates us.

She pulled open the dresser drawers and mindlessly grabbed several T-shirts and shorts and placed them in the suitcase. Next she packed a couple of pairs of jeans and a few sweaters. Growing up in Nova Scotia, she knew it wasn't unusual to change your clothes more than once a day. There was a running joke that went: 'If you don't like the weather, wait five minutes.' She absent-mindedly added socks and underwear as she contemplated the life she was living now. They were fortunate to live only a few blocks away from Angus and Isobel, her mother's brother and his wife: the aunt and uncle she adored. If it hadn't been for them they could never have made a decent go of it when they had first arrived, when Abby was still an infant. Isobel had always found some excuse to drop by and she never came empty-handed; her basket usually contained a casserole or some fresh-baked goodies, along with baby supplies like diapers and wet wipes. They would enjoy a cup of tea and Isobel would sneak off to throw on a load of laundry while she was there. Maggie was so grateful for all they had done, and the relationship her girls had developed with them was as special as hers had been as a child.

Maggie optimistically chose a couple of sundresses from the closet and did a final inventory of her case. She paused for a moment, trying to decide if she should bring along the flask that Val had given her. It might come in handy when I need some fortitude, she thought to herself, and ran downstairs to get it. She added it to her cosmetic bag and also threw in her copy of *She's Come Undone*. The book had been on the bestseller list for months and she just hadn't had time to read it. The title seemed appropriate, considering all that was going on with her at the moment. It was hard to believe that she and Glen had lived in Ontario for more than 16 years now — ever since Abby was born — and almost as long as she had lived in Halifax. The town of Brickton, where they lived, was small enough

Treading Water

to get to know people and yet close enough to Toronto that you could get there in less than an hour. Lucky for Maggie, it was big enough to have its own newspaper, and that was where she logged her hours. It even had a decent-sized lake and Maggie biked along the trails whenever she could find the time. But somehow living near the lake made her feel more melancholy than happy. It was never quite where she wanted to be. She missed the ocean terribly. Moving back East was a subject that she and Glen had stopped discussing, and yet Maggie considered the possibility every time she came home. She would do anything to trade places with the life she had now.

Chapter 12

Abby tapped her fingers on the kitchen countertop as the phone at the other end rang endlessly. She pictured her father lying on his back on the garage floor, tinkering around with a Harley Softail, singing along to his favourite artist. It might take a few minutes before he actually heard the phone over the music, and then another few minutes for him to roll over to the workbench on his dolly to reach the phone. Abby would often hang out in the garage with him, the conversation constantly being interrupted by him asking Abby to pass him another tool. She had to admit she missed him already. She heard the phone pick up.

"Hey Dad, how are you?"

"Hey, Abby! Hold on while I go turn the music down." Abby could hear Bob Seger wailing from the compact disc player in the background and then the volume dropping considerably.

"Now I can hear you. How's it going?" Abby could hear the excitement in his voice.

"Great — it's so great to be here. I'm already having the best time ever!" Abby said.

"What's his name?" Glen asked.

"Oh Dad, why do you always think it's about a guy?"

"Isn't it always?" Glen chuckled.

"Anyways, I've only been here a few days so I haven't had a chance to meet anyone yet!" Abby said.

"Have you done anything exciting?"

"Sarah and I have been hanging out. You know, just catching up and all."

"I hope you come up for air once in a while," Glen teased. "Things have been pretty quiet around here since you girls left."

Abby was notorious for chatting away endlessly about anything and everything. It was a running joke between them that if Abby was relating a story that dragged on for a while, Glen would clutch at his throat as though he were running short of air. That was Abby's cue to slow down and take a breath. GG used to say that her words spilled out of her like a waterfall.

Abby just giggled. "Yeah, we talk a lot, but it's so great to have a good friend to talk to."

"I'll bet it is. And what's Penny been up to?"

"You know Penny. The first day she was already conspiring with Mr. Jack. Apparently he has something new in the works for her this summer, something about saving the harbour or something. Penny is ready to save the world, I swear."

"I can just picture Penny looking all official with her clipboard, madly taking down notes," Glen laughed.

"Yeah, that's pretty much it. Hey Dad, I can't talk long. Sarah's coming over to pick us up soon. We're going down to the waterfront for the Canada Day fireworks. They shoot them off from George's Island and they reflect in the water in the harbour. Penny's coming too."

"I remember. I guess you'll be heading up to Citadel Hill to watch them?" Glen asked.

"Yeah, that's the plan. So I just called to see how you were doing. I hope you don't spend too many lonely nights out in the garage with your wailing guitars! You and Mom should do something special while we're gone."

"Oh. That reminds me — there is something I need to tell you. Did you talk to your mother the other night when she called?" Glen asked.

"No, I wasn't here, why?"

"Well ... she's decided to come out to Nova Scotia for a couple of weeks too," Glen said.

"What? Here? Why?" Abby couldn't believe what she was hearing. She broke out in goosebumps as a feeling of dread crept over her skin like a veil.

"She figured she could use the break from work and um ... wanted to spend a little more time with you girls." Glen felt uncomfortable with the lie, even though it was perfectly reasonable for Maggie to be in Nova Scotia with her daughters. Deep down though, he felt as though he was withholding the truth from Abby.

"I thought she was too busy at work?" She felt as though the veil had turned into a cloak and it hung heavily across her shoulders. Abby prayed she didn't sound as desperate as she felt. Please don't let this be happening, she thought to herself.

"Well, yes ... but she's hoping to do some research for an article she's working on for the paper. I guess she'll just pick up where she left off when she gets back," Glen said.

"Wow, that sucks," Abby finally blurted out, a

feeling of gloom taking away from her excitement to see the fireworks.

"What?" Glen asked.

She suddenly realized what she had said and made a quick attempt to cover it up. "I mean ... it's too bad that ... you know ... you'll be home on your own. Maybe you should come too?" Her dad was always a great buffer between her and her mother, stepping in to calm things down when they were having an argument. On her own, her mother would be like a warrior on a warpath, and Abby would be her sacrifice.

"Thanks, Abby. I'd love to, but I just can't afford the time right now. You know the summer is our busiest time in construction. We have at least 10 houses on the go in this new subdivision. It would be a bad move for me to leave now. Plus, I promised a friend I'd get his Harley detailed before the end of next week and I just haven't had any time to work on it."

"I get it. So, when is Mom coming?" Abby asked, even though she didn't really want to know the answer.

"She'll be flying in late Friday afternoon." Glen said.

"Great," she said sarcastically under her breath. She heard the front porch door slam and voices carried up the stairs. "I gotta go, Dad — I think they're here. I'll call you again soon, okay?"

"Okay babe, 'night. And go easy on your mother," Glen joked.

She put the heavy black phone back in its cradle

and dragged her fingers through her hair. She just couldn't believe it. Why did her mother have to pick this summer to come to Nova Scotia with them? She was going to ruin everything.

Chapter 13

Memories came rushing back like a wave rolling into shore, as Maggie drove down the grassy drive. Had it been almost five years since she had been back? Why had she waited so long? If she'd had her way she would have come every summer, but somehow it hadn't happened. She rolled down the window and inhaled deeply, savouring the stinky scent of seaweed and salt. It would always be the smell of home.

She was happy to see that the house hadn't changed much. Perhaps a little more weather-beaten than the last time she had seen it, but otherwise not a whole lot worse for wear. Her brother Danny would have noticed all the things that needed repair right away. In fact, if he were here he would have looked after the place for Mom. He was a real stickler when it came to keeping things up, repairing things when they needed to be fixed. He got that from their father. As the head carpenter at Neptune Theatre, her father had always been involved with woodworking, and as a result took pride in making sure things were always in working order. Danny had taken a job at Keltic Lodge in Cape Breton as maintenance and groundskeeper at the golf resort. It wasn't exactly a high-paying job, but he made enough to keep himself in golf fees and lobster, and he loved being outside. The five-hour drive prevented him from dropping in on Gil more often, but he would usually make it over to see Gil in the off-season. Maggie hadn't seen him in years. She made a mental note to get in touch with him while she was here.

Maggie loved the way the house seemed to welcome you. Her girls had always thought the two gabled windows looked like eyes, the screen door the nose and the wraparound porch was the smiling mouth, together creating a face that was watching for your arrival. Maggie always thought of it as a happy house. The olive-green paint was starting to peel in spots but was holding up well, despite the beating it got from the salt winds. The white trim could use a fresh coat, too. She should mention it as a potential project for Penny. She and Simon would probably love to do some painting.

Maggie slid out of the car and pulled her skirt away from her damp skin. The sticky air circled her legs and she could feel her hair frizzing as it blew around her face. She walked towards the house, the grass on either side of the drive reaching almost up to her waist. It always surprised her that things grew so wild here from the mist and rain. Everything smelled vibrant and healthy, like fresh-cut grass. The house created a dead end at the end of the laneway, the ocean just barely visible beyond it on either side, and another laneway continued off to the right, leading to several other houses along the shore. She wandered around to the back of the house, surprised that no one had heard her pull in, but savouring the initial reunion on her own.

It was funny how things turned out. If someone had told her when she was young that she would move away from Nova Scotia, she never would have believed them in a million years. This was home. God knows how much she loved it here, and yet that was exactly what had happened. Finding herself back in Nova Scotia brought back a flood of memories that she hadn't realized were so strong. For now, she was going to enjoy the fact that she was here, and deal with her mixed-up emotions later.

The house stood at the edge of a bluff, and the ocean lay beyond for as far as the eye could see, the horizon marking the edge of the earth in the distance. The view was as picturesque as you could imagine — a photographer's delight. Maggie vaguely wondered what had become of her old camera. As a teenager she had been a real shutterbug, but then after Abby was born she didn't really have any extra time for her own hobbies anymore. Maybe she'd splurge for a new camera on this trip. She deserved to spoil herself a little, and it would be fun to see her home through the lens of a camera again. She watched as a container ship slowly edged its way out to sea, getting slowly smaller in the distance. A fine mist hung close to the shoreline and she could hear the surf crashing onto the rocks below. Maggie loved that sound. The natural rhythm had lulled her to sleep on countless summer nights.

Despite all her worrying, Maggie had to admit she was glad her mom had decided to stay here, in this house. She couldn't begin to imagine coming home to any place but here. The house originally belonged to Uncle Angus and Aunt Isobel and she and Danny had spent most of their summers here. They practically lived outdoors and learned everything they needed to know about the beach from their aunt and uncle. And then when Angus announced that they were selling the house and moving to Ontario, her parents had jumped at the chance to live on the beach, and had bought it for themselves. For Maggie it was both a relief and a dream come true.

Still, Maggie didn't like the idea of her mom living all alone in the old house. She worried that it would be too much for her to look after on her own. They had offered the idea of moving into a residence or condo in town, closer to her friends, and close to the shops, but she had flatly refused to live anywhere else. She had no shortage of friends and no shortage of energy and as for being alone, she said, she couldn't ask for better company than Jep. She would comment that he didn't eat much, didn't give her any flak, and didn't go around moaning and complaining like some women's husbands did. Maggie was sure that Mr. Jack had been helping Gil take care of things, too. She'd have to make a point of thanking him even though he'd never admit to doing anything special.

Mr. Jack must have known she was coming - now here he was, taking his time walking down the path over from his place. He looked like he might have gained a few pounds since last time she saw him, probably from enjoying a few too many of her mom's butter tarts. She remembered him as always having been a lanky guy with prominent cheekbones and wiry arms. Now his face was fuller and he looked healthy and happy. Maggie knew that he had been married once but she could barely remember a time when he hadn't lived down the lane on his own. It gave Maggie peace of mind to know someone was watching out for her mother. Maggie ran to Jack and gave him a big squeeze. She heard her mother come out of the house, the wooden screen door slapping against the frame as it swung back.

"Hey, careful, hon, don't break me in two," Mr. Jack laughed as he squeezed her back. Despite his age he looked good, perhaps a little weather-beaten from being out in the sun but still strong, and always grinning. His blue eyes stood out against his tanned face. It was hard to believe that he was 10 years older than her mother.

"It's so good to see you. You've been taking care of yourself." Maggie held him at arm's length as they surveyed each other. She was glad that her mother had managed to find such a wonderful man.

"Well no, I think I can give your mom credit for that." He winked in Gil's direction as she came up to join them. Gil would have none of it, and just pretended she hadn't heard.

"Hey, Mom."

Maggie gave her mother a tentative embrace, and then stepped back to look into her eyes. At age 65, Gil looked good too. Her face was tanned from gardening, and her cheeks had a healthy rosy glow. Her white hair was cut just below her jawline and she attempted to tuck it behind her ear, but the wind teased it out again. Maggie was sure that there were a few more wrinkles since last time, but that was a good sign that she had been laughing more lately. Chalk another one up for

Mr. Jack.

"How are you, dear? I was surprised to hear that you were coming home, but then I never figured you would go this long without seeing hide nor hair of the ocean either," Gil said.

"It hasn't been that long, Mom," Maggie replied defensively. Her mother had a way of making her feel as though she had done something wrong, like she should be apologizing for something. She swallowed her pride and attempted to sound cheerful.

"Things don't always go as planned, I guess," Maggie said. "Oh, just leave those, Mr. Jack, the girls can get the bags for me. I didn't bring much. By the way, where are the girls?" Maggie looked around to see where they might be. She wasn't entirely sure what kind of reception she was going to get from Abby, and secretly wanted to delay any confrontation for as long as possible.

"Oh, they're around here someplace. Probably down the beach as always." Gil wiped her forehead with the back of her hand. "It's so hot and sticky. I have some cold lemonade. Why don't we sit on the porch and see if we can catch some of that breeze?"

"Sure, Mom. Just give me a sec, will you? I just need to do my arrival ritual," Maggie said.

"Okay, you know where to find us," Gil said.

Gil and Mr. Jack looked like a charming old couple as they sauntered arm in arm back to the house. Mr. Jack collapsed into a wicker chair, and Gil went inside to prepare a tray of drinks. Maggie felt the scratchy grass whipping against her ankles as she walked to the edge of the bluff. She looked down to the beach and could make out the figures of her two daughters running in and out of the waves, Jep close at their heels. They were searching for beach stuff along the water's edge. She smiled, knowing their rooms were probably already full of jars and dishes of miscellaneous treasures. Every so often they would pick up a piece of driftwood and send it flying across the waves. Always eager for a challenge, Jep would dive headlong into the surf to retrieve his prize. Once on the beach he would do a full-body shake, soaking the girls completely and looking to go again. She could just make out their laughter carried along on the breeze. She felt anxious as she anticipated Abby's reaction to her arrival. She pushed her worry away and focussed on the view before her. She still couldn't believe that anything could have taken her away from here. This was home and always would be. When they were saying their goodbyes so many years ago, her friend Val had said: 'You can take the girl out of Nova Scotia but you can't take Nova Scotia out of the girl.' She had been absolutely right.

Chapter 14

Abby curled up in the armchair in the front room, her latest book open in her lap, alternately reading and dozing. Her thoughts kept coming back to yesterday. She and Penny had been enjoying themselves on the beach, and when they had started back to the house, their mother had been standing on the path waiting for them. The last thing she wanted was her mother as a chaperone on her vacation. Their eyes had met and Abby had seen the hopeful look on her mother's face. She had given her mother a hug and whispered 'why are you even here?' and had walked off, leaving her mother to watch after her with a stunned expression on her face. Abby had felt bad, and yet she needed to make it clear that she wanted her space.

She was suddenly pulled back to the present at the sound of the front door opening. Penny wedged her way awkwardly through the screen door, her tousled red hair crowning the pile of papers that loaded her down. She scurried over to the kitchen and unleashed everything onto the counter with a big sigh. She poured herself a tall glass of lemonade that she downed in one long gulp, wiped her mouth and quickly poured herself another.

"What have you got there, kiddo"? Abby asked, turning the book over on her lap.

"My latest project," Penny beamed as she pushed her curly hair out of her eyes.

"What project is that?"

Abby feigned complete ignorance, totally playing

into Penny's obvious excitement even though Mr. Jack had mentioned it over dinner the other night.

"Well, these are the flyers that I have to fold for the Save the Harbour project," Penny said.

"Save the Harbour? What's that?" Abby asked. She came over to the counter and glanced at the papers that Penny had brought in. Penny started folding and Abby joined her. Soon they fell into an easy rhythm together, and as the piles grew, Penny bunched them together and boxed them.

"This summer they've started on an awareness campaign called Save the Harbour. There is so much pollution that it's affecting the fish and everything else that lives in the ocean. Did you know you can't even swim at beaches like Point Pleasant Park or Horseshoe Island anymore? If you do, your bathing suit will turn black. It's a big problem."

"So, how did you end up on this project?"

"Mr. Jack's been working with the Department of Fisheries and they got him involved with this project — and of course that's how I ended up on it!" She grinned. "They hired an engineer to study the problem and develop a plan to start changing things. These are all the flyers we just printed. I'm going to fold them and hand them out down the laneways near GG's place and then later in the week, Mr. Jack said we'd go downtown to the waterfront and pass them out. It'll be a great way to make people aware of what the problem is, and what we need to do to fix it. There's always a ton of people down at the waterfront in the summer."

Abby couldn't help but be impressed by her

enthusiasm. "Sounds like its right up your alley."

Penny was all freckles and gumption and pretty much any project was up her alley. She had had a thing for money for as long as Abby could remember. Even when she was really small she would hoard coins, especially ones from different places, her ultimate goal being to collect coins from every country on the planet. She had a bunch of little plastic envelopes with a penny for every year dating back as far as 1920. I guess with a name like Penny, we could have seen that coming, Abby mused. Her actual name was Penelope, after her great-aunt. This family of women felt strongly about passing along the female names, but they were equally good about shortening them. Margaret had become Maggie, and Penelope became Penny. Abby couldn't even imagine Penny being called Penelope. She was too spunky for an antique name like that. Even Grandma Gil, whose real name was Abigail, had gotten shortened to Gil and Abby, who had been named after her grandmother, had luckily become Abby. It kept things simple.

"And Simon, he's working on the project too. You know, he's gotten even taller since last summer, like that was even possible." Penny's cheeks flushed pink through her freckles.

"I think you have a crush on Simon," Abby teased.

"No, I just got too much sun today, I think. We sat outside for lunch." She quickly got up to start folding more flyers. "You know, you really should come and help us on the project. You'd have a blast. It's really a lot of fun."

"Fun?" Abby was sceptical. She had no intention of working while she was on vacation. It would be beach time and book time for her.

"Well, for starters it would give you something to do besides reading all day. Plus you'd be doing something good for the beaches. You know how much you love the beach."

That was certainly true. Abby spent the first hour of every single day at the beach. It didn't matter if it was cool, windy, foggy, or misty: Abby would pour coffee into her favourite mug with the seagulls on it, and head down the steps to the beach, Jep usually bringing up the rear. She knew full well what Penny was talking about. It disgusted her to see what floated up onto the beach: pop cans, bottles, chip bags, even tampon tubes. Why would anyone toss that stuff into the ocean?

"Besides, there is this really cute guy working on the project too." Penny looked up from her folding for Abby's reaction. "He looks a lot like Lance Bass from NSync. His dad is the project manager and he's here to help him out for the summer. Oh, and did I mention he was cute?"

Abby stopped what she was doing and looked directly at Penny. She certainly had her interest now.

Chapter 15

Maggie and Val had agreed to meet for dinner at McKelvie's, their favourite restaurant close to the waterfront. McKelvie's was famous for their crab cakes and Maggie made sure she had some at least once when she was in town. Maggie wasn't sure she'd had anything else on the menu except maybe the lobster, but why mess with a sure thing?

Val had promised to join her as soon as she finished with her last client. Val had inherited her mother's salon, Streaks and Cowlicks, on Quinpool Road. The name left a little to be desired, but everyone had associated the name with Val for so long now that she thought it would be bad karma to change it. Maggie decided to make an appointment while she was visiting. She had a tendency to just let her long hair grow longer and couldn't remember the last time she'd been to the hairdresser's. Maybe Val could find a style that would pick up her look a little — God knows she needed it. Maggie looked up to see Val, a flourish of blonde hair and leopard spots, her heels clicking as she made her way across the restaurant.

"It's *so* good to see you," Maggie said, hugging her friend tight. Val still smelled of Shalimar, the same scent she had been wearing since forever. If Maggie ever caught a whiff of it anywhere else, she immediately thought of Val. It suited her. It was spicy and feisty, just like Val.

"It's good to see you too, and tempting me with crab cakes will do it every time," Val said.

Val surveyed her friend with a critical eye. She lifted a handful of Maggie's hair and let it drop with a snicker. "What the heck have you done with your hair? Are you sure there aren't any birds hiding in that nest?"

"Yeah, I should have known you would comment on that right off the bat."

"And a little skinnier than last time I saw you too, doll. Don't they have real food where you live? I think we need to fatten you up a little while you are here; give a guy something to hold onto!"

Val had curves going in every direction and was proud of them. She had put on a little weight but she carried it well, her ample breasts distracting you from any other flaws she might have. She tended towards bright clothes, tightly fitted over her curvy figure, animal prints being her favourite. Maggie didn't think she had lost that much weight since they last saw each other. But then again, because of her diabetes her consumption of sweets had dropped considerably, even though she still had a tough time keeping away from chocolate.

"I didn't think you were coming out this summer," Val said.

"Well I wasn't, but then ... well, it's a long story. Let's order some wine first."

She was looking forward to being able to talk to Val but she was also nervous about what she might think. But she was just being silly. When they were in Grade 2, Val had come into the class as the new kid. The teacher had put her in the empty seat right in front of Maggie. She had been totally intrigued with Val's white-blonde hair. It had been tied back into two long braids and Maggie had resisted the urge to pull one just so she could get her to turn around and see her face. But right in the middle of copying down the cursive alphabet, Val had turned around and made some crack about this writing being a curse and it had sent them into uncontrollable laughter. They'd both kept their bobbing heads down, intent on their work, and hoped the teacher wouldn't notice. But then Val dropped something on the floor, and when she bent over to pick it up she had glanced up at Maggie, and they went into fits of laughter again. They had been best friends ever since.

Val had had a tough go of things over the years but had never let it drag her down. She was on her third husband with five kids between them, and it seemed she had finally hit the jackpot as far as guys were concerned. Val was one of the most cheerful and optimistic people she knew. Carpe diem was her mantra. Seize the moment, seize the day, seize the guy!

"Cheers!" said Maggie, lifting her wine glass.

"Cheers back." They clinked glasses and smiled at each other, happy to be in each other's company again. "I'm so glad you decided to come this summer. It's been too long. So what changed your mind?" Val asked.

"Well, actually there's a little bit of a story to tell." She paused to take a sip of wine, tucked her hair behind her ears and leaned in, her voice low. "Last week I was helping Abby get ready for her trip, like I always do. She hadn't done any packing yet so I was helping her with laundry. I was picking up dirty clothes in her room when I came across her journal."

"And you read it?" Val raised her eyebrows with interest, questions written all over her face.

Maggie glanced around to see if anyone had heard, but thankfully they were absorbed in their own conversations. "Not exactly. I mean I never had any intention of reading it. Every kid deserves her privacy, right? It was what caught my eye that sucked me in like an undertow. It was a list of things she wants to do the year she turns 16. Things like smoke a cigarette, have her first beer ... have sex."

"So, it's like every teenage girl's wish list. We all had things that we secretly wanted to try. What's the big deal?"

Val leaned back in her chair, casually hanging one arm over the back as though she had had this conversation a hundred times before. Being a hairdresser, there wasn't much that Val hadn't already heard.

"But did you ever consciously say, 'I'm going to have sex'?" Maggie asked.

"Well ... maybe not exactly like that. But we sure talked about what it might be like. Don't you remember all those sleepovers we used to have? We spent many a night in your room talking about sex and who we might like to 'do' it with. It could easily have been something you had on your list at that age." She winked knowingly at Maggie.

"*Exactly*," Maggie replied. "That's exactly what

I'm getting at. I'm scared to death that Abby is going to do something stupid, and she turns 17 in August, so time is running out."

"Do you seriously think she plans to check off this list while she's here on vacation?" Val's brows furrowed at Maggie, intent on the discussion. That's what Maggie liked about Val. She didn't hold anything back, and if anyone could give her a good reading on the right thing to do, it would be Val.

"I don't know. I know it sounds stupid. I just didn't think Mom was capable of keeping an eye on her while she's here. She can be so naive about teenage things," Maggie said.

"And that's why you decided to come? So you could protect her? Give your mom some credit. After everything she went through with you, she does know a thing or two," Val said, swirling her wine around in the glass.

"But Abby's different than I was at that age. She's always bucking the system. We're always locking horns about something."

Maggie pulled her hair together and lifted it up off the back of her neck before letting it fall. All this talk about doing the right thing always made her nervous and she was getting warm. The wine was probably playing a part as well, as she noticed her glass was almost empty.

"She's supposed to do that. You're her mother," Val commented.

"I know, but it happens *all* the *time*. And I'm not sure if Abby challenged Gil that she would stand up to her. Abby can be pretty bold and sneaky when she wants to be." Maggie sighed.

"What do you plan to do, hold her hand everywhere she goes?" Val kidded her. "You know, most parents have blinders on. They'll say 'Oh, my kid's not having sex,' or 'my kid's not doing drugs,' when everyone knows darn well that they are. You, on the other hand, have gone to the whole other end of the spectrum. You think your kid is into *everything*." She laughed that husky laugh of hers as though it were as simple as anything. "I think you need to relax a little, girlfriend."

The waiter arrived with their dinner and Maggie accepted his offer of a refill on her wine.

"I swear to God, Val. I feel like I've been treading water since I left Nova Scotia. My job — I keep hoping for a break that never seems to come and if I have to do one more assignment on a local event that no one gives a shit about, I'm going to scream. I've been waiting for a break for five years but nothing *ever* changes. Things have been distant between Glen and me. And now this thing with Abby ..." She dabbed at her eyes but the tears kept coming like a tap that wouldn't turn off. Val stood up and put her arms around her. Maggie took a few deep breaths and her sobbing subsided. She lifted her mascara-smudged eyes to look at Val, and could barely squeeze the words out.

"It's just that I would be absolutely devastated if Abby ended up in the same predicament I was in when I was her age."

Chapter 16

Abby bounded up the wooden stairs, leaving remnants of sand and watery footprints on every step. No matter how hard you tried to brush off the sand, there was always some left clinging to you somewhere. Sometimes Abby didn't even bother trying. She closed the door behind her and gave her hair a shake, bits of sand flying onto the bed and the hardwood floor. Jep had done the same thing, giving a full-body shake that made ticking noises on the wall, but luckily had been contained to the mud room.

They'd had a great run along the beach, and Abby had found a few more pieces of sea glass. Collecting sea glass was one of her favourite things to do while she was in Nova Scotia. There were several old Mason jars on the dresser nearly full with layers of coloured glass that she had collected over the years. She was always amazed at the variety of colours, wondering what the item had been before it had been surrendered to the ocean. Sometimes she was lucky enough to find some interesting shapes. She pulled a handful out of her shorts pocket and dusted away the sand for a closer look. One piece was a royal blue, a blue so deep you could just barely see through it. It reminded her of the Nivea jar that her mom always had on her dresser and she could almost smell the medicinal white face cream just from looking at it. The other piece of glass was brown and when you flipped it over it looked like a misshapen heart. One side was flatter than the other, so it wasn't perfect, but definitely a heart. Abby put it in the little ceramic dish beside the jar to keep it separate from all of the other pieces. Maybe this piece could bring her some good luck.

She was excited about Sarah coming over for a sleepover tonight. She could hardly wait to catch up on all those things they would never put in a letter, in case someone else got their hands on it. She was hoping Sarah could help her make some sense of all that was wrong with her life and what she should do about Tyson.

Abby and Sarah had been friends for as long as she had been coming out to Nova Scotia. When she was only about five years old, GG had taken her along to one of the bazaars at the hospital in Halifax. GG had plunked Abby in the corner near the book table so she could keep an eye on her while she attended her sewing table. Abby loved looking through the boxes for books she could read while she waited. It was like having her own personal library under the table and she could pick whatever she wanted. Maybe it was GG's fault that she loved reading so much. All Abby could see from her vantage point under the table were anonymous legs and feet moving back and forth, but at one point she had looked up from her book and found she was face to face with another girl just about her size. She had two pigtails that stuck straight out from her head, and a huge grin that would make anybody smile. She didn't say anything but just sat there grinning at Abby, so Abby smiled back. She had showed the girl her book and asked her if she wanted to read with her. Sarah had quickly scooted through the dust until she was directly beside Abby, legs touching, and then she smiled at Abby some more. When Sarah had heard her mother's frantic voice calling her, she jumped out from under the table announcing "Here I am, Mommy," like everything was hunky dory. They had become instant friends, begging GG for play dates at every opportunity, and that's the way it still was. They were inseparable all summer. What Abby wouldn't do to have a friend like Sarah back home.

Her jeans sat in a pile on the floor where she had dropped them after this morning's walk on the beach. They were still a bit damp, but she wanted to show Sarah the new jeans she had gotten for the trip. She'd have to remember to hang them over the back of the chair after the beach, or they would never dry. It seemed as though everything here was in perpetual dampness. Even the dresser drawer stuck from the humidity. She had to use two hands to pull it open as she searched for a T-shirt. She chose a plain white T-shirt and a funky purple zippered hoodie and surveyed her summer-vacation look in the mirror. She flicked her hair again and still more sand tinkled to the floor. She pulled it into a messy bun with one of the many elastics that were always bunched on her wrist like bracelets, and surveyed herself in the mirror again. She had some pink spots from being out in the sun, and some freckles had popped out as well. She looked healthier than she had looked in weeks, and a little mascara was all she really needed. Happy with the way she looked, she picked the salty-smelling towel off the floor and temporarily hooked it onto the latch of the casement window, knowing GG would have a fit if she found wet towels on the hardwood.

She grabbed her book and made her way over to the window seat to kill time until Sarah got there. She gasped as a dagger of pain shot through her foot. Her big toe had caught on a jagged edge of a floorboard that had worked itself loose. It felt as though her toenail had been ripped off and she hopped around for a minute, trying to divert herself from the pain. Tears stung her eyes as she bent down to check for blood and noticed that the floorboard beside the other one was also loose. It came up easily and when she lifted it off, she could see something lying below the floorboards. Her toe now forgotten, she reached down between the dusty boards and carefully pulled out a small book. The cover was pale pink and it had a small, rusty clasp on the side, with tiny keys hanging from a thin pink ribbon to unlock it. The key turned easily and Abby opened it gently, feeling as though she was invading someone's privacy, but that didn't stop her. The cover made a crunching sound from being closed for too long, and the pages were warped from the dampness, but the writing was still legible. Totally intrigued about who this book belonged to, Abby flipped the pages randomly, gently pulling them apart in spots where they had stuck together.

Dear Diary,

I'm so excited. Val and I went to the sock hop at the school last night and it was SO much fun! She came over after school and we got all dolled up. It was an American Graffiti theme and Mom had made these old-fashioned skirts for us. They go out into a complete circle when you spin around. Mom even stitched a picture of a poodle on mine. It felt like we had stepped straight out of the movie. We had our hair pulled up in pony tails and the skirts were so cool. We were the best-looking girls at the dance. We were hanging out along the back wall when I saw Glen come in with some of his friends. I waved when I saw him, and he smiled back at me but didn't come over. I wasn't sure what to do because I really wanted to talk to him, but I didn't want to just walk over to him like I was being pushy or anything. The DJ was playing all these great songs and it was killing me just waiting for him to come over. I thought maybe he was shy and I didn't know what to do. Then they started playing "Rock Around the Clock" and I could see him bopping his way over to me. Thank goodness. I was getting so worried! We danced so many songs after that one that we had to go and get some pop. It was so hot in the gym, they had to prop the back doors open. I didn't want him to go back to his friends because I thought if a slow dance came on he wouldn't want to leave them again to come back to get me, so I tried to keep him dancing. And then they started playing "Stairway to Heaven" and I kept looking over at him. I think every couple was on the dance floor and I just had my fingers crossed that he would want to dance a slow dance with me. He took my hand and pulled me out onto the floor and it was the most romantic dance I've ever had! He held me really close and then moved us over near the doors and I could feel the breeze on my bare legs and his tongue was licking my ear and oh ... it was the best!

Abby held her breath when she saw the writing at the bottom of the page. It was signed off with "Maggie" and the reality of who this diary belonged to hit her like a wave.

Chapter 17

A little bell jingled as Maggie stepped through the door of Streaks and Cowlicks and the pungent smell of perm chemicals hit her nostrils. Back when they were in school, Val and Maggie would catch the bus to Quinpool Road and hang out until Val's mother was finished for the day. Most days it was just an excuse to stop in at the Candy Bowl; it sold every kind of candy your heart desired. They could have spent days just deciding what to buy. It was a wonder they didn't both have rotten teeth for all the candy they ate back then. She'd have to make a point of stopping in at the Freak Lunchbox downtown; it was an updated version of the Candy Bowl, but with a vintage look.

Maggie glanced around for Val and noticed that the shop hadn't changed one bit; the walls still a sad beige colour that had gotten even softer with age and the sinks at the back still a godawful turquoise, with matching towels. On the far wall sat three antiquated over-the-head blow-dryers under which a couple of platinum-haired women tried to carry on a conversation over the noise. The only sign of keeping up with the times was a reception area at the front, complete with a computerized scheduler for appointments.

Val, wearing her trademark leopard-print pumps, came over to greet Maggie. "Hey, there you are! I was ready to send out a search party!"

"Sorry about that. I was just driving around the neighbourhood, reminiscing. I think I may have to stop

Treading Water

in at the Ardmore Tea Room for lunch afterwards. I can't believe that place is still here after all these years. Too bad the Candy Bowl is gone."

"Not too bad for me!" Val laughed as she patted her generous hips. "So, what are we doing today? Are you feeling adventurous?" She grabbed a handful of Maggie's hair and let it slip slowly out of her fingers, and then zoomed in for a closer look at her roots. She wrinkled her forehead in distaste and beckoned over her shoulder for Maggie to follow her to the row of sinks.

"Maybe not adventurous, but I sure could use a boost. It's been awhile," Maggie said.

"You're not kidding! I think I'll add some blonde highlights to brighten you up a little, and that will accentuate the red. How would you feel about a cute bob to tidy things up? By the time I'm done you'll look like a new woman."

"I like the sound of that." It was a good thing she trusted Val as much as she did. If anyone else had suggested a totally new hairdo she would have been more than a little nervous. Even so, she was still a little anxious about changing her hair, but it had been ages since she'd done anything exciting with it. After all, what did she have to lose?

Val threw a black plastic cape around Maggie's shoulders with a flourish as she caught her eye in the mirror.

"What else have you got planned for today? Anything exciting?"

"I was hoping to catch up with Abby. She wants to

wander around Spring Garden Road for a while and maybe even take a stroll through the Public Gardens. She's on a mission to take the winning shot for her school photography contest. I just never know what her reaction is going to be when I ask her to do something. I feel like I'm on the defensive before she even speaks."

"Ever stop to think that maybe she feels the same way? Don't worry about it so much, girlfriend. Just keep doing what you're doing. Things will be fine. Trust me." She wheeled a little trolley up beside Maggie and started painting her roots, every so often flattening the foil with her comb with a slap before moving onto the next clump of hair. It was mesmerizing watching her work, giving her a moment to collect her thoughts.

"I hope you're right." Maggie paused and lowered her voice before she spoke again. "You know, sometimes I still think I made the wrong decision back then."

"What the heck are you talking about?" Val leaned over Maggie's shoulder to hear her better.

"Once Abby was born, we really had no choice but to get away from here. It was *so* difficult. But you know, I never really wanted to leave." They eyed each other in the mirror as Val continued with her slapping as though they couldn't possibly be engrossed in deep conversation.

"I know, hon, but you weren't on your own — you had Glen," Val said.

"Yes, and he's been amazing," Maggie said.

Maggie thought back to those beginning years. Gil's brother Angus had moved to Ontario with his wife Isobel, and he was looking for fresh recruits for his construction company. Glen was fresh out of trade school, so it was the perfect opportunity for them. Maggie was very close to her aunt and uncle after all those summers she had spent at their beach house, the same one her mother lived in now, so they couldn't say no. Isobel was a kind soul and had promised to keep a close eye on the young family. So off they had gone. They had been so busy trying to figure out this little baby of theirs while trying to make ends meet, that they hadn't really had time to think twice about their decision to leave.

Once in Ontario, Glen had insisted that Maggie finish high school. There was no way he was letting her out of that and she was thankful, although there were days when she would fall asleep face down on her books after putting Abby to bed. Glen would gently shake her awake and say, "C'mon kiddo, hang in there, you have to do this," and she'd go right back at it again. And Maggie adored Abby. They would spend their days hanging out, just the two of them, and when Glen came home he would take over so that Maggie could concentrate on her courses. Nothing was ever too much for Glen, and Maggie soon realized just how much he loved her; how much he loved them both. Once she had finished high school, he had encouraged her to go on to do some journalism courses and when she landed the job at the local newspaper she felt like she was finally contributing to their family.

Around that time Penny had come along and they figured they had been away from Nova Scotia long enough. So after several years of being away, they had finally decided to go back East on a regular basis. They had been coming back almost every summer since, or had at least sent the girls. Except for the recent drought, Maggie vowed to never let work interfere with her trip home again. Maggie and Glen would come for only a week or so at a time, but the girls usually stayed for weeks, and when they were little they sometimes begged to stay all summer. Maggie often wondered if the ocean wasn't an ointment for all of them. Even Glen was different when he was in Nova Scotia, giving him a chance to catch up with family and old buddies. But she knew he still worried about her and the old memories that must surely cross her mind when she came back. Maggie's train of thought prompted her to ask Val something she had been thinking about for a long time.

"Do you ever hear anything about Rick?" Maggie asked hesitantly.

"Actually, no, I haven't heard much other than that he'd moved to Ottawa. No one has seen or heard from him in years," Val replied. "Now just sit tight while this sets and I'll be back in a jiff." Val was off to greet another customer. Maggie shut her eyes while she waited for the colour to take. She could hear snippets of conversation from other stations, some of which she would have loved to join in on, but then they would know she had been eavesdropping. Maggie listened to the buzz around her: female conversations punctuated by exclamations of laughter. A comment from the lady across from her interrupted her thoughts. "...and I guess they've even brought in this big-shot engineer from Ottawa to oversee the project ... His name is Rick something ... apparently grew up here, so he must know a thing or two about our beaches and harbour."

Maggie's stomach flipped and she felt a chill run down her spine underneath the cape. She was glad that no one was able to see the goosebumps on her arms. What were the chances that she would hear about him, here, today, right after she'd just asked Val about him? Maggie worriedly turned to look for Val, and when they made eye contact, Val put a finger to her lips as if to say: your secret is safe with me. It was a shock hearing his name after all these years. She thought about him every time she came home, secretly hoping she might bump into him, but then not sure if she really wanted to, either. And yet she just couldn't stop herself from asking questions she should never have asked; from wondering, *What if?*

Chapter 18

Abby and Sarah snuggled together on the bed in their pyjamas, stuffing their faces with buttered popcorn, and giggling with every sentence. Back when they were small they would scavenge around the house for every blanket, pillow and chair cushion they could find, and make amazing forts. They would take flashlights and put fabric over the top to soften the glow, and hoard cookies and chips from the kitchen. They would each take a turn telling part of a story, each one adding a piece as they went along, entertaining themselves for hours on rainy afternoons.

Things hadn't changed a lot since then. The bed was piled with quilts and pillows as they caught up on their own stories. A portable TV sat on the trunk at the end of the bed, the VCR player tottering precariously on top, waiting for them in case they ever stopped talking long enough to watch a movie. Penny was off somewhere with Mr. Jack, and her mom was watching TV downstairs. Abby thought she could hear GG busy in the kitchen and if they were lucky there might be some brownies for them. This was their first sleepover of the holidays, and they would probably stay up all night to catch up on each other's news.

"This is so great, hanging out again. I've missed you so much!" Abby hugged her friend again as though she couldn't really believe that she was here. It really was great to be together. Abby truly missed this easy friendship. Her friends at home always made her feel like she was walking on eggshells or worse, hot

Treading Water

stones — like you were going to get burned. She felt she had to always be on her guard to make sure that she didn't hurt anyone's feelings. It was frustrating. It was so nice to just be comfortable in each other's space; to just be yourself.

"Wouldn't it be great if we lived closer to each other?" Sarah asked.

"You know I would move here in a second," Abby replied without hesitation.

"So why don't you?" Sarah asked.

"I just don't think it's ever going to happen. Not anytime soon, anyway. Mom has mentioned it once or twice because she worries about GG living here all by herself, but GG seems to be doing just fine on her own."

"So, do you ever ask your folks about it — about moving here?"

"Not really. It comes up every time we come to Nova Scotia, but I don't think they're seriously thinking about it. They're always saying how hard it is to find jobs here. Plus they are always too busy to deal with it anyway."

"Maybe you should work on them again. You never know, right?" Sarah suggested. "Your mom could work pretty much anywhere, and your dad knows enough people he could probably find something, too. Then when you move here, we could hang out all the time. We could even go to school together."

"I know; that would be great!" The girls stopped to give each other a high-five. "I don't know. My mom always goes on and on about how Ontario is nothing like Nova Scotia, and how much she misses it and everything, but between her job and my dad's job ..." Her voice trailed off. She envisioned the piles of file folders covering the dining room table, and the remnants of sawdust and dirt that collected in the kitchen from various construction sites. *That* wasn't going to change anytime soon. She and Sarah had this conversation every time she came to visit, but maybe she *should* talk to her parents about it again. Maybe she could at least consider going to university here after she graduated high school.

"What about Tyson? Would you want to leave if you two were still going out together?" Sarah raised her eyebrows at Abby as though asking the million-dollar question. They wasted no time getting around to discussing boyfriends and boy stuff.

"I wouldn't really have a choice, would I? Would I care? Seriously, I don't know. He was acting kind of strange before I left. He showed up the day I left with a present and a note. I have no idea what it's supposed to mean." She pulled the chain out from under her T-shirt and showed it to Sarah. Abby lay back on the pillows, staring at the ceiling as though the answer might reveal itself in the water spots on the ceiling.

"That's pretty cool, the way it forms into a knot, but it's all connected. What did the note say?" Sarah asked.

"It said, '*Enjoy the summer but I know you'll save yourself for me.*'"

"What's that supposed to mean?"

"That's what I wondered. Either he wants to make us official when I get back, or he expects us to have sex when I get back." She held out the palms of both her hands, lifting each side as though imitating a scale. "Commitment or casual sex? Pretty big difference between the two, huh? What bothers me is that you would think he would have gone about things differently if he wanted us to be a couple. That's not something that just happens by chance; you should *know* it's going to happen, and then he just leaves me wondering by giving me this last-minute gift. I don't really know what to think. And the other option, well ... that's not the kind of relationship that I want."

Sarah leaned in closer to her friend and asked the question she'd been dying to ask since she first knew Abby was seeing Tyson. Some things you just didn't talk about in a letter.

"Haven't you guys done anything yet?" she asked.

"No, we haven't. I've been kind of waiting," Abby said.

"But he's older than you are, isn't he? And he hasn't asked you to do anything yet?" Sarah asked.

"Yes, he is ... but no, he hasn't ..."

"Is he still a virgin?"

"Of course not." Abby sat up again.

"And he's still okay waiting for you?" Sarah asked.

"He seems okay with it. With waiting, I mean. I don't know. It's so complicated." Abby threw herself back on the pile of pillows and rolled her eyes. "I'm not even sure I want to, I just think maybe I *should*, you know? What would you do?" She leaned up on one elbow, waiting for a response to her last question.

"Josh and I have been going out for six months now and I'm so glad he talked me into it. But I was really scared the first time." Sarah was grinning like she had just let out the biggest secret of her life. Clearly she had been just bursting to tell Abby about it.

Abby bolted upright and threw a handful of popcorn at Sarah. "Shut up! You never told me any of this before."

Sarah attempted to cover her grin with both hands, her eyes popping with glee above them. "I certainly wasn't going to tell you in a letter, and risk that someone might get their hands on it! Besides, this way is much more fun!" she retorted, throwing some popcorn back at Abby.

They both laughed and Abby wiggled herself closer to Sarah to get the full scoop. They were inches apart on the bed, popcorn bits strewn between them, foreheads almost touching as they spoke in animated whispers. "Wow. So what was it like? Where do you do it?"

"Usually after school at my house before everyone gets home from work," Sarah continued matter-of-factly.

"In your bedroom?" Abby raised her voice and her eyebrows to match. She had a hard time imagining that. She wouldn't even have the guts to try it at her place. She could hardly believe that Sarah had.

"They just think I'm studying if I'm up there when they get home. They can be so naive sometimes," Sarah said. She waved her hand nonchalantly as though it were the most normal thing in the world to be having sex with your boyfriend in your bedroom. Abby wouldn't even dream of trying it; her mother would probably sense that she had done something wrong, whereas Sarah's parents seemed to be oblivious. Abby wasn't sure which was better.

Abby shook her head, as though it were full of too many questions to handle all at once. "Don't you worry about getting pregnant?" Abby asked.

Sarah started to respond but Abby suddenly put her finger to her lips to shush the conversation. "Sh! Did you hear something?"

"No, did you?" Sarah's voice squeaked a little.

"I think someone's in the washroom — probably my mom. Don't say anything for a minute." They both sat up, leaning in the direction of the door, anticipating any possibility of being interrupted. They heard the toilet flush and the creaking of the floorboards as someone crossed the landing. Suddenly there was a light tap on the door, and the girls both covered their mouths at the same time in panic. The tension was too much for them and they collapsed in a heap of giggles onto the pillows.

"Are you girls having fun in there?" Maggie asked, peeking through the crack in the door.

"Yeah, Mom, we're having a blast. Can't you tell?" They broke into giggles again. Maggie shook her head hopelessly and closed the door again.

The girls waited until the footsteps receded to the main floor and Abby let out her breath. "Whew, *that* was close. Where were we? Oh, that reminds me. You'll never guess what I found ... my mother's diary!"

"Big deal. What could possibly be worth reading in your mother's diary?" Sarah laughed.

"No silly, not *that* diary! Her diary from when she was a teenager, when she was *our* age." Abby lowered her voice again, speaking in heated whispers for fear that her mother might be eavesdropping outside the door. "I found her diary underneath the floorboards in my room. This is the house she practically grew up in. She must have hidden it there and forgotten about it."

She had Sarah's attention now. "That sounds like it could be interesting. Did you read anything juicy?"

"Actually I haven't had much time to read it without people being around. I don't want anyone else to know that I've found it. I read some stuff about hanging out with guys so maybe I'll find out about her old boyfriends. She was a teenager when she had me so I hope she wrote something about that."

They giggled. It was hard to even imagine your own mother having a boyfriend. "But wait — getting back to boyfriends — you never answered my question. Aren't you scared you might get pregnant?" Abby asked.

Sarah picked up some stray kernels of popcorn and absentmindedly threw them one by one into the bowl as she collected her thoughts. "Maybe I'm a little scared, but you know if I did get pregnant, it would still be okay. Josh is crazy about me and I'm crazy about him, so I know we'd be together no matter what." Sarah looked up at Abby with a dreamy look on her face, her hands clasped in front of her chest, totally enraptured by the thought of it.

"You're crazy. You're only 16!" Abby was shocked to hear her friend talking this way. She took a whack at Sarah's shoulder to show how serious this was and continued. "And if it actually did happen, he'd probably run like a scared rabbit."

"Well, I think you're wrong. Besides, we do use condoms when we have them," Sarah said.

"You mean you've had sex *without* one?" Abby was feeling more and more exasperated with the conversation. She was genuinely concerned for her friend and was also having trouble processing the idea that Sarah had already had sex and she hadn't, as though she had broken their unspoken agreement of learning about everything together. And now she was feeling even more pressure, because Sarah was making it sound like sex was the most casual thing in the world, and as far as she was concerned, it most certainly wasn't. She had a wish to have sex, and yet she still wasn't sure that Tyson was "the one," and maybe that was why she was so nervous about it. At least now she had someone she could talk to about it.

"Sure, maybe once or twice. We didn't even know we were going to actually do it the first time. Everybody knows those things aren't foolproof, anyway. They break sometimes, too."

Abby didn't know what to say, but one thing she knew for sure was that the last thing she wanted for Sarah was for her to get pregnant now. It would ruin her life. Heck, it would ruin *their* lives.

Abby sat up on her knees and leaned in to look her friend right in the eyes, her mood suddenly serious.

"Promise me — from now on you'll *always* use a condom — and better yet, go on the pill. *Promise me!* We have way too many things to do before you or I start having babies!"

"Okay, I promise." And they put their palms together in affirmation.

Abby put her hands on her face and shook her head back and forth. "Jeez, Sarah, you've had sex with a guy!"

"Yes. I. Have!" Sarah responded and they broke into another fit of giggles.

"Okay, I have to get my head around all of this ... I want to know about Josh, and where you met him, and ..." She put her hands up to her forehead as though it were bursting. "I have *way* too many questions!"

Sarah fanned a collection of old movies in front of Abby's face to change the subject.

"So, maybe it's time for a movie, then? What's it going to be? *Dirty Dancing* or *Grease*?

Abby picked up the pillow and grabbed it to her chest, like she was dancing with someone, and dramatically pointed to *Dirty Dancing*.

"Oh, Patrick, you're so dreamy!" she crooned and they fell back onto the pillows, laughing hysterically.

Chapter 19

Maggie wondered, not for the first time, why such a rambling house had only one bathroom. She was sure it wasn't an issue for Gil, who lived in the house on her own with Mr. Jack as her main visitor. It became a problem when you had a house full of women. The number of females had increased to four now that she had arrived, and some days that was a challenge. It was also a problem if you had to go to the bathroom and someone was already in there. Maggie could still picture her brother Danny jumping up and down in the hallway yelling "Hurry up" to whoever was behind the closed door. It wasn't so funny when you were the one waiting. Maggie had seen many versions of the bathroom dance.

Maggie had tiptoed up the hardwood stairs as quietly as she could, not wanting to disturb the girls in Abby's room. Abby and Sarah were having a sleepover and the talking and laughing hadn't stopped since Sarah had arrived. She could hear the girls whispering and giggling between themselves. What she wouldn't do for Abby to have this kind of friendship back in Ontario. Everyone deserved a girlfriend that you could rely on. And then she realized that her best friend Val lived in Nova Scotia too. She wondered if there was something in a Bluenoser's blood that made them stick together like family.

It had warmed her heart to hear them talking about everything under the sun, from boys to books, from school to movies. Maybe Sarah would be the person to offer Abby a different perspective on her boyfriend. As she turned to enter the bathroom, though, the word "pregnant" snuck out through the crack in the door like a snake. Maggie covered her mouth in shock and leaned in a little closer to try to hear what the hell they were talking about. She could only hear snippets without giving herself away. The floorboard creaked under her foot as she tried to back up quietly to the bathroom. The conversation stopped dead and Maggie knew she'd been caught. She quickly flushed the toilet to cover her tracks, then knocked on the bedroom door and nonchalantly said hello to the girls. She wouldn't be hearing the end of that conversation.

Maggie had made her way back down the stairs, noisily emphasizing her departure. How long would she have to wait before she could realistically go to the bathroom again without raising suspicion? What a dumb idea that had been. She plunked herself back down on the sofa and turned off the TV. She glanced over at the liquor cabinet and decided a drink would go nicely right about now. A lone bottle of Cabernet Sauvignon sat amongst the vodka and whisky bottles. She uncorked the bottle and made a mental note to pick up some more wine next time she was in town. Her mother had never been much of a drinker: the other bottles were clearly more to Mr. Jack's tastes. She took a satisfying sip and sat back down on the couch, mulling over what she had just heard. This only confirmed what she had thought after reading Abby's journal. She needed to be here to keep an eye on Abby.

Maybe she'd give Alice, Sarah's mother, a call and just have a little chat. After all, she might want to keep an eye on Sarah too.

She rubbed between her eyes, and tried to shake the bad feeling she had. Why would the word "pregnant" come up in their conversation? Did Sarah think she was pregnant? Or, God forbid, Abby? Was it possible? Should she ask Abby about it? This was not the time for a wait-and-see attitude. But surely she was jumping to conclusions? The house was quiet except for the murmur of voices from upstairs. It went against every nerve in Maggie's body to not sneak back up and listen to what they were saying. She tried to push it out of her mind, knowing she couldn't do anything about it tonight. She turned the TV back on and snuggled into the couch, rubbing Jeopardy with one hand and holding her wine in the other.

Chapter 20

The church basement was desperately hot. The room was filled with people, mostly teenagers, who worked tirelessly despite the sweltering heat. Air conditioning was an unknown entity in old rural churches. Tables were lined up in the centre of the room lengthwise, and stacks of paper were piled periodically all the way down both sides. The chairs had all been pushed back against the walls so that everyone could stand and work efficiently at their spots. They folded and stacked flyers until they looked like accordions, their eyes glazed from the monotony and daydreaming of a quick dip in the ocean across the street. As the piles got bigger, someone else would come and slide them back together into a neat pile, elasticize them and deposit them neatly in the boxes near the doors. Everyone had a job to do, with the youngest helpers, usually younger siblings who were being babysat, in charge of making sure the water jugs stayed full.

Penny had been working on the project with Mr. Jack for the past week. He was one of the supervisors and every morning he arrived bright and early to pick her up and head off to the church, and every night she came home full of stories of what they had done that day. Only Penny could make work sound like fun, but she often mentioned one particular boy who was always there. After a few days, Abby couldn't stand it anymore. After all, what did she have to lose? Penny told her about a community meeting where the project manager was going to outline the project, while drumming up more support. It seemed like the perfect opportunity to check things out without being too obvious.

The meeting had been in the church basement, people fanning themselves with their programs to create a bit of air movement in the stifling basement. Abby had sat in the front row with Sarah, Penny and Mr. Jack, listening intently. Abby had had no idea the beaches had reached such a desperate state and the news had brought her to tears. The boy sitting behind Abby had noticed her crying and had leaned forward to offer her a Kleenex. She was embarrassed and pleased at the same time, and when she had turned to thank him, her heart had literally skipped a beat. His longish blond hair could only be described as tousled and messy, like he had just come back from a swim and hadn't bothered to comb it. He reminded her of a rock star, and the way he had looked at her with those piercing grey eyes made her catch her breath.

"I'm Jake," he said softly. "It was in my jeans pocket but it's clean."

"No problem. Thanks! I'm Abby and this is my friend Sarah," Abby said.

"Hey. It's great that you came. It looks like we have a really great turnout. How did you hear about it?" Jake asked.

"Oh, my Grandma Gil is good friends with Mr. Jack here. He has been an ocean activist his entire life, right, Mr. Jack?" Abby asked.

"I guess you could say that!" he chuckled and they

had continued listening to the presentation.

Abby had been appalled when the speaker described the rotting garbage that floated up onto the beaches and into the docks at the Harbourfront every day. Not only was it a disgusting sight, but it was also polluting the waters, and harming the natural wildlife that lived in the waters. Certain beaches had become infested with bacteria that discouraged swimming. Abby just couldn't imagine her beloved beaches becoming black and spoiled to the point where she wouldn't even be able to go swimming. It would be disastrous. As soon as Abby and Sarah had heard how serious the problem was, they had gone to the back of the church to sign up. Voices bantered back and forth about the problem, the list of names filling page after page, as though everyone in the room had volunteered. The enthusiasm had been contagious.

Ever since that night they had been out to the church every other day to fold flyers and help with anything else that needed to be done, and a couple of afternoons they would head into downtown Halifax and pass out information at the waterfront. They had met lots of other kids their age and lately spent their free time together, too. Suddenly Abby couldn't imagine a better way of spending her summer, especially since Jake had come into the picture. She was amazed at how easily they had become friends. It seemed that every time Abby found a spot to work from, Jake would end up across from her as if by magic, and they would spend much of their time stealing glances at each other. Every so often a pamphlet would turn into a paper airplane heading right for her head. It broke the monotony until someone coaxed them back to work, laughing all the while. Jake was always up to something, making it hard for them to continue working.

Abby and Jake sat on the fallen-down tree trunk, surveying the ocean as they licked their cones. They were taking an afternoon break and had gotten an ice cream at the Tastee Freez truck that was parked close to the beach. The cold ice cream was refreshing after being in the stuffy basement, but their cones were melting so quickly they had trouble licking them fast enough to keep them from dripping.

Jake pointed over towards the water. "Check out that pelican!"

Abby turned quickly to look and as she did, Jake zeroed in to bite off the top of her chocolate dip cone.

"I don't see ... Hey! You can't do that!"

"Why not? All is fair in love and ice cream."

She just couldn't get mad at him. He was such a joker. All day long he would be telling jokes that would have them all in stitches. Most were ones he had made up himself and they were so bad that it made them laugh even harder. Just yesterday he had been telling a fairly long, involved story and everyone had stopped what they were doing to listen. Mr. Jack had come over to see if anything was wrong and made Jake start the joke over so he would know what it was about. Before long everyone was hanging onto his every word, and then they groaned in unison when he reached the punchline. He was a great guy to be around. Abby started laughing again.

"What now?" Jake asked innocently.

"You have chocolate all over your face now. Serves you right!" She was barely able to squeeze the words out.

"Want to lick it off for me?" he half-teased, but proceeded to wipe his face with the napkins she offered, watching her through his messy bangs.

Abby blushed and lowered her eyes. Tyson never said things like that. It made her feel shy and attractive at the same time. They were interrupted by others from the church also looking for refreshments, lining up one by one in the intense heat. Penny plopped down beside Abby, licking away voraciously, like a dog on a fresh bone.

"Hey, take it easy, kiddo," Abby said.

"I know." Penny attempted to talk between licks. "I just" — *lick* — "don't want" — *lick* — "it to melt" — *lick* — "all over me." They all nodded in agreement and then Penny stopped licking long enough to laugh and point at Abby and Jake.

"You two should see yourselves. You're so cute. You look like teddy bears with little black noses. Maybe you should stick to plain cones next time." Abby and Jake rubbed their noses at the same time and their hands came away sticky with chocolate.

"It looks like we might have a good excuse to take a dip in the ocean before we have to go back to work!" Jake said. He was off, making a run for the beach.

For the first time ever, Abby wasn't embarrassed to have food all over her face. In fact it had actually been fun. Everything about Jake was fun. Abby felt she could be herself and Jake would still like her. They talked about anything and everything: school, parents, what they wanted to do with their lives after school, and Abby was surprised at how easy it was. Jake had her talking about things she had never dreamed she would share with anyone else, like he was opening a clamshell to find the pearl inside for the first time. It felt pretty darn good. She watched him run across the beach, his hair blowing wildly in the wind.

"So, you like him, huh?" a voice spoke beside her.

In her daydreaming she had forgotten that Penny was still sitting there, finishing her ice cream. She looked at Penny and hesitated for only a split second.

"Yeah, kiddo. I really do," Abby said, breaking into a big smile.

"Well, I think he's pretty cool, too."

And if Penny thought so, it definitely counted for something and Abby took off running after him.

Chapter 21

Maggie surveyed herself in the old, slightly frosted bedroom mirror over the dresser. It was a bit of a challenge putting on makeup when parts of your face were hazy, but she was tired of the interruptions in the single bathroom. She dabbed on a little extra mascara and ran a brush through her hair. She and Val had decided to catch a movie and go out for a drink afterwards. She glanced around, looking for her sweater, and chuckled to herself. There was that old adage when you lived on the East Coast: "Always bring a sweater." She still lived by that mantra. The phrase had been so ingrained that she always took along a sweater when she went out. Her friends in Ontario would tease her ruthlessly about it, saying that the temperature wasn't likely to drop very much in the middle of a heat wave. She'd just smile and say "You never know," and bring it along anyway.

There was a loud knock on the screen door and Maggie glanced at her watch. She wasn't expecting Val for another hour. Maybe she had changed her mind about dropping by for a drink before they left. Maggie couldn't imagine who else it could be, since her mother rarely received unexpected visitors. She ran down the stairs and tugged hard on the inside door. The humidity wreaked havoc with anything made of wood and it was giving Maggie a workout every time. She pushed open the screen door to let Val inside, and looked into a face she hadn't seen in more than 16 years. Maggie gasped and her hand flew to her mouth

Treading Water

as she tried to find her voice.

"Oh, my God. Rick?"

He smiled his winning smile as though no time had passed. Maggie's legs were shaking beneath her but she somehow managed to maintain her composure. All these years she had imagined this moment and now she could hardly believe her eyes. She could feel the colour rising to her cheeks. She certainly hadn't expected this. He hadn't changed much, perhaps a few more laugh lines, but his deep grey eyes still held her gaze as if she were in an undertow with no hope of catching air. But what was most distracting was his head. There wasn't a hair on it. Gone was the bleached blond mop from his lifeguarding days, replaced with a smooth, very touchable-looking bald head. Fine lines parenthesized his mouth and his dimples still showed when he smiled. Damn, he looked good. She self-consciously tucked her hair neatly behind her ear and tried to catch her breath. It dawned on her how his looks were such a stark contrast to Glen's. Glen was someone who made her feel safe, with his deep brown eyes and scruffy goatee. She had chosen safe because she had needed safe. And now here was Rick, standing right in front of her, looking edgy and, well, dangerous.

She stared at him and then turned away, unsure of what to do next. She couldn't remember ever being in a situation that had caught her so totally off guard. He had some nerve, just showing up here unannounced. And yet she had always wondered what had truly happened between them; she'd wished things had turned out differently. Now here he was at her door, looking just as good as he had all those years ago.

"What the hell are you doing here?"

She crossed her arms and frowned with all the seriousness she could muster, while inside her stomach was turning and twisting. She tucked her hair behind her ear again, and shoved her hands into her jeans, trying to hide the shaking, and waited for him to say something. She glanced around nervously, praying her mother wouldn't appear out of nowhere. She wasn't sure she could handle that confrontation.

He ignored her question totally and just grinned at her. He still had that wicked grin that made her weak at the knees. She leaned against the door frame for support. She wouldn't exactly impress him if she collapsed on the spot. She had to sit down. She stepped outside, pulling the heavy door shut behind her, and sat down on one of the big wicker chairs on the porch. Rick sat in the chair opposite her, leaning forward on his elbows, as confident as ever.

"You look great, Maggie — you really haven't changed a bit."

He grinned at her in that intrusive way, looking relaxed and comfortable, and "cool as a cucumber," as her mother would have said. If someone were watching this scene, she thought, they would think their conversation was the most normal thing in the world, and yet the tension was as thick as a Nova Scotia fog.

Maggie really wasn't sure what to say. She was still so shocked by his appearance from out of nowhere that she couldn't stop looking at him. Here he was in the flesh. All these years, she had tried to conjure up that beautiful tanned face, with the white paste on his nose to prevent sunburn and the straw-like tousled hair. Every time she had tried to visualize him, she just couldn't do it. It seemed a lifetime ago and her memory of him had vanished just as quickly as he had. In one sense she was still trying to put that time behind her, and in another it nearly broke her heart to think about him.

"You know, Rick — I really don't think it's a good idea for you to be here. Mom's just in the side garden and ..." Her mother wouldn't be too happy to find this man on her front porch. She'd as likely shoot him on the spot and worry about the consequences later. As far as Gil was concerned, it was Rick's fault that she and Maggie had developed a rift between them, never mind how it had changed all of their lives.

"I was hoping we could grab a coffee together — you know — try to catch up?"

He raised his eyebrows in cheerful anticipation, as though he had just asked her to go to the fair. Maggie couldn't believe how nonchalant he was being. Grab a coffee, like it was something they did every day. But this was her chance to talk to him, to somehow make some sense of what had happened. She paused, not making eye contact, playing with the fringe on her sweater, knowing she might never get this opportunity again.

"I guess that would be fine — nice, actually — sure." She worked up the nerve to look at him again.

Her cheeks flushed. She had given in, as she knew she would, but she felt she deserved some answers to the questions that had been sneaking into her thoughts when she least expected it over the past 16 years.

"But you really need to go before I have to start explaining ..." Maggie glanced worriedly to the side of the house again, dreading the thought of her mother seeing him. "Oh, but when?" Maggie asked.

"When what? Coffee? I don't know — tomorrow? 10:30?"

"I already have plans for tomorrow. How about the day after?"

"Great. How about I meet you at Perks at the waterfront? At 10:30, then?"

"Sure. That sounds good." She pulled her eyes away for fear of agreeing to anything more. She wanted him to leave now.

"Okay, I'll see you then." Without another word, he turned and sauntered back to the car. Maggie stepped onto the porch steps to watch the white rental car turn around and follow the grassy track back up to the main road. Maggie didn't hear Gil coming up behind her and she almost jumped out of her skin when Gil spoke.

"Who was that? I don't recognize the car," Gil said, putting on her glasses for a better look.

"Oh just someone looking for the beach cottages," Maggie answered more calmly than she felt.

Chapter 22

There was nothing like the smell of coffee brewing, especially on a cool summer morning. Abby went to the pantry to find her favourite mug, the one with the seagulls on it, and wondered what treats might be suitable for breakfast. GG was always baking and everything she made was to die for. The funny thing was that she never put anything where you would expect to find it; her fudge was often in the fruit drawer of the fridge, and, as was the case now, the bread bin held some freshly made butter tarts. GG always hid the cookie tins in the bottom drawer of the pantry, but as kids they had figured that out right away, as it was the only treat spot they could actually reach. Abby opened the tarts and a waft of sugary sweetness met her nose. She inhaled deeply. She pulled out a tart and savoured the first bite, its syrupy stickiness dripping onto her chin.

Abby had been thinking about her mother's diary ever since she had found it under the floorboards. She'd barely had any time to read it, short of the few pages she had flipped through before bed last night. She had planned to read into the wee hours, her flashlight ready in case anyone might see her light, but she had been so tired she had fallen asleep with the book on her chest. She had been so angry with herself she had made up her mind to find a secluded spot to continue this morning. She'd been so busy with the project the last few days that she hadn't even been home and when she was, she had been accused of being anti-social when she went up to her room to read. The coffee pot started gurgling and Abby popped the rest of the tart in her mouth, licking her fingers clean of every last morsel. She grabbed her towel, wrapping the diary inside, and tucked it under her arm. She took her coffee and headed for the beach, a quick bark reminding her that Jep refused to be left behind. She smiled at his eagerness, and held the door open for him to follow.

Abby and Jep looked like they were heading out on an adventure: Abby trudging along the path towards the beach, and Jep scampering ahead to lead the way. Abby cradled the blanket and diary close to her chest as she followed Jep down the steep incline. She remembered the day they had found Jep, and it was lucky for him they had. The whole family had been sitting on the front porch, fanning themselves with any piece of cardboard they could find, to try to take the edge off the heat. It had been desperately hot and they were all lounging around in various degrees of laziness when they heard mewing sounds. Penny, never missing a beat, sprang off the swing to investigate. Abby had spotted something moving at the water's edge that looked like rats, but the sounds suggested otherwise. They made their way down the rocky trail to the beach and as they got closer Abby had discovered they were puppies. Two of the scrawny bodies were hardly moving but one was still mewing loudly, begging to be rescued. Their tiny paws were tangled in seaweed, and the incoming tide doused their tiny faces. Jep had turned his little snout upward to try to get away from the water but the effort was proving too much even for him. Her mother had scooped him up easily and tucked him inside her T-shirt for warmth. Her mom had done everything in her power to nurse Jeopardy back to health and now, almost eight years later, he was still going strong. Abby remembered her mother crying when they had found him. She had said he reminded her of Stinker, the dog she'd had as a teenager. Abby reminded herself to ask her mom more about him.

"You would have made a great sailor dog, Jep," Abby said, giving him an affectionate scratch behind the ears, before he took off at full speed for the waves. "You were born with sea legs."

Abby found a spot just out of the wind in a little alcove of dune grass, and out of sight from the bluff. A large piece of driftwood served as a bench, and she wrapped the towel around her shoulders to fend off the early-morning chill. This is sweet justice, she thought to herself as she gazed at the cover of the diary. She felt as though her mom always needed to be one up on her, and now she might learn something that she could use as ammunition against her. Jep was already amusing himself trying to outwit the waves. Abby shivered, watching him, and gently flipped to a random page.

Dear Diary,

We went over to Val's place after lunch. It was so stinking hot we went down to the lake to go swimming. When we walk through the small brush of trees at the end of her street and down the embankment, we come out at the cove down by Chocolate Lake. Cindy came with us and we spread our towels out on the rocks to catch a few rays. And then you'll never guess who showed up! Tim, Mike and Glen! I almost died to see Glen there. I guess the guys hang out there a lot because they all live close. We started off not saying a whole lot, and me sucking in my tummy the whole time. The guys were in cut-offs so they just threw off their shirts and jumped in. We didn't want to just jump right in after them like we were part of their group or anything, but we wanted to! Tim swam over to me and splashed me so I'm totally soaked and my towel too! He says — Aren't you guys coming in? I said — Why bother, I'm already all wet! (I thought that was a pretty good comeback.) Next thing I know Glen is pulling Cindy into the water. I couldn't believe she let him do that when she knows I like him, but I guess it wasn't her fault. The guys had inner tubes so we all jumped on and started having water fights. Somehow I ended up on the one with Tim so I tried to paddle closer to the one with Glen and Cindy on it. We started splashing each other so much I could hardly see. Next thing I know the whole thing flipped and the tire came down on my head. By the time I came up, Glen & Cindy were in the water. We all started scrambling to get back into a tube, and when I looked up through the hole, Glen was sitting on the edge of the one I'm in, grinning down at me. "C'mon, hurry up, let's get them back," he says. He reached down to help me up and the next thing I know he reached into my bathing suit top and he's got his hand on my boob! I know it wasn't an accident because he squeezed my nipple before he gave me his other hand. When I looked at Glen he just grinned and started paddling. Yikes, what does this mean? Do you think he might actually like me?

It sounded like something she might have written herself, although she hated to admit it. It was hard to imagine her mother being so young. And here she was reading about her dad, too. How many people could say that they knew details about the first time their parents started going out together? She flipped a little further to another entry ...

Dear Diary,

Glen asked me if I wanted to go bike riding after school today. He's so CUTE. It's weird too that we've been going to school together all these years and now he wants to hang out with me! We went over to his house, had a snack and then took off on the bikes. We biked all around Armdale, up and down streets that I had never even been on before and ended up back at Chocolate Lake. We went down to the water and sat on the boulders. I was so nervous. He put his hand on my bare leg and I thought I was going to jump out of my skin. We both turned to talk at the same time and our faces were really close. He looked into my eyes and I thought he might try to kiss me. I think I might have died on the spot if he did. I had never been so close to him before. He kept looking at me and I started to get all hot so I just had to look away. He held my hand and I thought I was going to melt. I might never wash that hand again!

Yvonne Leslie

It felt strange to be reading about her mother's intimate thoughts. Abby double-checked the dates and figured out that Maggie would have been 16 when she wrote this diary. The same age as Abby was now, go figure. How many people ever stopped to think about what their parents were like as teenagers? It was cool and creepy at the same time. Wondering what else she might find out, she took a sip of her now-cold coffee and started at the beginning ...

Chapter 23

Maggie loved wandering along the waterfront and after Rick's impromptu appearance, being near the water helped to clear her head. It felt good to be somewhere familiar. She walked along the pier and glanced down at the seaweed tangled up in rubbery-looking bunches, slapping against the dock with the ebb and flow of the tide. Tourists sat in the outdoor cafes enjoying lobster dipped in melted butter and a nice cold Moosehead beer. The seagulls soared against a brilliant blue sky, crying loudly for an opportunity to zoom in on some of the food scraps. And there was the familiar stench of sea salt and low tide that only a true Maritimer could appreciate. Maggie breathed in deeply, savouring it all.

She had spent the morning on her own, poking around the shops at the Historic Properties and now made her way up towards the ferry terminal with the intention of grabbing a coffee. It was a perfect day for sitting on the pier and watching the sailboats communing with the wind. Who knew? If she sat there long enough she might even run into somebody she knew. The waterfront was busy with tourists, cameras ready, and the hint of sunburns starting to appear. It was deceiving being down by the water where there was always a breeze. Even on the hottest days it was easy to forget that the sun was still beating down on your skin. Maggie was glad she had splurged for a sun hat. She wasn't typically a hat person, but her fair skin seemed to burn more easily these days, and it just wasn't a pretty sight. The hat didn't look half bad. It gave her a kind of jaunty look.

She heard the blast of the *Haligonian II* announcing its arrival at the ferry dock from Dartmouth. A flock of people scuttled across the platform and dispersed in various directions. The waterfront was the hub of activity for Halifax, especially during the summer months, and most days there was some form of entertainment to enjoy. It might be a Scottish piper wailing on his bagpipes, street performers busking in hopes of a tip, or artisans selling their crafts. Maggie noticed some activity near the terminal and made her way over to have a look. There was a large display of billboards indicating all of the beaches along the South and North shores, the names instantly familiar: Blandford, Fox Point, Hubbards, Queensland; and heading north, Lawrencetown, Cow Bay and Martinique. Some of her favourite memories took place on these beaches.

She remembered going to the annual lifeguard competitions at Queensland Beach. The lifeguards from all of the beaches would compete. Rick worked at the YMCA during the winter and at the waterfront beaches in the summer. You had to be extremely fit and Maggie had felt like she was drowning herself as she watched them perform rescues in the frigid surf. The challenges were intense. Her heart swelled, watching Rick's strong arms bring someone to safety. Afterwards there were parties on the beach and at the lifeguard house. The lifeguards had rented a tired-looking cottage where they stayed when the weather turned bad. She laughed, remembering one time when so many people had been leaning against the rickety porch railing that it had snapped and everyone had fallen backwards off the deck. Luckily no one had been hurt.

She was pulled out of her reverie by voices shouting "Mom!" She turned to see her daughters running toward her, beaming excitedly. They each grabbed an arm and dragged her over to the displays. The tables were covered with an array of garbage and bottles of dark liquids. Maggie couldn't make any sense of what they were showing her. What did this have to do with the beaches she had been looking at earlier?

"What's all this?" she asked.

"This is our project!" they both exclaimed together. "We're so glad you came by to check it out! We've been waiting to show you."

"Your project?" Maggie hadn't realized that it was so important.

"Yeah, you know, Mom, the Save the Harbour project. We've been helping Mr. Jack with it since we got here," Penny piped up.

"Of course! *This* is what you've been doing?" Maggie took a closer look at the display on the table and quickly realized that it showed the future of their beaches. The beaches they all loved so much. How could she have been so stupid? "I had no idea that what you were doing involved coming into town and approaching the public," Maggie said.

"We're trying to educate people about the

potential problems with the beaches if we don't take action now," Abby said, her face both serious and excited at the same time. This was a different Abby. One that Maggie hadn't seen before. She liked what she was seeing. "It's been really interesting and fun too. And we've made so many friends. It's been a blast. We're doing a good thing getting the word out."

"Plus, we get to hang out by the waterfront! This is where the action is!" Penny beamed. Her freckles were really starting to show after spending so much time outside. She looked healthy and happy. Penny loved being the centre of activity and if she had a cause that she could share, all the better. Maggie was starting to see more of herself in her girls, and wondered whatever had happened to her own enthusiasm and zest for life. It was like she had left it all behind on the beach when she moved away, like pieces of stranded driftwood, waiting to be found and turned into something worthwhile.

"We should be getting back, Mom. Mr. Jack will be looking for us. He makes sure we stay close, Grandma's orders. Thanks for coming to check it out!" and they were off again.

Maggie had to laugh. At least someone was keeping an eye on them. She'd make a point of getting some more details over supper tonight. Maggie knew the girls had been working on a project that Mr. Jack was involved in and had pretty much left that up to him. She was happy that they had something else to occupy their time besides going to the beach every day. It would keep them, especially Abby, out of trouble.

But she had to admit she had only been half paying attention when they had told her about it. She hadn't realized what a big deal it was to them.

It was encouraging to see Abby looking so confident and excited about something. It could only be a good thing for her to develop her self-esteem a little. Maggie took a closer look at the rest of the displays before continuing on to get her coffee. The project was well represented, the displays clearly outlining the issues and potential changes and the tables full of information that apparently her girls had helped to produce. Maggie picked up a flyer to read with her coffee. She waved at the girls again and as she turned away, she saw a face that literally made her stop in her tracks. Every time she came back to Halifax, she felt that everyone she saw looked like someone she knew. She would often find herself looking more closely at a face, thinking it was someone she had gone to school with, but of course it never turned out to be that person. She'd been away far too long for that to happen, but she had always hoped. She really had to stop looking at everyone as though they might be familiar to her. But this young man, who was animatedly passing out information flyers to passersby, looked disturbingly familiar. She glanced over at him again and shook her head as she walked away. It wasn't possible. She must be crazy.

Chapter 24

Abby couldn't remember when she had enjoyed herself so much. They had been working on the Save the Harbour project several days a week, depending on the opportunities and jobs that needed to be done. Sarah had decided to stick with it, too. She was glad to be busy while Josh was away so she wouldn't miss him so much. At first Abby wasn't sure if she wanted to spend her summer working, but once they got involved, it didn't feel like work at all. They had both made new friends and when they weren't at the church, they were hanging out together, at the beach or the mall on their off-days. Abby didn't even mind that she was spending her days with her little sister. She had to admit Penny was a good kid. She was pretty sharp and had a real knack for keeping the younger kids focused on what they were doing. Penny was right in her element.

And of course there was Jake. Abby had to give her sister Penny full marks for picking out the good ones. Jake was funny and easy to talk to, and she was pretty sure he liked her. Yesterday they had been in one of the classrooms together, packing up all the components for the displays. At one point they were packing the box and they bumped into each other. Jake had carried on working as if nothing had happened, but when Abby glanced at him she could see that he was still grinning. She tried to hide the fact that she was blushing, but inside she was bursting with happiness.

Today they were back in the assembly line again, folding more flyers for distribution. They didn't mind this job at all, because it gave them all a chance to talk together while they worked. Jake stood beside Abby and they had been rubbing elbows all afternoon. It was an interesting coincidence how Jake always managed to position himself either beside her or across from her, but Abby wasn't complaining. Sometimes they were so close she could smell his lemony shampoo and she loved inhaling the clean scent of it.

"Hey, do you think you would like to go see a movie with me one night?" Jake asked. He leaned over to put some more flyers into the box at their feet, and Abby's heart skipped a beat.

"Sure, that would be great. Our only problem is getting into town."

"Do you think your Grandma would mind if you asked for the car?"

GG was pretty good about letting Abby use the car, but she had to have a good reason. She wouldn't just let Abby take it whenever she wanted, but she'd been allowed to use it to get to the church, and a couple of times to bring supplies down to the waterfront.

"I'm not sure going to a movie with you would be a good enough reason for GG." Abby wasn't sure she could talk GG into letting her use the car in the evening, especially if she was going to go out with a boy. She knew she had to figure out a different way to make this work. She really wanted to go out with Jake without all these other people around. Suddenly her face lit up. "What about if we tell her we need it for the project again?" Abby asked.

"Well, maybe we could do both — that way you wouldn't really be lying about why you need the car, and we'd be helping out at the same time. We could deliver the display unit to the museum and then head out to the movie after that," Jake reiterated, obviously pleased with his plan.

"That's a great idea. I'll try to get Mr. Jack onside too, that will help. GG's a real softie when it comes to doing stuff for Mr. Jack." Abby waved over to Mr. Jack who returned her wave and started walking in their direction.

"Hey kids, how's it going? We're keeping you hard at it, are we?" Mr. Jack wiped his forehead with the back of his hand, but within seconds he was sweating again. "This darn heat is really taking the wind out of my sails today," he chuckled.

Mr. Jack was one of those people who wasn't afraid of hard work, doing whatever needed to be done, and never complaining about the heat. The past few days he'd been working outside cutting the wood for the displays, so he was getting some fresh air, but the sun was still hot and the air was sticky. He had a good farmer's tan, his face and neck brown and leathery and the white of his chest just visible below his collar. He always had a smile on his face, and took the time to share a joke with anyone who stopped to chat. Abby couldn't ever remember seeing Mr. Jack unhappy or upset. She was glad GG had him as her friend. She felt a twinge of guilt for coercing him into their plan to get the car.

"Yeah, it's pretty hot but we're actually having fun. In fact, we were going to offer to take the displays in to the museum for the exhibit tomorrow, if that would help? Maybe we could drop them off tonight?" Abby asked.

"Sure, that would be swell. That way everything will be all set up and ready when the others arrive to work the booth. That'll save 'em some time and work tomorrow morning," said Mr. Jack.

"Do you think GG would let me use the car so we could look after it ourselves?" Abby asked. She tried to keep her voice nonchalant but was sure her eagerness was written all over her face. She bent down to rearrange the flyers in case he got wise to their plan.

"Well, that would certainly relieve me of the trip. I'm feeling pretty tuckered out. I'll put in a good word for you, how's that?" Mr. Jack laughed, knowingly. "I'm just heading out myself. I'll give you a lift home, shall I?"

"Sure, Mr. Jack. Thanks! That way we can grab a bite to eat, get the car and come right back to load everything up," Abby said.

Mr. Jack slowly made his way up the stairs. "Hmmm, maybe I can wrangle a bite of something to eat for myself," he chuckled. Abby and Jake followed him up the stairs and gave each other a high-five.

"Mission accomplished," whispered Jake.

Chapter 25

Maggie gripped the steering wheel to keep her hands from shaking. She hadn't been this nervous since her last job interview, but this was hardly the same thing. Her hands were clammy and her stomach felt like she was on a ship in rough seas, flipping and turning every time she thought about Rick. On the one hand she was excited to see him, but on the other, she was scared to death of being close to him again. She shook her head, remembering the other night and how shocked she had been when she opened the door to see him standing there. She certainly hadn't seen that coming, even though she may have wished it a million times. Once she had gotten over the initial shock, she was surprised at the way he had made her feel. She hadn't expected him to still have an effect on her. After all, she wasn't a teenager anymore. So much had changed since then, but apparently some things hadn't. She was going to have to get a grip on herself before she got to the coffee shop. If she was lucky she might still have some Gravol in her purse from the flight.

Despite her anxiousness, Maggie thoroughly enjoyed the drive, the fresh air filling her lungs. The sky was a brilliant blue accented with puffy cotton-ball clouds. She rolled the window all the way down, catching a whiff of the sea as she followed the winding road along the shoreline heading into town. The wind and humidity weren't doing her hair any favours; stray curls and frizz were just visible out of the corner of her eye. Hopefully she'd have time to do a quick fix-up when she got there.

By the time she reached the waterfront, she had calmed down considerably and she was lucky enough to find a parking space one block away from the ferry terminal. She considered this to be a good omen and made her way to the coffee shop. A wave of cool air hit her as she entered the coffee shop, a welcome reprieve from the humidity. No Rick in sight, she headed straight for the restroom to survey her hair and makeup. She brushed it out gently, tucking the loose ends behind her ears, and applied a touch of pink lipstick. It didn't look as good as when Val had styled it, but it was better than usual. She smiled when she saw the retro flask peeking out from the bottom of her purse. That would help to calm her down a bit. Happy with the results, she went back out to find a seat.

She grabbed herself a cup of coffee and found a spot at the window so she could see him coming. She discreetly added a shot of Baileys to her cup. The combination of coffee and liquor was calming and she relaxed a little as she turned her gaze to the waterfront.

A flutter of panic seized her again as she scanned the faces of people walking by. Was she really going to go through with this? Rick had really caught her off guard by showing up like that. How had he even known that she was in town? She briefly contemplated leaving when suddenly there he was, walking briskly as always, across the promenade. Wearing a dark grey suit that looked pressed and crisp despite the heat, he stood out amidst the crowd of tourists in bright-coloured T-shirts. Rick had always been the confident, assertive type. She remembered the way their friends responded to him when they went to parties. He would pat his friends on the back like a politician working the room. The girls also anticipated his attention, and if they were among the lucky ones, he'd lean in and bite their earlobes — his signature move for the girls he liked. Always the charmer, she thought, as she took another swig of coffee and tried to keep her hands still. He spotted her at the window and waved casually as he strode over to the entrance. Maggie was thankful she was sitting down. How was she ever going to carry on a normal conversation with him?

"Hey, how are you? Good to see you," he said, taking the chair beside her and running a hand over his smooth head. "Whew, it's going to be another hot one." He grinned. Maggie let her thoughts wander to thoughts of shaving her own head. Ridiculous, yes, but it would be so much simpler than fighting her hair in this muggy weather. Even with a fresh haircut, the humidity still turned her hair frizzy in no time. His voice drew her back to the conversation. She frowned, trying to understand what he was really saying to her.

"Listen, I hate to do this to you ... but I'm going to have to reschedule." He placed a hand on her arm as he spoke but when Maggie gave him a puzzled look, he quickly pulled it away. "The mayor scheduled a meeting at the last minute about this project that I'm working on. I'm sorry to make you come all the way into town for nothing. I wanted to call you, but I didn't want to risk getting your mother on the phone."

Maggie's emotions flipped from relief to

Treading Water

disappointment to anger all in the space of five seconds. She paused to hide all of those emotions before speaking. What could she say? "Oh, it's no problem. I had plans to go shopping afterwards anyway," she half-lied. It had taken every ounce of courage to actually go through with this, and now he was dumping her. How typical. But in a way she was relieved.

"Listen, could we do dinner instead? How about tomorrow night? I could pick you up at seven?" Rick leaned forward with his famous smile, waiting eagerly for her response.

Maggie felt flustered, but nodded. "Sure, that should work. I'll just need to double-check to see what the girls are doing." She should really be doing something with Penny instead of going out on her own again, but she probably had something on the go with Mr. Jack anyway.

"Well, if anything comes up, you can give me a call. Here's my business card." And he was gone.

She finished the last of her coffee and absent-mindedly turned the business card over. It read:

Rick Morrison
Consulting Engineer
Save the Harbour
ENVIRO Industries
Ottawa, ON

She drew her breath in sharply. Wasn't that the name of the project Abby and Penny were working on with Mr. Jack? Did that mean that Abby was working on the same project with Rick? The idea of that was more than she could handle. She knew she would have to tell Abby about Rick sooner or later, but she wasn't prepared to explain things now. She and Glen had agreed to tell her the circumstances around her birth when she was older, but when was that, exactly? It was something they kept meaning to do but somehow they just never got around to it. Up to now, there had been no urgency to tell her and Maggie had needed to move on and forget.

But she had never really forgotten.

Chapter 26

Abby lay on her bed, staring at the ceiling. She just wanted to be alone to think about the past few days. They had been doing a lot of preparation for the project but they didn't usually work on the weekends, so she had slept in for a change, and by the time she got up, her mom was already out. She was probably out doing something with Val again. And any day that her mom wasn't around was a day that she wasn't bugging Abby. She had been looking forward to getting away from everything, including her parents. GG was pretty good about letting Abby do what she wanted when she visited. She was so thankful that GG was the way she was. They had an understanding that as long as Abby got home when she said she would, all was good. No third degree like with her mom. She got along fine with Penny, too.

But now her mother was here, breathing down her neck like always. Abby was so frustrated. It seemed like her mother was always trying to catch her at something. And Tyson was upsetting her too. Abby never knew where she stood with him. One minute he was great and the next he was being a jerk. Between her mom and her boyfriend, life sucked.

And yet she had met Jake. Jake was an amazing guy. They'd had so much fun together at the movie last night. They had told each other jokes and had a hard time keeping their laughter under control. And then when Jake started making creatures with red licorice, Abby had thought she was going to lose it. The people sitting behind them had gotten a little annoyed but they hadn't cared. Abby couldn't remember the last time she'd felt so comfortable being with someone. It wasn't anything like the relationship she had with Tyson. When she was with Tyson, she felt like she was just tagging along, whereas with Jake, it was like they belonged together. She never realized that two people could get along so well.

Abby heard a light knock and Penny poked her curly head around the door.

"Hey," Abby said.

"Can I come in?"

"Sure." Abby sat up to make room for her sister. Penny sat cross-legged at the end of bed, grinning at her. Her cheeks were rosy and her eyes were dancing. Abby couldn't help but smile back.

"What are you grinning at?"

"Didn't you go to the movie last night? With Jake?" Penny raised her eyebrows knowingly.

"How did you know?" Abby asked. "And you better not tell Mom or she'll kill me for taking the car on a date!"

"Don't worry. Your secret is safe with me. So ... how was it?"

Abby threw herself back on the pillows and sighed.

"It was great. He's *such* a great guy."

"Did he hold your hand?" Penny asked.

"What is this? An interrogation?" Abby sat back up and wagged a finger at Penny who just giggled.

"So, is he officially your boyfriend now?"

"No, not officially, but I guess he is." Abby mulled this over for a moment. She sat up and looked Penny in the eye. "It's complicated, Penny. You're too young to understand."

"Try me. What's the problem?"

"Tyson. That's the problem."

"Well, I think it's pretty simple, actually. Why are you worried about Mr. Idiot at home when Mr. Amazing is right here?" She shrugged her shoulders as if it were the most logical thing in the world.

Abby punched the pillow and rolled over, Tyson's chain slipping out of her T-shirt to hang below her nose. She held the knot in her hand, flipped back onto her back and sighed deeply. What the heck was she supposed to make of this? One minute he forgot to call her and the next minute he wanted her all to himself. Just like a guy. She suddenly sat bolt upright on the bed, a look of determination on her face. She had made up her mind.

She left behind a startled Penny as she jumped off the bed and tore down the stairs, the screen door slamming loudly behind her. Maggie and GG both looked up to see Abby running full tilt towards the bluff, windmilling her arms at the edge to slow herself down. She took a moment to catch her breath and reached inside her shirt for the chain, her hand clasping the knot tightly in her fist. With a sharp tug, the necklace broke and came free in her hand. She looked at it one more time and hurled it into the sea before she had a chance to change her mind.

Yvonne Leslie

Chapter 27

Maggie was stunned. She looked silly in her heels, walking up the steep sidewalk to Barrington Street, and trying to make sense of what had just happened. He'd done it again — controlled the situation, controlled her, the way he always had, in his usual charming way. Damn him. She wasn't sure if she should feel upset or disappointed after his brush-off, but she did have an invite for dinner. Now that she'd had some time to think about it, she wasn't even sure if she should go. She was a nervous wreck just being close to him, how was she ever going to make it through dinner?

Chocolate always made her feel better, and she detoured to the Freak Lunchbox. She walked through the door and was immediately bombarded with every type of candy she could imagine. Kids were screaming and pointing to the largest lollipop in the stand, its swirls and bright colours enough to tempt anyone. Did anyone ever actually make it through one of those suckers in its entirety? She stood dreamily in the colourful confection of a room, pausing to reflect on what a great word lollipop was. Didn't you just want to eat something that sounded as good as it tasted? Adults exclaimed about things they had enjoyed themselves as children: Thrills gum, the one that tasted like soap — Maggie never understood why some people liked that stuff — Gold Rush gum, in a little cloth pouch that looked like a small bag of gold, licorice whips, Cracker Jacks and Pixy Stix. Maggie was in heaven. Didn't everyone want to go back to their childhood by devouring the sweets they had loved as a child? They obviously did, because the store was packed with people walking around with baskets of memories.

Maggie could have easily bought everything in the store with the mood she was in, but settled on some Jelly Belly jelly beans, Penny's favourite; some red licorice for Abby; and threw in some licorice allsorts for her mother. She chose a Peanut Butter Cup for herself. That will go nicely with the bit of Baileys I have left, she mused. She left the coolness of the store and stepped back out into the muggy heat. The heat was so oppressive it was like walking into a wall. She crossed the street to sit for a little while at the Grand Parade. It was starting to get busy with the lunchtime crowd, with people in suits and heels vying for spots in the shade to enjoy their lunches. A brass band had set up in the centre area and the atmosphere was light and entertaining. She was lucky enough to share a bench with another lunchie and welcomed the opportunity to sit in the shade. Her feet were killing her and she could feel the start of a blister on one foot. She had elected to go without pantyhose because of the heat but regretted it now as she surveyed the red skin dangling from her baby toe. She rubbed her feet in the cool grass, thinking that she might never get the shoes back on her feet from the swelling. She'd walk barefoot back to the car if she had to. She pulled out the Peanut Butter Cup and enjoyed its gooey sweetness, the chocolate immediately melting all over her hands. She took a sip of the Baileys, savouring the combination of flavours.

Her thoughts returned to Rick and her stomach did another flip. She really needed to talk to Val and hoped she might have time to sneak out for a coffee between clients. It looked like she was going to have to head back to the ferry terminal to find a pay phone, which conveniently was in the direction of her car. She finished her chocolate and found a shrivelled Kleenex in the bottom of her purse to wipe the melted mess off her fingers. With some difficulty she squeezed her feet back into her shoes and the throbbing started immediately. If she could just make it back to the car, she would be all right.

She walked through the entranceway out of the square, when suddenly a sound like a gunshot ripped through the air, catching her totally off guard. She went over on her ankle and fell onto the sidewalk. She lay crumpled on the ground, her ankle throbbing, her skirt rising above her knees and her elbow badly scraped. She tried to sit up, but a wave of dizziness overcame her and she lay back down on the grimy pavement.

Within seconds people had gathered around to help. She wasn't sure she could walk: certainly not in these stupid heels.

"Are you okay?" a concerned voice came from behind her. She looked up to a sea of concerned faces, and attempted to fix her skirt.

"Yes, yes, I'll be fine." She felt so stupid. Clearly the combination of heat, shoes and Rick had been too much for her. "But I heard a gunshot ... ?" she started.

Everyone laughed despite themselves.

"That was the noon cannon. It goes off every day from Citadel Hill at precisely twelve." A young man wearing dress pants and rolled-up shirt sleeves smiled and helped her sit up. He wasn't making fun of her but she felt like an idiot.

"Of course." She raised her hand to shield her eyes from the interested crowd that was quickly growing. "My heel must have caught on the sidewalk," she attempted to explain. This was all so humiliating.

"Can we help you? Could we call someone for you?"

She gave a fleeting thought to the business card Rick had given her but immediately thought better of it.

"Actually, my friend Val would probably come and help me out. Could you call her for me?"

A suited businessman volunteered to run over to the shop to use the phone and came back to say Val was on her way. The young man handed her a fresh bottle of water that she drank eagerly. A silver-haired lady with a fresh blue perm eyed Maggie with concern. She was fretting over the blood on Maggie's arm, digging around in her Mary Poppins bag until she managed to find a Band-Aid for her elbow. It didn't quite cover it but it helped. Maggie, embarrassed at all the attention, thanked everyone, and attempted to stand up. Only in Nova Scotia would people be so quick to come to her aid. She was assisted over to the shade where she sat on a park bench facing the street to wait for Val.

It wasn't long before Val pulled up with a screech, putting on her flashers and jumping out of the car. She surveyed Maggie, clucking at the ridiculousness of the situation, and carefully helped her into the car. They drove up to Spring Garden Road where Val found a little coffee shop. They were now sitting in air-conditioned coolness enjoying some cold lemonade and a bit of lunch. The waiter had brought some ice for her ankle and even though it was a bit swollen, it felt a lot better.

"What the hell were you doing?" Val asked.

"I was walking ... up to the Grand Parade ..."

"In *those* heels? Are you crazy, girlfriend? Next time you are planning to go gallivanting around the hills of downtown Halifax, wear your sneakers or flip flops, please!"

Val looked as fresh and cool as if she had just stepped out of the shower, wearing a yellow sundress that set off her tanned legs. She wore her hair high on her head in a style that would have made anyone else look like Peg Bundy on *Married with Children*, but it suited Val perfectly. Maggie noted that Val was wearing heels, and started to comment but thought better of it when she realized that she had never seen Val in anything but heels. No sense starting that argument.

"I know, it was stupid of me, but there was a reason I was wearing heels." She paused before dropping the bomb. "I met Rick for coffee ..."

Val slapped both hands on the table at once, everyone in the restaurant turning to the noise. "No

Treading Water

way! You aren't serious?" Her eyebrows almost touched her hairline.

"I'm dead serious. He showed up at Mom's, just out of the blue. Just about gave me a heart attack. And Val, he's still gorgeous. He's as bald as a cue ball but it's so attractive. It really brings out his eyes. That's all you notice when you look at him."

"That's no surprise. He was a looker even when we were teenagers. All the girls had the hots for him."

Maggie looked up quickly. "They did?"

"Oh, never mind," Val said, waving her hand like she was swatting away a fly. "Tell me more."

Maggie described everything, from the time when Rick had showed up at her door to the escapade that had ended at the Grand Parade. By the time she was finished she was feeling a little light-headed again. She sighed and took another long drink of tart lemonade. She felt as though she had just hiked a mountain or, more appropriately, the hills of Halifax in heels. She had to laugh at the absurdity of it all.

"That's quite a story, girlfriend. So, what are you going to do? It sounds like you're not sure about going for dinner?" Val looked seriously into Maggie's face, reading her worry like no one else could.

"No, I'm not sure. But then I have so many questions. All these years I've been asking myself — what if?"

"So what are you worried about?"

Val seemed to take everything in stride and brought every situation down to its simplest form. Nothing was a big deal to Val.

"I guess I'm worried about what he's going to say; what he's going to tell me. Plus somehow it feels like I'm cheating on Glen. Do you think I'm cheating on Glen?" Maggie nibbled on her thumbnail.

"Don't be silly. You're just going out for dinner."

Maggie wondered if it was really that simple.

"What's a girl to do, huh? Listen, tell you what. Your hair already looks fabulous, thanks to moi. Why don't we stop into a couple of shops on Spring Garden Road and see if we can find a dress that will knock him off his feet? Think your ankle is up for the challenge?"

Maggie ran her hand gently over her ankle and decided it felt much better. "I think it will be all right as long as I don't walk on it too much. It would be great if I could find something nice to wear. I didn't really bring anything dressy. Val, what would I do without you?"

Val just shrugged her shoulders. She started to collect her purse but stopped when she noticed that Maggie hadn't moved. Maggie was sitting very still, tracing her finger along the edge of the placemat before she looked up again at Val.

"So, you're sure I'm doing the right thing?"

Val plunked herself back down in her chair and put both of her soft hands over Maggie's. "If you ask me, I think you need to get him out of your system, once and for all."

Maggie nodded slowly.

"If I don't go, I'll never forgive myself. And if I do, I might never forgive myself!"

Chapter 28

Abby sat on the front porch enjoying the gentle breeze, and the rare opportunity of some time by herself. She had to admit that her mom hadn't been all that bad, but she still questioned Abby about where she was going, what she was doing and with whom. Even when GG had agreed to let her and Jake have the car for delivering the display to the museum, her mom had given them a hard time. Little did she know she had a right to, but all they wanted to do was go to a movie together. Her mom hadn't said much to Jake, but commented later that he seemed like a polite young man. She was probably relieved that Abby was spending time with someone other than Tyson.

Abby was happy to have a chance to read in her favourite wicker rocker. She could just barely hear the sound of the surf, and she couldn't imagine anywhere else she would rather be. She was still on cloud nine after her night with Jake and thought she might have some time to write about it in her journal. She had also contemplated taking her mom's diary down to the beach, but GG was baking and she intended to be the first taste-tester. She could hear her beyond the screen door, bustling around with mixing bowls and measuring cups and singing to herself. Instead Abby had grabbed the latest book in the series she was reading, and wrapped it up in the crazy quilt along with her mom's diary. That way if anyone interrupted her she could just switch books and no one would be the wiser. Abby loved this quilt. She rubbed the blanket against her cheek, feeling the softness that comes from years of washing. Patches of different fabrics were all randomly quilted together and stitched with an edging of soft ribbon. When she was young she had dragged the quilt everywhere with her, often falling asleep on this very porch, the heaviness of the quilt keeping her warm. She still dragged it with her everywhere. When she put it back on her bed at night, she could smell the freshness of the sea air in its folds.

She pulled out the diary, trying to imagine her mother as a teenager. She caught a whiff of ginger coming from the pantry and her mouth starting watering in anticipation. She paused to picture her mother as a child in the same kitchen, Gil rolling out cookies, her face splotched with flour, her mother sticking her fingers in the bowl to lick the leftovers. Her mom hardly baked at all anymore. Maybe she could get her mom to teach her how to bake when they got back home. Abby knew that she would jump at the opportunity to do something together. She was all about that mother-daughter bonding stuff.

As Abby flipped through the pages, a ticket stub fell onto her lap. It had faded but she could still make out the details: April Wine - Halifax Forum. This must have been one of her mom's first concerts, she thought, looking at the date. 1978. The memorabilia was proving just as interesting as the diary itself, as every so often something would flutter from between the pages. She arranged herself comfortably in the chair, tucking the quilt around her toes. She opened the diary again when something else fell out. It appeared to be a sheet of loose-leaf paper, folded enough to fit perfectly into the back of the diary. She opened it up carefully to find a letter written in the same loopy scrawl, the edges decorated with flower and heart doodles like the cover.

Dear Baby,

I'm going to miss this place. It's been so nice waking up to the sound of seagulls and waves on the beach. This morning I sat on the cottage porch watching the sandpipers scurrying around. They looked so funny trying to keep from getting their feet wet. There were some little kids playing in the surf and they made me smile because I can see you doing the same thing one day. I can't wait. I know you are coming soon because you keep pushing your little fist into my belly as if to say "Hello, are you there?" And then you start your little flips again even though there isn't much room for you to flip anymore. It's like you are playing at the beach but in my tummy.

Abby sat back somewhat flabbergasted. She was reading a letter that her mother had written when she was pregnant — with her. It was strange and cool at the same time, knowing the baby she had been writing to was her. She read on ...

This summer has been really great, even though I've gotten so big. I look like I'm carrying a beach ball underneath my shirt, but it's you! Most days I take a walk along the beach with Stinker. He loves to run in and out of the water with me. Mom comes out to see me but not very often — it's been a bit of a catch-22 with her because she wants to see that I'm all right but she doesn't want to be reminded that I'm having a baby. Every time she comes, she brings something to eat – usually fresh fruit and some of her baking. I could sit here all day eating her fresh-baked bread – maybe that's why I'm so fat! She has also been making some clothes for me since nothing else fits. She has made some really pretty sundresses, out of really colourful fabric. About a month ago I asked her what she did with the leftover pieces and she said she had a basket full of them. Some days I'm going out of my mind I'm so bored, so I decided to start sewing.

Mom brought out the basket of scraps, and a bunch of needles and thread. I think the only time I had ever tried sewing before was in Home Ec but I wasn't half bad at it, so I'm making a small quilt for you. I've been working away at it every day, usually out on the porch where I can catch a breeze, and Stinker is usually curled up in the chair right beside me. I sure hope I can finish it by the time you come.

Abby stopped and fingered the quilt on her lap. Her mother had made this? She had never bothered to consider where it had come from. It had always been hers to use when she came to visit here, and now she knew why. But why would her mother not have mentioned it before?

I never imagined that I would be a mother at 16, but then who does? And right now it feels like the most natural thing in the world. Your dad and I love each other very much and even though people don't think that we can make it work, I know we can. Love makes everything work out.

I am looking forward to holding you in my arms, looking into your eyes, and playing with your little toes. I can't wait to meet you, pumpkin.

Love,
Mommy (Maggie)

Abby sat back and let the page fall onto her lap. Wow. It gave her goosebumps to think of her mother writing this to her. It was actually pretty cool. The one thing that still bugged Abby was the cottage. Her mother kept mentioning the cottage in the diary and she had no idea where it was or even whether or not it still existed. It couldn't have been very far from here. How was she going to find out without letting on that she knew from reading the diary? The screen door opened and the scent of gingerbread came wafting towards her. She quickly tucked the diary under the quilt and replaced her own novel on her lap, as GG appeared with a plate of fresh-baked gingerbread piled high with whipped cream.

"Oh, GG, that smells amazing," Abby drooled.

"If I recall correctly, it's one of your favourites." GG smiled.

"It sure is. And it's best when it is still warm." Abby sat up in the chair and eagerly accepted the floral plate from her grandmother.

"Would you like a cup of tea to go with it?"

"Umm, yes," Abby mumbled, her mouth already full of cake, crumbs littering the edge of her lips.

"Thanks, GG."

Gil returned carrying a tray with two china tea cups, and sugar for them both. She set the tray gently on the wicker table and lowered herself into the opposite chair with a sigh.

"It's almost too hot to be baking, but I have to look after my girls, don't I?" She winked. "I'd better put some away for Penny, or she'll miss out."

"You know, GG, I don't understand how drinking hot tea on a hot day can cool you down, but it does," Abby said.

"I know. I can't quite figure that one out myself, but tea and gingerbread sure go good together. So, what have you been doing out here all morning?" GG asked.

Abby took a moment to swallow. She could devour this whole thing in one bite, it was so good, but she tried to act like a lady in front of her grandmother. She took a sip of tea and cleared her throat before beginning. She figured now was as good an opportunity as any to find out more about the cottage.

"Grandma, can I ask you something?"

"Sure, what is it?"

Abby thought about how she was going to ask this. She wasn't really sure how GG would react if she knew she had her mom's diary, so she decided to go the vaguely curious route instead.

"Every once in a while Mom and Dad mention a cottage: someplace they went when they were going out together. They never said a lot about it, but I thought maybe you would know. I was just wondering."

Gil paused to take a sip of her tea and sighed. "Well, yes, actually there is a cottage. It's not far from here, and it's right on the beach. It belonged to my brother Hamish, your mom's uncle, and his wife Marjorie. They went there often when their family was small, but years later, when Marjorie broke her hip, it was difficult for her to get around and they stopped going out. It wasn't being used, so when your mom was pregnant with you she liked to spend time out there. It was quiet and your mother loved being near the beach. She was out there most of the summer you were born, and your dad was out there a lot too, of course."

"So it's still there, then?" Abby asked.

"Oh it's still there, but I don't know what kind of shape it's in. I don't think anyone has been out there in years," Gil replied.

"Do you think I could go and check it out sometime?" After all Abby had read in her mom's diary, she was dying to see the place for herself.

"I don't see why not. I'll see if there are any old keys still hanging in the pantry for it, but you probably wouldn't need them anyway. I would imagine the sea air has rusted the lock right off by now." She laughed as she stepped back inside.

Well, that was easy, Abby thought to herself. She sat on her hands to conceal her excitement.

Chapter 29

It was hard to believe that she was really sitting here having dinner with Rick, the man who had ruined everything. But that was a long time ago. People change. She had changed. And seeing him again was something she had been dreaming about for a long time. It was like unfinished business. She'd been a little stunned when he had blown in to the coffee shop to reschedule, and yet here they were. She had to admit she was curious. She wanted to know what he had been doing all these years, and find out more about why he was in Halifax this summer.

They sat in a touristy spot on the waterfront called Salty's. The outdoor patio faced the harbour and they had a magnificent view of sailboats and other watercraft sailing back and forth on the water. The conversation was interrupted by gulls squawking overhead, hoping to snag some leftovers for themselves. Every so often, a waiter would shoo a particularly bold bird away from a table. Tourists enjoyed their fill of lobster. The couple next to them was having fun putting on each other's bibs before tackling the messy but rewarding task of cracking their lobster meals. Maggie would have loved to have lobster herself but thought the seafood chowder was a safer choice, since there was less risk of getting it all over herself. She took a sip of wine and as she listened to his smooth voice, she allowed her mind to wander back to the time they met.

Rick had been a swim instructor and lifeguard at

the YMCA. He was the type of guy that all the girls looked at twice — longish blond hair, steel-grey eyes and a grin that made you weak at the knees. Maggie had done her volunteer teaching there and when she took her Bronze Cross — guess who was teaching the class? Maggie kept hoping that she would have to perform artificial respiration on him but the instructor never had to do that with his students. They had chatted a bit during classes but she hoped it might turn into more than that. Then one day when she was teaching her class, she had caught sight of Rick getting ready to lifeguard the family swim. She had stuck around and chatted with him while he patrolled the deck, and then swam some lengths so it wouldn't seem too obvious that she had been waiting for him. After getting dressed and taking her time with her hair, she had slowly started up the stairs to get her bike. She had been digging in her knapsack for something when he had come up behind her. He had looked at her the way he was looking at her now. He had grinned and asked her to go to a party with him that Friday night. She had almost melted on the spot, saying yes, and the rest, as they say, was history.

Flash forward 16 years, and here she was sitting at dinner with him like it was the most normal thing in the world. She had forgotten how he made her feel, her skin tingling in his presence. He didn't so much look at her, as look through her, like he was taking in every inch of her. She had to admit it was great to see him. Damn, he looked good. His bald head actually added to his appeal, making him sexy in a totally different way from when he was a teenager. He still made her nervous, with his piercing grey eyes and that smile. She wondered what he was thinking. Did he like the way she looked? After her catastrophe at the Grand Parade yesterday, she and Val had made a stop at Mills Brothers where she had found a simple but classy sleeveless teal-blue dress that accented her red hair. She'd even surprised herself when she looked in the mirror. She hadn't looked this good in years. It gave her the extra confidence she needed.

She had often tried to envision this moment, wondering whether she would even go through with it if he ever showed up and asked to see her, deep down knowing all along that she would. Every time she came home she would scan people's faces, hoping she might recognize someone she knew, to reaffirm that she still belonged here and really hadn't been gone all that long. She had anticipated running into Rick on the street or at a coffee shop, but it never happened. Strangely enough, it seemed the most natural thing in the world to be sitting here with him again, the conversation flowing as easily as the wine they were drinking. Maggie pushed away thoughts of Glen, wondering what he would think if he knew they were out together.

"So, what have you been up to, Mags? What brings you back to Nova Scotia this summer?"

Maggie blushed at his familiar use of her nickname. He looked at her as if he were reading her thoughts. Could he possibly know what she was thinking? How she had always wondered about him?

She tried to clear her head, stop thinking about the past and carry on a normal conversation in the present.

"As a matter of fact, we've been coming back every year since Abby was five, but I actually haven't been home myself for the past few years." She chuckled at the use of the word "home," since she had lived in Ontario now as long as she had lived here. But then the place you grow up will always be home, the memories making you the person you turn out to be.

"I've been so busy at work that I hadn't really even planned on coming this summer. Then I decided to come after all and just moved some things around and ... well, here I am." She paused, thinking about the list in Abby's journal, her real reason for coming. "Actually, I've been worried about Abby, so I decided it might be wise to keep an eye on her." She couldn't believe she was talking about Abby barely five minutes into the conversation. Rick furrowed his brows and his eyes deepened. She was secretly pleased to see he still had some feelings of concern for Abby, despite his lack of contact.

"Oh, nothing serious, just teenager stuff," Maggie continued, seeing his reaction. She certainly wasn't prepared to tell Rick all of her daughter's secrets. Maggie wondered if he had ever really cared. He hadn't even tried to get in touch with her. Not once. Which was probably just as well, she thought.

"It wouldn't have anything to do with me, would it?" he asked, his expression totally serious, as though he had been dealing with these family issues forever.

"With you? Why would you think that it has

anything to do with you?" Maggie's stomach twisted. Arrogant bugger. She could feel where this was going. He assumed that Abby knew. She had never told Abby about him to protect her, when all along she had been protecting herself. She blurted out the words before she lost the nerve to say them. "Rick ... Abby doesn't know about you ... about us."

Rick blinked his eyes furiously, his frown deepening. "Why not?" His eyes clouded over and he looked at her with an intensity that was becoming uncomfortable.

Maggie pulled her eyes away and started pleating the napkin on her lap as she tried to explain. She felt as though she was in a sinking boat, the water level rising quickly. "We just never told her. There was no need when she was small, and when she got older ... well, we just forgot." She couldn't bring herself to look at him; the boat was taking on water with every word she spoke, dragging her down.

"Forgot?" He took a mouthful of wine the way a runner gulps water after a race. "You just forgot?"

"Well, not forgot, just ... We always planned on telling her eventually, but there never seemed to be a good opportunity. Plus, I wasn't sure how she would take it, finding out that Glen wasn't her real dad but that someone else — you — were. We didn't want to risk upsetting her for no reason."

Rick ran his hand over his smooth head. "I guess I just figured you would have told her at some point."

"Lord knows I've thought about it and I am reminded every time we come back," Maggie said.

"Maybe you'll have a chance to tell her this summer." He looked past her, out over the water, his demeanour suddenly cool and dejected. Was she actually starting to feel sorry for him?

Her words tumbled out to fill the empty spaces. "Yeah, maybe — maybe it's time. But Glen will need to be part of that conversation." Glen's name hung in the air like the fog that was starting to creep in along the shoreline, but neither one of them seemed prepared to acknowledge him. Maggie took a sip of wine and excused herself to go to the ladies' room. She looked at herself in the mirror and ran some cool water over her wrists to cool herself down. Her eyes looked wild and frightened, like the eyes of an animal that had been backed into a corner. She needed to turn the conversation around before she became a nervous wreck. Serves you right for bringing Abby up in the first place, she told herself. She checked her reflection, smoothed the front of her dress and, taking a deep breath, walked back to their table. Rick jumped up to pull out her chair. Always the gentleman, she thought as she sat down slowly.

She took a deep breath as she sat down, intending to divert the topic of conversation from Abby. "So, are you married?" She hadn't meant to just blurt out the question but now it lay like a dead thing on the table.

"No. Not at the moment. I was, though. Seems like a long time ago now," Rick said.

"Anyone I know?" Maggie batted her eyes teasingly. Now it was Rick's turn to be uncomfortable.

Rick looked down and brushed some nonexistent

crumbs off the tablecloth. He was suddenly embarrassed, which was totally out of character for him. She had never seen him as anything but calm, cool and in control.

"As a matter of fact, I married Vicki."

Maggie raised her eyebrows. She had to give him credit for being honest. "Wow, Vicki? I always knew she had a thing for you."

"Yeah well, it only lasted two years, so I guess it really wasn't meant to be," Rick said, obviously relieved that the waiter chose that moment to refill their glasses. Maggie mulled that over. It was no surprise that he had ended up with Vicki. Vicki had always been trying to move in on Rick, even when Maggie and Rick were dating. She remembered being at a party together one time. Maggie had gone to the bathroom and when she came back she couldn't find Rick anywhere. She had wandered through the house, nonchalantly peeking into rooms as she passed, but couldn't find him. Then she had heard giggling from the bedroom at the end of the hall, and when she peered in she saw Vicki sitting in Rick's lap, with her arm around his shoulder. Rick had gotten up quickly, saying it wasn't what it looked like, but Vicki had just laughed. The fact that they had eventually hooked up was no surprise. Maggie turned her attention back to Rick. She had so many questions, but Rick beat her to it, deftly changing the subject again.

"So, how are you really, Maggie?" Rick asked. Those eyes were once again piercing into her to her soul.

"I'm okay," Maggie replied, feeling like the whole conversation was a tennis match and it was her turn to be on the defensive again.

"Just okay?"

"No, really, I'm good." She nodded as though trying to convince herself. "I'm just a little frustrated with my job right now — but who isn't, right? I've been waiting for the next opportunity to come along. The deadlines are killing me. I would much rather be freelancing, and then I'd have the freedom to go where I want and work when I want. And I could probably come up with some good excuse to come out here more often and visit with Mom."

"How is your mom?"

"She's great. We've mentioned the idea of moving her up to be near us in Ontario, but she won't hear of it. It's like trying to take the salt out of the sea. We worry about her but, as she often reminds us, she has more friends here than you can shake a stick at. And for selfish reasons we're secretly glad that she wants to stay, because we love coming back here so much. I can't imagine not coming on a regular basis — the girls would really miss it."

"So why don't you?" Rick asked.

"Why don't I what?"

"Come out here on a regular basis."

"Well, I do. Almost every summer."

"You know what I mean. I've seen some of your articles. You're good. And some of those commentaries you used to write for the school paper? Talk about a rebel with a cause. Maybe it's time to break out on your own, do some more freelancing. You could even do a piece covering our environmental project. It'd be right up your alley and you'd be just the type of person that could generate some interest."

Maggie grinned, remembering her passionate contributions to the paper. Her editorials were legendary. She had always felt the need to voice her opinion. Once in English class, she had gotten so involved in her discussion that the teacher had taken a seat in one of the empty desks and Maggie had moved to the teacher's spot at the front. She wasn't sure she had the guts to be that outspoken now, but maybe if she tried to find that Maggie again, she might get that promotion sooner than later.

"I did have a hard time keeping my opinions to myself, didn't I?" she laughed.

She swirled the wine around in her glass, considering the possibilities. Maybe Rick was right. Maybe that was exactly what she was looking for — a new job opportunity, a chance to spend more time with the girls and a chance to be home again. Her cheeks were hot from excitement and wine. He had sparked something in her that hadn't been there in a long time. Did he really understand her better than anyone or was he just telling her what she wanted to hear? When she looked up his eyes were on her, serious and intense, as he raised his glass. She felt her stomach do a triple flip.

"Welcome home, kiddo," and he leaned in and kissed her.

Chapter 30

Swinging was one of those sensations where the steady rhythm made you feel as though you were on a sailboat rocking gently on the sea, the movement so addictive that you never wanted to stop. Abby and Sarah pushed their bare feet off the deck, pushing the porch swing back and forth with enough momentum to create a lovely breeze. When they were little they would go to the playground and always race directly for the swings. Showing no fear, they would stand on the seats of the swings to get their momentum going and then quickly sit down and start pumping furiously to see who could get her swing the highest. Sometimes they went so high it looked as though they might actually circle the bar at the top. GG would supervise from the nearest bench, with her hand half-covering her eyes, afraid to look. The porch swing didn't exactly have the range of the playground swings, but the girls were certainly giving it a run for its money. The swing creaked back and forth like a melody. Penny sat in the big white wicker chair across from the girls, offering every possible bribe she could think of to convince them to let her come with them to the beach.

"We just want to hang out at the beach by ourselves for a change. We'll take you with us next time, I promise."

"You always say that!" Penny retorted. "You haven't taken me once yet!"

"Well, you've been so busy hanging out with your boyfriend, Simon, you haven't been around much,"

Abby teased.

Penny's cheeks bloomed red at the mention of Simon.

"See, I told you, you like him," Abby said.

"Maybe I do, but he's not around today, so why won't you take me to the beach with you? I promise I won't be in your way," Penny pleaded.

"Yes, you will. We want to swim out to the sandbar and that's too far for you. Besides, we have a lot of things to talk about." Abby winked at Sarah, and Sarah nodded.

"How about if I do the dishes on the night it's your turn?"

"Nah, that's no big deal."

"How about if I make your bed for you every morning?"

"Tempting, but no, thanks."

Sarah picked up her towel and beckoned for Abby to follow while Penny continued shooting out bribes. She jumped out of her chair and called to their backs.

"Okay, okay, I know — I'll bring you coffee in bed every morning so you can stay in bed and read."

Abby turned. *That* one had gotten her attention for a moment. There was nothing nicer than lying around in bed on a summer morning, the sun streaming in, the pillows propped behind your head, and a coffee steaming on the nightstand beside you.

"Seriously, Penny, we just want to hang out together. I promise we'll take you next time. Maybe GG will do some baking with you? Why don't you go ask her? We'll see you later."

Penny pressed her bottom lip into an impressive pout that Abby pretended not to notice. Normally she wouldn't mind Penny tagging along, but she and Sarah still had so much to talk about. The girls headed off to the beach without a backward glance at Penny. They walked down to the beach and were happy to find that the tide had left behind a collection of treasures. The girls engaged in comfortable conversation while scavenging for pieces of sea glass and driftwood.

"So tell me more about Josh. Do you miss him?" Abby asked.

"Of course I do, but it helps that you are here. His family should be back before you leave, so at least you'll be able to meet him."

"Yes, I'll need to check him out before I can offer my stamp of approval."

Sarah laughed. "I'm not sure what Josh will do if you don't approve! Have you thought any more about what you are going to do about Tyson?"

Abby found several flat stones and started skimming them across the water. Little splashes appeared every time the rock sliced through the water. She and her dad always had rock-skimming competitions. He had taught her how to bend her body and turn her arm sideways to get a maximum cut into the water. Her record was five times, but that didn't usually happen unless she found the perfect rock.

"Did you see that? Four times. Try it!"

"So ... what about Tyson?"

"I'm done with him for good." Abby continued skipping stones with intense concentration.

"What? Have you talked to him?" Sarah attempted to skip a rock herself but it merely hit the water with a kerplunk and disappeared. "Man, I'm just no good at this!"

"I have been having such an amazing time with Jake, you know? I just started thinking about how much fun we have, and how easy he is to be with. It's nothing like it is with Tyson. So you know that knot and chain that Tyson gave me before I left?"

"The one he gave you with the note about 'saving yourself'?" Sarah made quotes in the air with her fingers.

"Yeah, that. So the other night Jake and I went to the movies together and we had such a good time. When I got home, Penny and I were sitting on the bed talking. I told her how confused I was about Tyson, especially now that I've met Jake. All of a sudden Penny says, 'So what's the problem?' and I thought, 'She's right!' And right after that I ran down to the bluff, yanked off the necklace and heaved it into the ocean."

"You didn't!" Sarah said.

"I did! I knew right away that I had done the right thing. Maybe I should have talked to Penny about it sooner!" Abby chuckled. "She's a pretty bright kid."

"C'mon, let's swim. I'm getting hot. Race you to the sandbar."

The water never actually got warm on the East Coast. In fact, the cold absolutely took your breath away. The only way to get in was to dive right in or you would never convince yourself to do it. They counted to three and made the plunge, coming up screaming and laughing from the cold. The waves challenged them every stroke of the way and they were grateful to be able to stand on the sandbar. Abby flicked her hair out of her eyes and looked back to shore. She could have sworn she saw something bobbing around in the water, but the waves were making it difficult to tell.

"Do you see something out there?" Abby asked Sarah. Sarah squinted to look and that was when they both heard screams. "Oh my God, I think it's Penny! What the heck is she doing?"

Abby dove back into the water and swam as fast as she could in Penny's direction, her lungs bursting with the effort. She kept losing sight of Penny as wave after wave swelled and crashed into shore, but was able to call to her as she got closer. Penny was so tired from trying to keep her head above water that she surrendered into Abby's arms. Abby held Penny in a rescue hold and slowly pulled her back to shore. The waves tossed them around and it took all of Abby's strength to get Penny back to the beach. When they reached the shore they collapsed on the beach, Penny coughing and Abby breathing heavily from the effort. Sarah swam along with them and when she reached the shore she ran ahead to grab the towels. She immediately wrapped one around Penny.

"Are you okay?" Abby asked. She pulled Penny's matted hair away from her face. Penny was still breathing hard.

"Yeah, I think so." Penny coughed and burped up

some water. "I don't feel so good."

"No kidding! What the heck were you doing?" Abby admonished.

"Well, you guys were taking so long, and I was so bored that I decided to come down to the beach and just watch you. When you started to swim out to the sandbar I thought I could keep up with you and surprise you. But a big wave hit me in the face and I went under and couldn't get my breath back. I swallowed so much water I thought I was going to drown. I'm sorry, Abby. I didn't mean to spoil your fun."

Abby sat back on her heels and breathed a deep sigh. She pulled the towel around Penny's shoulders and gave her a big hug. "Don't worry about it, kiddo. I'm just glad you're all right. Let's get you back up to the house and make sure you're okay before GG finds out you've gone missing."

They trudged slowly up the path, Sarah in front and Abby walking behind to make sure that Penny could make it on her own. Abby made hot chocolate for all of them and they curled up on the porch swing together. Penny complained of a stomach ache, but seemed to be enjoying the extra attention. Abby hoped the warm drink would calm her tummy and her nerves. They heard a car crunching across the gravel and looked up to see Maggie pulling in. She was all smiles and packages after her shopping trip. She walked up to the girls with a big grin on her face.

"Well, don't you girls look all cute and snuggly together on the swing!"

Abby's eyes threw daggers at her mother. Maggie looked from one girl to the other and saw that Penny had been crying. She sat down when she realized something was wrong. "Did something happen?"

"Yes, Penny almost drowned, but we got to her in time, thank goodness," Abby snapped. "She's still pretty shaken up about it. If you had been home, this never would have happened. Maybe if you did some things with Penny once in a while she wouldn't have to tag along with me and Sarah all the time!" She hugged Penny a little harder, letting her know there were no hard feelings, but her anger at Maggie never wavered.

"How can you say this is *my* fault? GG was home, wasn't she?"

Maggie glanced around as she heard GG coming through the screen door.

"Maggie, I'm so sorry. Penny had a bit of an accident, but she's going to be fine." GG stood wringing her hands, clearly upset about the turn of events. "When I came downstairs I couldn't find Penny, so I went outside to look for her. I heard yelling and saw the girls on the beach, their arms waving for help. Thank God Abby has been taking those lifesaving classes. I'll bet she never thought in a million years that she would actually have to save someone, let alone her little sister."

Maggie squatted in front of Penny and rubbed her legs through the towel. "Are you sure you're okay, honey?"

"Yeah, I'll be fine, Mom. Abby's got it under

control," Penny said.

Abby watched as her mother ran her hand along Penny's cheek. She saw her mother move in her direction, but turned her head away. She didn't feel like talking to her mother right now and she certainly didn't want any of her guilt. Let her feel bad, she thought.

Chapter 31

This vacation wasn't turning out quite the way Maggie had expected, but then what had she expected? That she could come down to Nova Scotia and put Abby in a chastity belt to keep her out of trouble? No, she had come so she could keep an eye on things; to make sure that Abby didn't get herself into trouble. And look how that was going. They hadn't even spent that much time together since she arrived, except for a shopping trip and some dinners out. The only time Abby seemed happy to be in her company was when they were going somewhere that *she* wanted to go. Just the other day Abby had begged her to go into town because she was dying for some french fries from Bud the Spud and Maggie had finally given in. They'd had a nice conversation while waiting in the line at the famous chip wagon, inhaling the mouth-watering scent of greasy fries cooking. Afterwards they had poked around Spring Garden Road together, so in hindsight, things had turned out pretty well. Maybe she should just stop over-thinking everything. Maggie realized that Abby wasn't going to spend every waking minute of her vacation with her mother, so maybe she should just take things as they happened. Abby had been spending a lot of time with Sarah, but Maggie hardly knew what they were up to from day to day. And Penny was such an independent child that it was easy to forget that she was in need of some attention too. It was as much her fault as Abby's that they hadn't done much together, what with her "gallivanting around" with Rick, as her mother would say. Maggie plunked herself into the wicker chair and put her face in her hands. She wanted to cry. Did she really think that she could hold their hands for the entire vacation and keep them with her all the time like two-year-olds? As if.

She decided to take a walk to clear her head. She seriously considered carrying the flask in her purse permanently if this was the way things were going to go. She needed to sort things out, both for herself and for the girls. Right now everything seemed to be going wrong. Except this thing with Rick — whatever that might be. Strangely enough, that felt right. She started walking aimlessly, seeing the lupines swaying along the drive. Lupines were her favourite flower. She had tried many times to grow them in her own garden in Ontario, but they had never survived. Her mother said it had something to do with the type of soil. It just goes to prove that some things just weren't meant to be taken away from Nova Scotia. Like me, she thought. She felt like she had merely existed after leaving, never quite feeling as though she belonged elsewhere.

Random thoughts collided in her head and before long she found herself down at the water's edge. She walked to the end of the pier and sat down, letting her legs dangle over the side. She watched the seaweed as it swished around like a mop. Water lapped against the boats as they bobbed on their moorings and ropes lay twisted in coils along the edge of the pier. Every so often a seagull would land on a post, squawk some words of advice and fly off.

"Hey, what's a pretty lady like you doing in a

place like this?"

Maggie squinted in the sun to make out Mr. Jack's tanned and smiling face. She sighed deeply. "Oh, just trying to figure out how to fix my life." She shrugged.

"Sounds serious." His brow furrowed as he sat down beside her. "You figure the answer is out there blowing in the wind, do ya?"

"Actually, I was hoping these seagulls might give me a little insight." Maggie laughed gently. She was glad she had run into him. Some people were good at making you feel better just being in their presence. Jack was one of those people: "The salt of the earth," her Grandma used to say.

"So, what brings you down here in the middle of the afternoon?" Maggie asked.

"You see that little blue boat over there? She's mine. I come down to visit with her a couple of times a week if I can manage. You know, keep her in shape."

Jack looked lovingly across the water at the small skiff. He had kept it tied up here for years, and everyone was accustomed to seeing him tinkering around on his boat. Maggie could see the name *Miss Kate* barely legible across the front bow. Maggie watched it bob around on the waves looking deserted and beaten-up. She wondered if he felt that way too, sometimes. She had seen that faraway look in Jack's eyes before.

Gil had told her that Mr. Jack had moved into the cottage just down from her place shortly after his wife died. Before that they'd had a place on the ocean where he worked as a lobster fisherman. Maggie remembered

Yvonne Leslie

the story of how one day, his young daughter Catherine had gone down to the beach on her own. By the time they realized she was missing, it was too late. They had found her floating face down on top of the waves. Grief-stricken, they had laid their only child to rest and struggled to continue on. And then one particular night, just a year later, a fierce storm had blown up, with a wind strong enough to blow the roofs off the houses. Mr. Jack and his wife Louise had gone out to moor the boats more securely. The waves had grown to a deadly height and had swept his wife off the dock and she had fallen between the boats. Mr. Jack had tried everything he could to reach her, but she had been dragged beneath the waves. Rumour had it that you could hear Mr. Jack howling for miles. It wasn't until a couple of days later that they were able to retrieve her body from the frigid water. The very next day Mr. Jack had announced his retirement from fishing, and not long after that had moved to the cottage inland. He had told Gil that every time the wind blew through the eaves, he could still hear the voices of his wife and his daughter and he just couldn't take it any longer. He figured that if the ocean was going to take away both his girls, he had nothing left to give. He had kept himself busy over the years, mostly doing odd jobs, but before long he had been lured back to fishing. It was as much a part of him as being a Maritimer, and it clearly did him good.

Maggie shook her head, reliving his story in her mind. He'd endured so much pain, and yet despite all the grief the ocean had caused him, he was still happiest when he was puttering around his boat. It was ironic to think that the things that bring you the most pain can often bring the most comfort.

Maggie remembered years ago when Val had split from her first husband. She had been devastated and Maggie had made the trip out on her own to make sure her friend was okay. She had stayed with her and her kids for a week, to try and get them through the worst of it. She had taken the kids to a movie so Val could deal with some things and when they got home there had been another car in the driveway. She had plunked the kids in front of the TV and gone to find Val. She knocked on the bedroom door to make sure Val was all right. Val had opened it a crack to talk to her and Maggie had caught a glimpse of Val's ex in the bed behind her. Maggie had been ready to tear a strip off both of them, but Val had put her finger to her lips and whispered that it was all right. She had just needed some comfort from someone who understood her and she had softly shut the door. At the time Maggie had been flabbergasted but now she thought she understood.

Wasn't it the same as what was happening between her and Rick? He was the only one who could comfort her because he was the only one who truly understood what had happened between them. And that was why she needed him, why she needed to talk to him. So she could make sense of it. And know once and for all that everything happened for a reason.

"So what seems to be bothering you, m'dear? Anything I can help you with?"

"Oh, I don't know, Mr. Jack. It's the same old stuff. I can't seem to get along with my daughters — they both hate me right now. And Mom and I just can't seem to get back on track, though Lord knows I've tried. It's like I can't do anything right for all the trying I'm doing. They are all pushing me away and I don't know what to do to fix it."

"Maybe that's half your problem."

"What do you mean?"

"You're trying too damn hard. I'll tell ya, some of the best times I had with my girls was doing things like we are doing here right now: sitting on the dock chatting about this and that, or taking the boat out for a nice ride on the waves. It's the simple stuff that makes everything work out. And it's worth it because you just never know when things are going to change. You think you have all the time in the world to fix things, but ya don't. If I could just be with my girls one more time, it would be enough to keep me going for the rest of my days. I miss them terribly, but I keep busy. And that's what you need to do. Be with them, spend some time. You've been so busy being off socializin' you ain't hardly been home. Now it's none of my business, but some of the best memories I have with my girls was being right here, doing nothin'."

Maggie looked into those bright blue eyes and knew he had it all figured out. She had to admit he was right. It really was that simple. Maybe she should just stop trying so hard, and just be there for her girls. Who would have ever thought she would glean such words of wisdom from a wizened old fisherman?

Chapter 32

It was another spectacular day on the waterfront. The sun overhead was hot and ice cream cones were melting quickly. Tourists carrying cameras and souvenirs wandered up and down the pier. A bright sunny day was enough of an excuse to be down by the water, but it was also Natal Day weekend and the buskers were in town. Crowds gathered to watch the street performers entertain and impress with unusual acts. Some performed magic, some did acrobatics, and some ate knives and fire.

Abby, Sarah and Penny wore their aqua-blue Save the Harbour T-shirts, or Project H, as they had begun to call it, with waves all over the front. They were attending a booth designed to increase awareness for the Save the Harbour project. Abby was disappointed that Jake wasn't with them today. He and some of the other guys were working a similar display at one of the malls. The guys were probably a lot cooler, but the girls were definitely having lots of fun. It was nice to be hanging out with just the girls for a change. There were always lots of activities going on around the city to celebrate Halifax's birthday. Jake was going to come with them to the parade on Monday, and Abby was excited to show him the pipe bands. Their location in the midst of all this activity was sure to attract interest in their cause. There were lots of other tents displaying jewelry, sunglasses, caps and clothing as part of the

Natal Day festivities.

"I'll watch your display table if you girls want to take a break for lunch," Mr. Jack offered. He was similarly dressed in his Project H T-shirt and matching blue baseball cap.

"Thanks, Mr. Jack. Let's go get some lunch and then maybe we'll get lucky and find a spot along the wall to sit and watch some of the buskers," Abby suggested.

"I think I saw a hot dog vendor setting up on the other side of the ferry terminal this morning. Want to go and check?" Sarah asked.

"And I saw someone making home-made lemonade. We should go there too," Penny said. "Man, it's hot!"

"Sounds like a great idea," Abby said.

They wove their way through the crowd, Abby holding tight to Penny's hand and constantly checking to make sure they were still together. After yesterday, she wasn't taking any chances of something else happening. Abby and Penny waited in line for hot dogs and Sarah offered to get the lemonades. Food in one hand and drinks in the other, they held their hands high to avoid getting bumped as they navigated their way back to the waterfront. They squeezed into a spot along the wooden wall as a busker was setting up his next act. A guy with dreadlocked hair was pulling torches and knives out of a large crate.

"Perfect timing!" Penny said. "I can't wait to see what this guy is going to do." She took a huge bite of her hot dog, sending a gush of mustard out of the other

Treading Water

end. She narrowly missed hitting a lady in the foot, and Abby had to apologize since Penny's mouth was so full. The whole incident had Penny choking with laughter.

"You're lucky, kiddo! Now, wise up before you choke to death," Abby said. Penny swallowed but when she looked at Abby she was lost in another fit of laughter. Her laugh was so contagious, Abby and Sarah couldn't help laughing too. Abby was happy to see Penny enjoying herself. She had given them quite a scare yesterday. She didn't dare think about what might have happened if she hadn't noticed Penny when she had.

After Sarah went home, the two of them had spent the rest of the day lazing around on the front porch. Penny had even fallen asleep on her lap for a while while she read. The whole escapade had really tuckered Penny out. Today she seemed to be back to her usual self, excitement playing across her face as she watched the busker throwing around flaming torches like they were matchsticks.

Abby looked up to see the busker motioning in their direction. Before she realized what was happening, Penny had jumped up to join him on stage. He told the crowd that his name was Loki and the next thing they knew, he was standing on stilts and Penny was passing flaming torches up to him. Sarah motioned for Abby to get some pictures and quickly pulled the camera out of her backpack. She quickly checked to see how many photos were left on her roll of film. Their mother was never going to believe this, she thought, as she snapped away. Penny looked thrilled to be his assistant, and with the water and the crowd in the background, Abby was getting some very cool shots. She might even consider using one of these for her contest entry. The crowd was spellbound as he performed various stunts, cheers erupting after every intense moment. Abby gasped as he threw the torches back to Penny and jumped down. He took the torches from Penny, blew out the flames, and raised her hand above her head. She bowed and the crowd went wild as Loki started passing around his hat for money. Abby shook her head as Penny returned to their spot.

"I can't believe you did that!" Abby said.

"It was *so* much fun! He makes it look so easy," Penny said.

"Don't you get any ideas," Abby said jokingly.

"Don't worry, I wouldn't even think of trying that on my own!" Penny said.

"I guess we should be getting back," Abby said. The girls dug into their pockets for some change before working their way back to their tent. When they returned, Mr. Jack was animatedly talking to some visitors and they quickly picked up some brochures to help him. The tent was crowded with people interested in Project H. Sarah's cheeks were turning pink from sitting in the sun, so she was happy to stay in the shade of the tent. Penny strapped an apron around her waist and started passing out buttons in front of the tent. Abby picked up the tin for donations and joined her outside.

"Thanks for letting me work with you guys

today," Penny said. "I'm really having a good time."

"No problem. You're a good kid," Abby grinned at her sister.

"You're not half bad either," Penny chuckled. "And tomorrow Mom's taking us out to Peggy's Cove. I can't wait. This vacation just keeps getting better and better!"

"I know. I'm having fun too." Abby winked at Penny. "It's such a great place for taking pictures." She shaded her eyes to look out over the water. Sailboats skirted across on the waves and seagulls swooped and cawed, scavenging for food. "You know, I'm really going to miss all this. Project H especially. It's been great making new friends, but it really feels good to be doing something worthwhile. I hate that we have to go back home before it's all done."

"Me too. What are they ever going to do without us?" Penny raised her shoulders emphatically.

"By the time we come back next summer, we should have a chance to see some of the results. Hopefully they'll want to have us back on the project." She felt tears stinging her eyes as she remembered that it was pretty unlikely that Jake would be back. He had mentioned that he was here for the summer to work with his dad. Sometimes she just couldn't believe her luck. She had finally met a great guy and after this summer she might never see him again.

"What's up?" Penny asked.

"Nothing." Abby wiped her nose with the back of her hand and tried to blink away the tears.

"You're thinking about Jake, aren't you?" Penny

said.

Abby was constantly amazed at how perceptive Penny was. She was so good at reading people. *Too bad I wasn't a little better at it myself,* she thought.

"Yeah, actually I am," Abby said.

"He's a really nice guy. I like him!"

Abby had to laugh at Penny's announcement, but her stomach flipped, thinking about next summer. She couldn't imagine working on Project H without Jake. Would he be back? A girl could always hope, couldn't she?

Chapter 33

Maggie pulled her sweatshirt over her head and tied her hair back into a short ponytail. The mist hung like a shroud and wouldn't be doing her hair any favours. Even with her new haircut, the humidity would bring out the frizz in no time. It was a typical early-morning fog and as on most summer days in Nova Scotia, it should burn off by lunchtime. They were heading out to Peggy's Cove early so that Abby could take some photos for her photography contest. There was nothing like a Maritime mist clinging to the rocks to add mood to a seaside shot.

"I've got lunch all packed, Mom," Penny said.

Penny helped Gil load up a wicker basket with all sorts of plastic containers, cans of pop and a checkered tablecloth. Gil was famous for her picnic lunches. She would prepare things that you always envisioned in a picnic basket but never bothered to make yourself: things like potato salad, fried chicken legs, sandwiches with the crusts cut off and brownies. Maggie drooled just thinking about it. She hoped that the sun would be shining on them by the time they were ready for their picnic. Abby sat on the couch, carefully packing everything into her camera bag. She threw it over her shoulder and walked over to peek into the picnic basket.

"Ooh, brownies for breakfast." Abby reached into the basket but her hand was gently slapped away by Gil.

"Not so fast, young lady. Help your mother put

some rain jackets into the car. You might need them yet, if only for the spray from the surf."

"Good idea, GG." And she disappeared into the pantry.

"Are you sure you won't come with us, Mom?" Maggie asked. She secretly wished her mother would take her up on it, especially for the girls' sake.

"No, no, you girls go and have fun. I have enough things to do around here to keep me busy."

"Okay, if you're sure. Let's go, girls," Maggie announced.

They loaded the car and waved out the windows to GG standing on the porch. The roads were still damp from last night's rain. They had been very lucky with the weather so far on this trip. Maggie remembered one particular vacation where they had spent the entire time inside playing board games and doing puzzles while the rain continued day after day. When you live on the ocean, it's hard to predict when the sun will make an appearance. Last night they had heard the rain pelting against the windows and that usually guaranteed some extra high surf, which was always very exciting at Peggy's Cove. Maggie took her time on the winding road and settled in for the scenic drive. Here and there pockets of sunlight tried to break through the fog. Penny had her eyes glued to the side of the road, totally intrigued with the changing scenery. "I still can't believe all these boulders were left here from the ice age," she said.

"I know. It's the only way they could have gotten here. They are so huge," Abby agreed.

The landscape became sparser as they got closer to Peggy's Cove, the trees and bushes being replaced by boulders and craggy moss. It had an eerie feeling in the mist, as though you were on the moon's surface, only with purple flowers welcoming you. They took the winding road into the village, passing colourful shacks and a small inlet with boats anchored to their docks. As they climbed the last stretch of narrow road, the historic lighthouse came into view, a lone beacon on the rocks.

"Look, Mom. There's the lighthouse!" Penny could hardly contain her excitement.

"Did you know that after it was no longer a functioning lighthouse, they turned it into a working post office? Tourists loved it because they could send postcards home with an actual postmark from Peggy's Cove. I wonder if it's still there," Maggie said.

"Wow, check out the surf! I'm going to get some amazing photos today," Abby said.

"Yes, it looks like you will," Maggie said, and pulled into a parking spot.

The famous lighthouse with the red roof sat at the edge of the rocks, having once played sentinel to the passing ships. There was nothing but rocks and boulders leading right to the water's edge. People navigated their way across the rocky surface, looking like ants on a blanket compared to the hulking size of the boulders. Every so often a wave would crash into shore, sending up a spray of water that reached high above their heads.

"It looks like last night's storm created some extra

big waves," Maggie said. "Just remember not to get too close to the edge. You'll see signs all over the rocks warning people. It's hard to imagine that a wave could come up and sweep you out to sea, but sadly it has happened. You need to be very careful."

"Don't mess with Mother Nature!" Penny said.

"That's exactly right," Maggie laughed. "Let's go."

Abby immediately pulled out her camera and started taking photos. Penny enjoyed the challenge of trying to climb up on a particularly large rock, finally giving up and trying from the other direction. Once she reached the top she spread her arms in jubilation, Abby capturing the victorious moment.

Maggie leaned against one of the rocks and watched her girls. She was enjoying herself immensely. It was wonderful watching Abby in action. Every so often she would crouch down on the rocks to get a different shot of the surf. *She reminds me of myself,* she mused. Penny was pleased to be the subject of Abby's photos, posing whenever the camera was aimed in her direction. Maggie had to laugh as she watched Penny hanging over the edge of a rock, her head just visible to Abby below, who continued to click away. Her heart skipped a beat, remembering yesterday's incident on the beach, but before she could say anything, Penny was off exploring again.

Maggie closed her eyes, feeling the spray on her face, and wrapped her scarf a little tighter around her neck. It was invigorating: the wind, the surf, the salt air. She just wanted to fill her lungs up with all of it, and never breathe out again. She climbed over the boulders to join Abby and Penny near the lighthouse. Penny ran in to look into the post office situation and Maggie chose the moment to chat with Abby.

"How're you enjoying your vacation so far, Abby?" she asked.

"It's been great." She beamed at her mother, cheeks flushed from the wind, eyes sparkling with happiness and her finger still poised above the shutter button. Maggie wanted to talk with Abby while she had the opportunity, but broached the subject carefully, so as not to spoil the moment.

"Have you heard anything from Tyson?"

"No. And I don't plan to, either. I'm done with him." Abby spoke matter-of-factly. It appeared that nothing was going to spoil her day. Her eyes continued to scan the landscape, not wanting to miss a photo opportunity. Maggie was surprised at her response. She'd had no idea that things had changed between Abby and Tyson. With a 16-year-old you never knew what was going to happen. Deep down, Maggie was pleased with this bit of information, but she didn't let on.

"What happened?"

"I finally figured out that he's a loser and I'm not, so I'm not going to waste my time anymore. Hang on a sec, Mom. I see another shot I want to take." Abby was off again, squatting down to get a shot of the sun making a valiant effort to break through the fog.

Penny came running out of the lighthouse to join her mother. "You were right, Mom. They *do* have a post office! Can I send a postcard to my friends at home?"

"Sure, why not?" Maggie handed Penny a pen and some change. "Hey, did you know Abby wasn't going out with Tyson anymore?"

"Yup, I told her he was a loser. Besides, she has a new boyfriend now." And Penny was off again to send her postcards.

Maggie chewed on this new bit of information for a moment. *Oh, she does, does she?*

Chapter 34

"So, where is this place?" Jake asked.

"I'm not exactly sure, but GG said it would be easy to spot because it's painted in crazy, bright colours. Apparently it's right on the beach, so if we just keep going along Beach Shore Road we should come across it. My mom spent a lot of time out here, so it can't be too far away."

Abby had told Jake all about her conversation with GG, specifically about the cottage she had read about in her mother's diary. GG had given her the keys and now they were driving slowly along the winding road that followed the beach, keeping their eyes peeled for the elusive cottage. The road ran so close to the beach that you could hear the surf crashing onto the sand. They passed several smaller beaches along the way, tucked into the corner of an inlet, and so small they were like private beaches. Every so often they could see cottages hidden among the grasses, most looking a little worse for wear, but happily facing the sea; but no signs yet of the colourful cottage.

"Isn't it cool how all the houses are painted a different colour? Look, that one is actually purple!" Jake pointed at the houses as they drove by. "The houses where we live are all boring brick or white siding."

"I know. That's one of the coolest things about being Down East. It's like a competition to see who can paint their house the most unique colour. I think our cottage will be the winner, though. GG said its colours were pretty psychedelic, and it's one of the few that is actually right on the beach," Abby said.

They scanned the beach, every so often seeing a small hut nestled amongst the dunes. Up ahead they spotted a petite cottage whose bright colours were hard to miss.

"That's got to be it!" Abby exclaimed. Her eyes widened as they approached, hardly believing that they had found it. She pulled the car off the road onto the grass-covered track, crushing the tall grass and weeds. Everything was wild and overgrown with neglect. Abby jumped out of the car and ran ahead, motioning for Jake to hurry up. The grasses tickled their legs as they made their way to the front of the cottage. Abby knew this was the place; she could feel it.

A battered sign just visible in the weeds confirmed that this was the spot. The faded tag had a lot number and Beach Shore Road written on it. A small lopsided outhouse at the back was perched at an odd angle to the ground. Abby secretly hoped they wouldn't need to use it. They held their noses as they peeked inside the outhouse. A 1978 Sears catalogue lay splayed on the floor.

"At least we have toilet paper if we need it," Abby laughed. "I remember a story Mr. Jack told me once from when he was a kid. Some kids had pushed over an outhouse with someone still inside, as a prank. I would be mortified if anyone ever did that to me. It's bad enough just holding your breath while you're in there, let alone getting pushed over unexpectedly. God knows what could be creeping around." She shuddered at the thought.

They walked back around to the front of the cottage. "C'mon, let's check it out!" Abby called out over the surf. The place looked more like a dollhouse than a cottage. Its bright yellow paint was weathered and peeling and the turquoise gingerbread trim gave it a whimsical look. Narrow steps led up to a small porch that looked barely strong enough to hold the weight of two chairs, the railing missing on one side. The screen door hung on one remaining hinge and every so often it would catch in the wind, banging loudly into the door frame. Two symmetrical windows faced out to the sea, so dirty with years of salt and sand that they couldn't see inside. A weather-beaten old sign, with a large rope knot at the bottom, hung lazily off the railing. It appeared to be a nautical weather guide. It read:

Rope moving — windy
Rope still — calm
Rope invisible — foggy
Rope wet — rainy
Rope dry — sunny
Rope missing — hurricane

They laughed at the unusual Nova Scotia sense of humour; it was corny, but true. Abby pulled the keys out of her pocket and fiddled with the lock. They clearly hadn't been used in some time, and the lock itself was flaking with rust.

"That lock isn't going to keep anybody out, is it?"

Jake asked.

"I don't think that's really the point, but they probably closed it up so not just anyone could walk in." The lock turned easily, and the door, having swelled to strange proportions after years of facing the ocean, protested loudly as they pushed to open it. Abby hesitated, peeking around the door before stepping across the small threshold, Jake right behind her. The room smelled damp and musty from being closed up for so long, and cobwebs hung from every corner. Water had stained the ceiling with brown spots, and the floor was covered with a fine coating of sand.

"Well, it certainly is a beach cottage!" Abby said.

They tiptoed around carefully as though they were invading someone's privacy. Faded blue gingham curtains hung limply from the windows, the hems frayed. A small bedroom was visible off the main room, and a small area at the back of the cottage served as a kitchen, but was essentially a counter with a hotplate. Two large white wicker chairs hobbled in the corners, and a low wooden table sat in the middle. A bookshelf rested against one wall, old books with curled corners on one shelf, random pieces of driftwood on another and a series of baskets on the bottom shelf.

But what shocked Abby the most was that almost every square inch of wall space was covered with photos. Some were roughly framed with bits of driftwood, while others were randomly taped to the wall, the edges curled and the tape yellow and brittle. Mom must have taken these photos, she thought. Most of the shots were of scenery — the beach, the surf, the dunes — and they were really quite good. Her mom clearly had an eye for a unique shot. Her mother had talked about wanting to be a photographer but had never really pursued it, focusing on journalism instead. But look at all these photos! Abby was surprised to know that her mother loved taking photos as much as she did. The only time she took photos now was to mark special family events. Abby wondered why she had stopped. Abby and Jake examined the photos one by one, and came across some shots of Maggie with her growing stomach.

"Look, I'm actually in some of these photos!" Abby laughed. "My mom's pregnant, so that has to be me!" She had to admit it was a strange thought now that she had said it out loud. It was uncanny how much her mother looked like her — or rather the other way around. Abby lingered on the photos, taking in all the details and trying to imagine her mother here at this cottage.

"So, how did you find out about this place, again?" Jake asked.

"I read about it in my mother's diary," she said, pausing at another shot taken at sunset. The colours had faded but the sea spray illuminated by the sun was stunning.

"Really?" Jake sounded intrigued. "And how did this particular item come into your possession?"

Abby was pleased that Jake actually seemed interested and continued her story. "I found it in my room at GG's. It's my mother's old bedroom, but I've always had that room, so I guess you could call it my room now. It has a cool gabled window and old hardwood floors that creak when you walk across them. I accidentally stubbed my toe on a piece of floorboard and when I bent over to check it out, I realized it was really loose. It lifted off easily, and there underneath the floorboard was a diary — her diary. My mom mentions that she spent most of the summer she was pregnant at a cottage. So next time I was talking to GG I just casually asked her about it. Of course, Mom never mentioned a cottage to me, but GG didn't know that. She seemed pretty cool about us checking it out, and here we are."

"Cool," he said, grinning. "It's like figuring out a mystery that you aren't supposed to know about. Hey, look. Some Hardy Boys books! Do you remember these? My dad was always trying to get me to read them, but I think it was just because he liked them as a kid. I never really got into them."

"Me too — my Mom was always trying to get *me* to read Nancy Drew! I do love a good mystery!" They both laughed. "Let's see what else we can find."

They moved into the bedroom. It was painted baby blue and the once-cheerful gingham curtains at the window looked sad with age. There was a double bed with a black metal frame and a couple of quilts lay at the end as though waiting to be used. There was just enough room beside the bed for a night table and light, but otherwise that was all that would fit in the small space. The walls were bare except for one large photo framed in driftwood pieces at odd angles. It was a photo of Maggie on the beach, smiling, with her arms around a guy on either side of her.

"Hey, that's my dad!" Abby said, pointing at Glen. "That's so cool."

Jake leaned in to take a closer look at the photo. He looked at Abby and back at the photo again. He seemed puzzled.

"What?" asked Abby.

"You're not going to believe this, but the other guy in the photo? That's *my* dad."

Chapter 35

Rick had chosen a classic spot for dinner. The Five Fishermen on Argyle was practically an icon in Halifax, well-known for their seafood dinners. Maggie had to admit she was enjoying herself. She couldn't quite believe that she was sitting across from him having dinner — again. She wasn't even sure that she wanted to be here. Well, that wasn't entirely true. But what *was* she doing here? Why had she said yes a second time? He was like an undertow pulling her out to the open sea. She still had a lot of unanswered questions, and she wasn't about to miss this opportunity. They were seated at a lovely table at the back, candlelight, white tablecloth and warm red surroundings. Maggie had insisted they sit in a secluded spot, worried that she might run into someone she knew. Maggie's mom knew nearly everyone in town and she didn't want it getting back to her mother that she had been out for dinner with some guy who was clearly not her husband. Rick poured some wine and raised his glass to make a toast.

"Cheers. To old memories."

They clinked their glasses together and Maggie thought about those memories. There were certainly lots of good ones, but if she were honest with herself she would have to say that the whole thing with Rick was one bad memory. Maybe after all this time she could finally let it go. Clearly he was trying to change her perception of it.

They had been so good together. They had often

worked together at the YMCA and the pool parties that the lifeguards had were legendary. They had quickly grown closer and were together most weekends. The weirdest part was the fact that Rick and Glen had been friends. After she had started going out with Rick, Glen had dropped out of the picture for a while. But they still crossed paths every so often at parties and over time it became easier for them to be in the same space together. Soon Rick and Glen had resumed their friendship and the three of them would sometimes hang out together. After Christmas Maggie had found out that she was pregnant. She knew her mother would be furious but Rick's reaction was so positive and loving, she hadn't worried. They had immediately started making plans for the baby and spent the summer together at the cottage. It had also been a romantic time for the two of them. And then everything had fallen apart. Maggie was still trying to make sense of it.

They enjoyed some more wine and he ordered for both of them, assuming his take-charge style. Maggie didn't care. She found herself opening up to him about her life. She was telling him things she had never intended to tell him, but he was drawing it out of her; he was peeling away layers to expose the real Maggie underneath. He was interested in everything she said, never taking his eyes off her, except to refill their glasses. She couldn't remember the last time she'd had a conversation like this with Glen, and immediately felt guilty for letting him creep into her thoughts. The other reason Maggie had come was to make Rick realize that she was doing fine. *They* — Glen, Abby, Penny too — were fine. If he thought that she had been pining for him all these years, he was sadly mistaken.

Rick suddenly placed his cutlery in perfect parallel on his plate, as though he were finished. He looked piercingly at Maggie, making her stop mid-sentence. The room seemed eerily quiet, as though everyone had stopped talking, like they were waiting for the punchline. He reached over and took both her hands in his, his eyes penetrating, sending a shiver down Maggie's spine. What was going on? Why the sudden change in him?

"Can you ever forgive me for what happened that summer?" Rick asked.

It was like he had punched her in the stomach. She had thought about him countless times over the years, always wondering what had gone wrong, and whether things might have been different had they stayed together. She certainly hadn't given any thought to the fact that he might be thinking the same way. And suddenly all the years had washed away and she was being sucked into the whirlpool again, with no way of stopping it.

"Forgive you? Rick, I was heartbroken. You left me nine months pregnant — with our baby!" Maggie bit her lip to keep the tears away. How dare he look to her for forgiveness when it was all his fault. She didn't trust herself to look up at him.

"I know. But you and Glen had reconnected, so I knew you were going to be okay. Glen was always the kind of guy who stepped up to the plate."

Maggie looked up again quickly. She twisted her napkin in an effort to control herself and took another drink of wine. "I thought you didn't care. You said you didn't love me."

"I know what I said ... but it wasn't true. It was never true." Rick's eyes locked on hers, daring her to waver. "I have always loved you."

Maggie choked on her wine. How dare he speak to her like this? After all that had happened? She felt like the breath was being squeezed out of her. Her words came out in a harsh whisper. "What exactly are you saying?"

"I thought it was the only way that you would let me go. If you thought I didn't care, you would do what you needed to do, for Abby's sake. And that's exactly what you did."

"So you lied to me?" Maggie raised her eyebrows.

"Well, not exactly." He looked down at his plate. It was a moment before he spoke again and when he raised his head slowly he had tears in his eyes. "Maggie, the hardest thing I have ever had to do was tell you that I didn't love you."

Maggie's stomach was doing flips. Her heart was battering in her chest like a creature wanting to escape. This couldn't be happening. Was it possible that he really did love her after all this time? And what did that really mean? Wasn't it what she had always wanted? Always secretly hoped for? Were these the feelings she had been trying to ignore all of these years?

"Why did you do it? Why did you leave, then?

How *could* you?" Maggie could barely control herself, her anger giving her the confidence she needed.

"My parents were coming down hard on me. I told them about the plans we had made, and about the job I was planning to get, but they wouldn't hear of it. I didn't have a choice. When my dad got his transfer, they figured the best thing was for me to go with them, and get on with my life."

"What about *my* life? We had everything all figured out and then you pulled the rug out from under me."

"I just knew that if I told you the real reason, you would never have let go. This way you were able to move on and make a life together with Glen. You could open your heart to someone else and get on with your life."

"But I wanted to be with *you*!"

She spat the words at him, red wine spraying from her lips. She glanced quickly around the restaurant, hoping none of the other patrons had heard her outburst, but they were engrossed in their own conversations. The room started to spin. Maggie felt faint. Did that mean that after all this time, he really *did* love her?

She was so confused. Despite all that Rick was telling her, she wanted to be here, with him. She was actually happy to know that he had always loved her. Emotions swirled around in her head. She tried to stand. She needed air. Everything was closing in on her. Suddenly the wine rose in her throat and she felt the room spin away.

Now Maggie sat slumped in the passenger seat, covering her eyes with her hand while Rick drove her home. They had hardly spoken a word to one another. Maggie was still embarrassed about the scene she had caused at the restaurant, not to mention the bomb Rick had dropped in her lap. It would have been enough to make anybody pass out. He had been very understanding, calmly helping her up as though nothing had happened. Once her head had stopped spinning, she had asked Rick to take her home. The combination of wine and Rick's confession had totally overwhelmed her.

The car seemed unnaturally quiet, so Maggie turned on the radio to break the tension. The strains of classical music were a welcome distraction and the drive passed quickly. The music allowed her to come back to the thoughts swimming around in her head, each one competing for attention and none of them winning. Before she knew it, they were turning into her mother's drive, and Maggie tried to think of what she could possibly say to Rick.

"I think we'd better say goodbye right here. I'm not in the mood to answer any questions tonight," she said.

In the half-light, Rick looked so dejected, Maggie actually felt sorry for him. He was so different from Glen, it was hard to believe she was attracted to them both. Glen was rugged-looking where Rick was clean-cut; Glen was safe where Rick was dangerous; and at this very moment, Rick was exciting. And she knew it. Rick was clearly waiting for the right moment to say something. "So, do you think we might try this again?" Rick asked.

Maggie paused before answering. A simple question loaded with possibilities. She still had so many things to ask him. Other than his shocking confession, Rick hadn't really told her anything. She needed to reconsider her feelings for him. Every time she looked at him, she was drawn into his gaze again. She wasn't sure she could trust herself.

"I don't think I can answer that right now. Can you give me a couple of days? You know, to think about things," Maggie said.

"Sure. I understand. Are you sure you're okay?" Rick asked for the hundredth time.

"I'll be fine." She opened the door and stepped out. "And thanks for dinner."

The passionate exchange of their earlier conversation was gone, replaced with awkwardness, like two strangers on their first date. She said goodnight, and watched as he turned the car around and drove away.

Maggie made her way carefully down the driveway in her black heels. Every so often a twinge shot up her calf, reminding her of the episode at the Grand Parade. She opened the door and the smell of popcorn hung in the air. Two empty bowls sat on the coffee table, and Penny lay in a heap at the end of the couch, sound asleep. Abby was nowhere in sight.

"How was dinner?" her mother asked.

Maggie ignored her question. "Why isn't Penny in bed?"

"She fell asleep before the movie was done and I didn't have the heart to wake her," Gil said.

"Where's Abby?" Maggie asked. She felt slightly nauseous and hoped it was the wine and not the anticipation of something more. Did she know what Abby's plans were for tonight?

"She went to that bonfire, remember? All the kids working on the project got together tonight at the beach. Jack went over to help them get the bonfire started."

"It's late. Why the hell isn't she home yet?" Maggie's voice sounded more distressed than she had intended but she didn't care.

"Oh, they're probably having fun and just lost track of time," Gil said with a wave of her hand, still watching her show.

"Yes, I know all about losing track of time!" Maggie said, the sinking feeling growing in her stomach.

Chapter 36

It was a perfect summer night at the beach. The setting sun painted the sky a million shades of orange as it sank lower on the horizon. The water was aflame with colour, enjoying one last moment in the spotlight before fading into darkness for another day. The Project H group shouted out words of encouragement as Jake busied himself with starting the bonfire. They had all scoured the beach for driftwood, and Mr. Jack had patiently showed Jake how to assemble the sticks and wood for maximum drag, as he called it.

Penny came up beside Mr. Jack, carrying an armful of twigs and branches that she had collected. She dropped them at the edge of the stones that they had laid in a circle to designate the bonfire spot. She brushed her hands on her shorts and looked eagerly at Mr. Jack. "What do you think, Mr. Jack? Will this be good for starting the bonfire?"

"Definitely. You've done a fine job. These smaller pieces will be perfect for getting the fire started, and then we'll add the bigger pieces once the flames are going strong."

Abby could tell that Penny was thrilled to be contributing to this important part of the evening. Penny had begged GG to let her stay for the bonfire, but GG had felt she was too young to be hanging out with the teenagers all night. They had agreed that she could stay for the pizza dinner, and once Mr. Jack got the bonfire going he would bring her home with him.

"You need to give the fire some room to breathe,"

Mr. Jack said. "If you just pile everything on top of itself, the flames can't get any air. Make it like a teepee and the flames have room to catch and grow."

Jake paid close attention to everything Mr. Jack was telling him. This was going to be the best bonfire ever, if he had anything to do with it. The driftwood crackled and snapped as the flames caught and spread through the smaller twigs. Everyone clapped and cheered as the flames reached higher. Couples linked arms and danced around the fire like tribal warriors.

"Well, that fire's looking mighty fine, son. Just keep feeding it some small twigs every now and again and it'll keep going just fine. Then you can start adding some larger pieces. I'll leave you kids to it." He waved over his shoulder as everyone thanked him. Penny ran to catch up and at the last minute she turned to yell to the group. "Have fun, everybody! Have some s'mores for me!"

Abby could see that it was all Penny could do to drag herself away, but she was glad she wouldn't have to watch out for her tonight. She had more important things on her mind. Abby hugged her arms to her chest. She was so excited. This was like an official start of summer holidays for her, the moment when all the fun began. They had ordered pizzas at the church for dinner and then come across to the beach to build the bonfire. People kept arriving, carrying blankets and hoodies to keep warm as the sun went down. Jake plunked himself beside her on a hunk of driftwood and admired his handiwork.

"It's awesome. People will see it for miles," Abby

said. She was genuinely impressed. The dry twigs crackled and the smoky smell instantly brought back memories of good times and good friends. He put his arm around her and Abby snuggled in close, thinking that she had never been happier.

Abby loved having bonfires on the beach. It reminded her of Halifax Natal Day weekends when they came Down East. Her family would build a bonfire worthy of competition in honour of Halifax's birthday. Neighbours and cottagers up and down the beach would join in and no one came empty-handed. She and Penny and Sarah would spend the whole day collecting driftwood and logs for the fire. She could still taste the slightly charred hotdogs that they cooked over the flames, and later they roasted marshmallows that turned out soft and gooey. It was always a challenge get it off the stick and into your mouth without getting all that sticky mess in your hair. And then when you crawled into bed that night smelling smoky from the fire, you slept like a baby from all the salt and fresh air. Abby sighed and hoped that someone had remembered to bring some marshmallows.

The sun had finally gone down beyond the horizon, setting the sky aflame with one final display of orange and maroon before it grew dark. Faces glowed in the brightness of the bonfire, and twilight cast the group in shadows as they danced around on the beach. The waves were a symphony in the background, rushing in to the sand and out again. Jake reached into his knapsack and pulled out two water bottles. He smiled as he passed one to Abby, and opened the other for himself. He took a satisfying swig and grinned at her.

"No, thanks," Abby said.

Jake looked at her like she had food on her face or something. Self-consciously she wiped her cheek, but he kept looking at her strangely and he offered the water bottle again.

"No, thanks. I'm not thirsty."

"Have a little drink. You'll be glad you did," Jake insisted. She took a drink and broke into a coughing fit as the liquid burned in her throat. When she recovered she started laughing, realizing how stupid she must have seemed when she didn't get it the first time. She caught her breath and took another sip, this one going down a lot more smoothly than the first.

"Oh, *that* kind of water," she said, and they started laughing.

The next thing she knew, Jake had grabbed her hand and they were dancing around the flames. They obviously weren't the only ones who had thrown a little moonshine into their knapsacks, as the air filled with laughter. Before long, the group had made a chain that trailed around the fire and down the beach. Abby grabbed Jake's waist but was laughing so hard she could barely keep up. Every so often Jake took off at greater speed, and Abby would lose her grip. She dragged the person behind with her as they fell into a heap in the sand. Soon the guitars came out and everyone started singing. They spread out the quilt Abby had brought and lay back to look up at the sky. It was a brilliant clear night and the stars shone like a million tiny diamonds.

What she wouldn't do to be able to live here all the time. She considered bringing the subject up again with her mother. Every so often the idea of moving back to Nova Scotia resurfaced but never seemed to get resolved. Even her mother was more relaxed and happy when she was here. Maybe it was the fact that her mom was on vacation that made the difference, but Abby was sure it was the sea air. She was convinced that the ocean was a cure for everything.

Abby was having an amazing time, with an amazing guy. They'd had a few more swigs of vodka, or beach water, as they had decided to call it, and Abby was feeling happy and warm inside. They stared at the flames, mesmerized by the orange glow. It was a delicious combination of warmth on your face from the fire and coolness on your back from the sea breeze. Abby's face glowed in the light of the bonfire. She looked over at Jake, wondering what he was thinking, and hoped that he was feeling as good about things as she was. She thought about the list she had written in her diary, and wondered if maybe they might find a secluded spot a little later on. She smiled to herself. They leaned close to each other, and rocked back and forth to the music.

"I haven't sung these songs in so long, I forgot that I knew them," Jake said. "My mom sent me away to camp for a month every summer when I was little. I always put up a fight about going, but it was a great camp. We would have a bonfire every night, and people would play guitars and sing along just like this. You didn't know that I knew the words to the hokey pokey, did you?" Jake stood up and put his hands on his hips and did a little sashay to prove his point. Abby fell back again laughing and holding her stomach.

Jake sat back down and started stroking the palm of her hand. It felt the most romantic thing anyone had ever done and she gave a little shiver of delight.

"Are you cold?" Jake asked.

"Just a little," Abby said. She snuggled in closer to Jake, putting her arms around his waist and leaning into his shoulder.

"Want to go for a walk?" Jake asked.

"Sure." Abby shivered again in anticipation.

Abby pulled up the hood of her sweatshirt and Jake threw the quilt around their shoulders as they walked away from the fire. The voices faded behind them as they progressed further into the darkness. Abby's eyes adjusted quickly, but the blackness ahead of them was intense. She could remember when she was small, sometimes sneaking out to the porch at night when she couldn't sleep. If all the lights in the house were out, she could raise her hand in front of her face and not be able to see a thing, even though she knew her hand was there. It was hard to conceive darkness so all-encompassing. Her dad always used the phrase "dark as pitch," and this certainly was. This time it was Abby who took Jake's hand, and he didn't object.

"Let's sit over here, out of the wind a bit." Jake pointed to an alcove on the beach where the dune grass

Yvonne Leslie

created a sheltered spot. Jake put the quilt on the sand, and after they sat down, he put his arm around Abby's shoulders. Abby dug her feet into the cool sand, then lifted her foot up to let the sand run between her toes. Her stomach did a flip as she thought about making out with Jake. They were far enough away from the group that no one would ever be able to see what they were doing. They glanced back at the glow of the bonfire in the distance, shadowy figures melting together and voices carrying across the breeze. They sat quietly looking out into the darkness, a faint glow on the water from the moon playing peekaboo with the clouds. The waves had calmed as the tide went out and the water lapped at the shore. Abby crossed her fingers, anticipating what might happen next.

"Are you having fun?" Jake asked.

"Oh yes, honestly, this is the best summer ever! I wish we could live here, instead of just coming in the summer. I guess we'll just have to make sure we have a bonfire every year to start the summer." She and Jake had developed a secret handshake which they performed every time they agreed on something. It was their equivalent of a high-five, only way better. She held her hand up to Jake's to do it now, but Jake pulled his hand away.

Abby tensed. Had she said something wrong?

"What's wrong?" She looked at Jake but she couldn't make out his features in the dark. She could kick herself for ruining this lovely moment. She reached out to turn his face to hers but he turned away. Now she was really worried. What could possibly be wrong? Jake scooped the sand at the edge of the blanket, as if digging for the answer. He didn't speak for a while, and when he did, his voice cracked a little.

"I won't be back next summer, remember? I'm working with my dad on this project, but after this summer he'll be on to something else."

He kept digging as though he wasn't sure what else he should do. Abby was quiet. She knew that he was only here for the summer, but she had tried not to let herself think about it. Not yet. She didn't want to accept the fact that she had finally met a guy that made her feel the way no one else ever had, and all they would have was this one summer together. Life just wasn't fair. She gently reached for his hands to stop his digging.

"Let's not worry about it now, okay?"

"Okay," Jake said, and he leaned in to kiss her. His lips were soft and warm and wet and Abby thought she might die on the spot. He ran his fingers through her hair and kissed her again. Abby gave in to it, not wanting this moment to end. Ever.

"Abby! Abb-eeee!" A voice carried across the beach, occasionally interrupted by the sound of the waves.

Abby's heart did a flip. She quickly sat up, trying to make out the figure advancing towards them on the beach. Why would anyone be looking for them? She was really annoyed at the interruption.

"Did you hear that? Someone's calling me. I can't make out who it is. Maybe we'd better find out what they want."

They grabbed the quilt and starting walking in the direction of the silhouette. As they got closer they finally met up with the person who had been running towards them. And with the sudden horror of recognition, Abby said, "Oh God, it's my mother."

Chapter 37

Today was not going well. Maggie rubbed her forehead to ease her throbbing headache. She had dragged herself to the bathroom to survey her bleary-eyed reflection in the mirror. Not pretty. Her eyes looked like someone had taken a red Sharpie marker and traced road maps on the whites. She didn't think she'd had that much to drink, so it must have been from all the crying. Oh, wait, she did remember having another glass after she had brought Abby home from the bonfire. Who wouldn't need a drink after all that she had been through last night? If she had to be truthful, she'd have to say that she'd been dipping into the bottle a little more lately, but considering her relationship with Abby, it was sometimes the only way she could deal with it. She would never admit that she had a problem, but her head was telling her a different story. Her doctor had warned her that she needed to keep an eye on her liquor intake. It could wreak havoc with her blood sugar levels, complicated by her diabetes, which probably had as much to do with the way she was feeling as anything. But her doctor didn't have a difficult teenage daughter and sometimes she just referred to it as self-medicating. As Val would say, "A girl's gotta do what a girl's gotta do." She was still shaking from the events of last night. She had popped a Tylenol with the tepid water on her bedside table and had shuffled downstairs. She had been pouring a coffee into an extra-large cup when Abby had stomped into the kitchen, hands on her hips, ready for battle.

"So, what the hell was all that about?" Abby had asked.

Maggie had felt the bands tightening on her forehead and had shuffled over to the family room in a feeble attempt at escape. She had needed to sit down. Abby had followed and had sat down directly opposite Maggie, waiting for a response. Maggie had appraised Abby over the rim of her coffee cup before taking a sip. How was it possible that a mother could love her kid to death one minute and just want to slap her, the next? she had thought to herself. Whenever she had argued with her own mother, Gil had often commented that she hoped Maggie would one day have a daughter like herself. It appeared she had gotten her wish.

"Excuse me?" Maggie had known what she was referring to but she had hardly been able to form the words with her thick tongue.

"Last night? You had to pick last night of all nights to be all high and mighty about my curfew?" Abby had sat arms crossed, with a look of indignation on her face.

"There was more to it than that, Abby. I was worried about you," Maggie had replied.

"That's crap! GG knew exactly where I was and who I was with. She wasn't worried." Abby's eyes had flared as she fired her comments at Maggie.

Well, she is not your mother. Maggie had bitten back her response, in an effort to keep the conversation from spiralling out of control. "I expected you would be home by the time I got home, and when you weren't, I came looking for you. How was I to know that nothing was wrong? I obviously couldn't call you at the beach." Maggie was fading quickly. She had been sure that she wasn't ready to handle the battle her daughter seemed ready to wage.

"There *wasn't* anything wrong. I was having a good time for a change. And not only did you ruin it, but you totally embarrassed me in front of my new friends. I hate you!"

Maggie had closed her eyes to better receive the barrage of remarks from Abby, but when she opened her eyes again, Abby had already stalked off. She sighed wearily and curled deeper into the corner of the couch, both hands around the cup, holding it steady. Her head was pounding with a vengeance. Maggie had expected that kind of reaction from Abby but she still felt that she had done the right thing.

Maggie lay back on the couch, letting her thoughts wander back to when she was pregnant with Abby. She remembered how upset her mother had been when she told her she was pregnant. She was sad that she hadn't been able to turn to her mother at that time, but her mother had pulled away from her. Maybe things would have been different if her father had still been alive. He had always been able to help her mother to see things more clearly, especially where Maggie was concerned. She'd had a terrible argument with her mother, and Maggie had yelled things she would never have dared say in front of her father. And Gil had slapped her. Her mother's expression was absolutely wretched afterwards, but she had walked away without another word. After that, Maggie figured she'd better keep quiet and listen to her mother's end of the deal. And now, all these years later, they were still trying to fix the rift.

She came back to the present and mulled over the events of the previous evening: her dinner with Rick, the wine, and the most incredible part where Rick told her he loved her and always had. She had been so overwhelmed and confused that when she came home to find Abby not there, she'd lost it. She wasn't cut out to deal with all of this. She needed to make some decisions about Rick and she needed to get some perspective on Abby. When she opened her eyes, her mother was sitting at the opposite end of the couch. Maggie wanted to close her eyes again. Here it comes, she thought, Round 2.

"Why do you have to be so hard on that child?" Gil asked.

"I don't know. I guess I learned it from you," Maggie shot back. The moment the words were out of her mouth she wanted to take them back. She wasn't going to score any points with her mother that way, and she could use her mother's help with all of this.

Her mother chose to ignore her comment. "Seriously, Maggie, she's a good kid. Why are you so protective of her?"

Maggie softened at her mother's words. For the first time in a long while it felt as though her mother was reaching out to her, really trying to talk to her. Maggie felt so emotionally drained that she let the walls come down and everything she had been feeling came pouring out. "Because she's 16 years old and teenagers do crazy things and I'm scared to death that something bad is going to happen to her. After everything that we've been through already, I just couldn't take it." She rubbed her fingers on her temples and her eyes filled with tears. She stifled a sob as she tried to say the words she feared most. "Mom, my worst fear is that she'll get pregnant like I did."

Gil slid closer to Maggie and rested her hand on Maggie's knee. "That's not going to happen. She's not you. If you would step back for a moment and look at her you'd see that. She's trying to fit in. She's just trying to figure out who she is, just like you did at that age. And you dragging her away from her friends last night didn't help any," Gil said gently.

Maggie looked at her mother, and she just couldn't contain herself any longer. She'd been worrying herself sick for years, and her mother might very well be the only person who could truly understand. The dam burst and everything came spilling out. Her mother wrapped her arms around her and held her as Maggie cried.

"Oh, Maggie. You are still so hung up on the past that you can't seem to move on to the future." It had been so long since her mother had held her that she sobbed even harder. She sobbed for years gone by, for opportunities lost, but most of all she sobbed for the love of a mother and her daughter.

Chapter 38

Abby lay curled up on the bed, the white chenille bedspread leaving little bumps on her bare legs. She had been so anxious about going to the project yesterday, after her mother's invasion at the bonfire. She had been afraid of what Jake would think, and whether he would even want to speak to her again. She had never been so mortified in all her life. And then when she and Penny had pulled into the church parking lot, she had seen Jake standing on the steps with a coffee in each hand and a big smile on his face, and she knew everything was going to be fine.

The gabled window was open and the curtains blew lazily in the breeze. She had been up here reading for hours — a unique mystery that had captured her interest right from the get-go. But this wasn't one of her typical mysteries. This was her mother's diary. This was one of those stories where she was pretty sure she knew how it ended but didn't quite know all the details that led up to that point. And it was proving to be very intriguing.

Penny and GG were watching *Jeopardy* downstairs. Every so often she could hear them yelling out their own guesses, and her mother was out with Val, further increasing her chances of being left alone. There were no locks on these doors, but Abby was seriously debating whether she should ask GG for one. Her mother seemed to think that she had the right to barge in on Abby at any and every moment. Ever since the night that Sarah had stayed over, and they had been pretty sure that her mother was eavesdropping, she hadn't been sure about how much privacy she really had. She was relieved to think she wouldn't have to deal with that tonight.

Abby had feigned a headache after supper as an excuse to come upstairs and read uninterrupted. She thought about all those photos she had found at the cottage with Jake. Jake was confused too, but she had begged him not to ask his dad anything about it just yet. She needed to figure this out. Why would Jake's dad be in photos with her mom and dad? It just didn't make sense. She knew Jake's dad had grown up here in Nova Scotia too, but her mother had never mentioned him. Then again, there were probably a lot of people Abby wouldn't know about. But wasn't it a really weird coincidence that Jake's dad, Rick, was in the photos? She hoped the answers might be written on these diary pages.

It was bizarre for Abby to be reading all this stuff about her mom when she was 16: the exact same age as Abby this summer. She tried to picture her mom sitting on this same bed as she wrote in her diary. What her mother had written could easily have been something she might have written in her own journal. Maybe all teenagers thought the same way. It was hard to believe that her mother ever was a teenager! More importantly, she was reading about when her mom was pregnant. Pregnant with *her*.

Abby pulled out the photo she had brought back with her from the cottage. She had slipped it out of its driftwood frame and wedged it between the covers of one of the books they had found on the shelf so it wouldn't get damaged. She looked at it closely, trying to compare the girl in the photo to the woman who was her mother. They couldn't possibly be the same person. Her mother was wearing a man's button-down shirt stretched tight across her big tummy, her long hair blowing across her face, as she hooked her arms over each of the guys on either side of her. Abby's dad had longer hair that blew haphazardly across his face as he looked over at Maggie. Jake's dad stood out in contrast to the other two, with his bleached blond hair, his vivid grey eyes and tanned face. They all looked young and innocent and ... happy, yet she knew there had to be more to the story.

Abby plumped up the pillows and leaned back with the diary on her legs. Every so often something would drop out — like a dried flower, or a poem scribbled on a piece of napkin, or a movie stub. So many mementos of a time so many years ago, a time that was dear to her mother in the same way her memories were special to her. Abby had her share of wrappers and stubs tucked between the pages of her journal. Maybe we aren't so different after all, she mused, and kept reading.

Dear Diary,

This morning I was sitting on the front porch reading and feeling kind of sorry for myself. I heard something on the beach and I looked up to see Rick and Glen walking along the beach. They were both holding onto a huge basket covered with a blanket. They both wore crazy yellow sou'westers — the kind of hats the fishermen wear — and their tummies were huge because they each had a beach ball under their T-shirts. I laughed so hard I almost cried. I got hugs from both of them and then we went inside to unpack the basket. They had everything in there — books that I had asked for from the library, a pile of magazines, a couple of bags of cheesies (my favourite), some more sewing supplies so I could keep working on the quilt, a checkerboard, and a whole pile of muffins, and squares and cupcakes — like I wasn't fat enough already! It was like Christmas for me! And the best part was that they stayed all afternoon. We tried to play toss with the beach balls but the wind wasn't helping. Then we sat on the porch pigging out and taking turns at checkers. I don't think I've ever had so much fun playing checkers — everybody was cheating! I love those guys more than anything, and I honestly think they would do anything for me. (sigh)

Abby couldn't stand it any longer and flipped to a section near the end of the diary. Some of the words were smudged, like tears had fallen onto the page. Intrigued, Abby continued reading.

Dear Diary,

I can't believe this is happening. Everything has changed — I'm so confused. I can hardly stand to write this but if I don't, I'm not sure how I'm ever going to make any sense of it.

Yesterday I was really enjoying being at the cottage, because I know we probably wouldn't be here much longer, from the way the baby is pushing to get out. Rick said he was coming out to see me and I was excited about the picnic lunch that he had planned. He seemed a little quiet when he got here but I figured we would talk when we got to our picnic spot. We walked down the beach to our favourite spot, the one that we christened Driftwood Cove. And then he dropped a bomb on me. He said he doesn't love me, that we can't be together. I'm suffocating him. I couldn't believe he was telling me the truth after all that we've been through already. I mean, we had PLANS. I was so upset I threw all the food at him and called him things I've never said to him before. It was so awful. And that wasn't even the worst of it. I was so mad at him I told him to leave and he did. I had to get across the boulders to the next beach by myself. Of course with my big belly I fell, and landed on the rocks. I felt like I couldn't move and all I could hear was Stinker barking on the other beach. I don't know how long I lay there but I was so worried about the baby. Then Glen appeared from nowhere. I was so glad to see him. He was so sweet. He put my arm around his neck and helped me walk back to the cottage. I was pretty banged up so Glen went to get my mom. She drove me back to the house and they called the doctor to make sure that the baby was okay. Thank goodness you are! I have some scrapes and bruises on my one side but I'm okay too. I have been crying a lot and I can't stop. Everyone thinks I'm still in shock and worried about the baby. But I'm really crying about Rick. What on earth am I going to do?

Abby realized she had been holding her breath.

Treading Water

She pushed the diary aside and picked up the photo again. She looked closely at the three faces in the photo and then the connections became horribly clear. Her mother had been crying over a boy named Rick Morrison. And that someone was her *real* father.

Chapter 39

"Hey, you want to take a little spin? You know, for old time's sake?"

Rick looked at her with those piercing eyes and she just couldn't say no. When he had called to see if she had any plans, she had hesitated. After the confession he had made at dinner the other night, she wasn't sure what to think anymore. But she still felt she wanted to find out what it all meant. What was behind it? Where would it go? If she didn't reconcile her feelings on this trip, while Rick was here, how was she ever going to move on? And whatever she decided, it would be the right thing. She just needed to know. And in some weird, twisted way it felt like the right thing to do. So she had said yes. She'd managed to answer the phone before Abby, who had been getting a lot of calls from Jake lately. Both she and Penny had been keeping themselves busy with their new friends and Project H. Their vacation was going by quickly. Just this morning they were commenting that they wished this summer wouldn't end, and Maggie felt the same way. It always took a couple of weeks to unwind, but now Maggie woke up happy and rested. She hadn't felt this good in a long time.

"Sure, why not, it's a beautiful evening. Just let me grab a sweater and a blanket." She was back in no time and jumped into the car, the wind blowing her hair around her face.

"Hey, that looks familiar," said Rick, eyeing the quilt.

Maggie ran her fingers over the soft-worn fabric, each patch telling its own story. She had made this quilt for the baby, as a way of wrapping it in another generation of love, and it had been the perfect project to fill her days when she was pregnant. It had even kept her legs warm while she worked on the deck, sitting in the cool sea breeze. Maggie remembered every agonizing little stitch. It had been a labour of love, with the emphasis on labour. Turned out she wasn't much of a seamstress, but with a little help from her mother, it had turned out just fine.

"Yup, Abby brings this ratty thing with her everywhere she goes. It's always on the bed here waiting for her when she comes to visit. I'm sure she won't mind if I soak up some more beach scent with it. She loves it when it smells of sea and salt. It's still holding together pretty well, considering."

They drove along without talking, enjoying the drive. Every now and again Rick would look over at her, smile and look away. Maggie had the feeling that he was gearing up to say something, but didn't know how to begin. Maggie bit her lip. She was amazed at how easy it was being with Rick. It was like they had picked up where they left off. After his confession, she wasn't sure what to think anymore. She had to admit she was considering spending more time with Rick. She just wanted to make sure she was doing the right thing a second time. Should she leave things open so that she could have time to think about it? But that was crazy. There was nothing to think about. Would she really ruin everything she had, her life with Glen, and her lovely daughters, to set everything into a spin again, just to be with Rick? It was ridiculous. *Was it? Wasn't it?*

Maggie was pulled from her reverie. She had been so wrapped up in her thoughts that she hadn't been paying much attention to where they were going, and as she looked up, the cottage came into view; the same cottage where she had spent her last summer in Nova Scotia waiting for Abby to be born. Tears sprang to her eyes and for a moment she couldn't breathe.

"Wow. It's still here," Maggie said softly. She hugged her arms to her chest as a wave of memories came flooding back. She had spent a whole summer here, watching her tummy grow, and lazily enjoying the ocean view every day. Every day she had walked the beach, her camera over her shoulder and Stinker close on her heels. She wondered if the photos were still hanging in the cottage. They must have all shrivelled up and fallen off by now. She realized she still hadn't followed up on her plan to pull out her camera again. Maybe she would even look into buying a newer one while she was still here so that she could go back to taking photos of her favourite subject — the beach.

She and Rick had spent countless hours here, curled up under a blanket, discussing their future and making plans. Glen had spent a fair bit of time with her here as well. As the summer wore on, Rick had not been able to make it out as often, and being the reliable guy that he was, Glen came by to make sure she was okay. It was one of the best summers she had ever had, right up to the point where Rick had walked out on her and Abby. The memories were overwhelming. Was that why Rick was bringing her here? So they could pick up where they left off?

"Well sure, why wouldn't it be?"

"I don't know, I guess I figured it would have disappeared into the ocean after I left. I guess that's what I would have secretly wished, to have everything from that time just wash away. But I'm glad it's still here."

"It's a cool place, but it could sure use a handyman to fix things up a bit," said Rick.

They grabbed the quilt and made their way up the front steps. They too were starting to rot away, the wood sagging in the middle where the footsteps left their mark. Rick was right. The cottage had seen better days, but in Maggie's mind it looked exactly the same.

She was transported back to days on the ocean, the damp sea air enveloping her and Stinker curled up in the rocker. She suddenly missed Stinker terribly. Stinker had been a border collie, like Jep, except that he had been all black. Rick had brought Stinker as a gift for Maggie on the first day she had officially moved her things into the cottage. They had taken him down to the beach one day to run in the waves. He was having a grand old time until suddenly he came running with something hanging off his back. As he got closer they saw that it was a clump of seaweed, and it had tangled around one of his paws. He had smelled of seaweed for days afterwards, and from then on they had called him Stinker. Maggie had insisted that

Stinker make the move to Ontario with them, but sadly he had been hit by a car a year later. It still broke Maggie's heart to think about him, wishing that he could have been around longer to get to know the baby he had lovingly protected.

She would never have made it through that summer without him. On the nights that she was alone at the cottage, Stinker nuzzled her neck lovingly and would curl up in front of her tummy, stretched out in perfect alignment with her body, like he was protecting the baby. And when they walked on the beach, Stinker never strayed very far, as though keeping a close eye on her, like he had a sixth sense to watch out for her.

Maggie's thoughts returned to the present, her stomach in knots. She hadn't planned on finding herself back at this cottage and the flood of memories, good and bad, took her by surprise. The two of them stood on the porch looking out over the water. Neither spoke for quite some time, each absorbed in their own thoughts.

"Seems like just yesterday," Maggie whispered, not daring to disturb the moment.

"I wasn't totally sure you'd want to come out here ... but I hoped you would." He put his arm around her shoulders and focused on the horizon again.

"I didn't really have any choice, did I? You fairly kidnapped me!" she laughed. "I certainly would never have come out here on my own." She hesitated, the knot in her stomach twisting a little more, and turned to Rick.

He took her in his arms and held her close. She

could feel his muscular chest through his shirt, and the alluring scent of his cologne. She gave herself in to the moment, enjoying his arms around her, and feeling his breath on her neck. She looked up into his eyes and suddenly his lips were on hers, warm and intense, like he was making up for lost time. She pulled away breathless, not really knowing what to say. They kissed again, more gently this time, and she felt herself disappearing into everything she had ever dreamed about. She had missed him, and now he was here. She pulled back to collect herself for a moment. She turned to look out over the ocean, hoping to find the right answers in the waves. She needed to be sure. She was about to cross a line and she might not be able to go back. She was so confused, and yet everything about this moment felt right — the beach, the cottage and of course Rick. Did she know what she was doing? She took a deep breath. "Rick, I'm not sure if I can do this," Maggie said.

"Do what?"

"You know — take this ... where it seems to be going."

"I'm not exactly sure what you mean," Rick said.

"You. Romancing me, again. It's been lovely. I haven't felt this way in a long time. I'm amazed at how easy it was to pick up where we left off. I wasn't sure that I could, but now ..." She turned and looked at him, his face just inches from hers. She held his gaze until he turned away.

He sat in the corner of the porch railing, wringing his hands and avoiding Maggie's eyes. He didn't say anything for a few minutes and his voice was soft when he spoke. "It's not what you think, Maggie. I'm sorry if you got the wrong idea."

Maggie's heart was hammering in her chest. The knots in her stomach were unfurling like snakes and quickly turning to anger. *How dare he bring her here, of all places, to let her down, again?* She tried to control her voice. "What are you saying?" She dug her nails into her palms, trying to calm herself down. He had successfully toyed with her emotions again.

"Well, for starters, I can't stay here. I have to get back to Ottawa. I'm only here working on the Save the Harbour project and doing research over the summer. Then I'll have to go back and work on some strategies for the project."

"Wait, what? What are you talking about? The Save the Harbour project?" Maggie felt as though she were on a roller-coaster ride.

"The project that Abby and Penny have been working on all summer. They haven't told you?"

"Well, of course they told me!" She had to admit she had only been half-listening. She had been so distracted with Rick that she hadn't really put the pieces together. Suddenly her eyes grew wide, like a deer in headlights. "So you have been working *with* Abby? All summer?"

"Yes. Well, sort of." He looked down at the railing, still not meeting her eyes. "I'm not actually working at the church. I just stop by on occasion to see how things are going."

"How could you not tell me that?" She shouted

the words and saw him wince. It was all she could do to keep herself from hammering her fists against his chest. She was furious. How could she have been so blind? So stupid?

"I intended to, but I didn't want you to take Abby off the project because of me. She doesn't know who I am, unless you told her. It was the last name that gave it away. Any time I hear the name Boutilier, I pay attention. After that it was pretty obvious. She is the spitting image of you, Maggie. And she has the independence you had as a teenager, too."

Maggie couldn't believe what she was hearing. No wonder he hadn't asked to meet Abby. He had been working with her all this time, for God's sake! She paced back and forth across the porch, and then stopped with her hands over her eyes. "I can't believe you didn't tell me!" She had never felt this angry, this betrayed, this lost. And Rick was acting as though it were the most normal thing in the world to be discussing it.

"Believe me, I wanted to. But it was wonderful being in her space; to see the girl she turned out to be. You've done an amazing job. She's a great kid. And it's so great that she and Jake get along so well."

"You had no right ... Wait, Jake?"

"My son."

"Jake is your *son*?" The words came out like a hiss between her teeth. Things were spiralling out of control.

"Yes, he's just a bit younger than Abby. You know I hooked up with Vickie. Anyway, she got pregnant —

yeah, I know, don't even say it — and we got married. Of course it didn't last, but at least I have a great kid to show for it. I'm sorry for not telling you."

"Does Abby know who you are?" Maggie asked.

"No, she doesn't have any idea. If she does, she certainly hasn't said anything."

Maggie slumped back against the rickety railing, not believing what she was hearing. Somehow Rick had managed to pull the rug out from under her feet again. And then all of a sudden, images started flipping along in her mind's eye, like an old slide show, coming into focus and moving on again: the list in Abby's journal, the boy who reminded her of Rick, Abby spending time with Jake, the half-empty water bottle in Abby's purse after the bonfire.

"Oh. My. God!" Maggie shrieked hysterically as the realization hit her full-force. "If she doesn't know about you — then she doesn't know that Jake ... is her half-brother."

Chapter 40

Abby closed her bedroom door and pulled out the diary and the photos she had found at the cottage. She studied the photo of her mom with the two guys and then dropped it on the bed as though it had stung her. If Rick was her real father, what did that make Glen? She couldn't believe it. It couldn't be true. Why wouldn't her parents have told her? She deserved to know. Was it possible she had it all wrong? And how was she going to find out for sure? This man who had been supervising the Save the Harbour project all summer was her real father! It was just too weird to think about. She felt as though she might throw up.

Abby fell back on her bed and tried to make sense of the questions swimming around in her head. Her thoughts went back to Glen: in his garage, on his motorcycle, playing piggyback with her. How could this person be anything but her father? She envisioned Rick looking efficient and in control, smiling at people, shaking hands and joking like Jake did. He didn't even seem like the fatherly type. But he was Jake's father, wasn't he?

She suddenly sat bolt upright on the bed. Jake! She'd have to talk to him right away. She snuck into GG's bedroom and picked up the pink phone beside her bed. She dug into her jeans pocket for the note with the name and number of the cottage where Jake and his dad were staying. She dialled the number, tapping her foot impatiently, praying Jake would pick up.

"Hello?"

"Jake? It's me, Abby."

"Hey, what's up? You sound upset. Is everything okay?"

"I have to talk to you, right away, but I can't talk about it over the phone. Can I come over?" Abby asked.

"Sure, do you know where the cottages are?" Jake asked.

"I think I can find them. I'll be there as soon as I can, okay?" Abby hung up the phone. He might think she was losing her mind, but she didn't want to risk anyone hearing their conversation on the phone. She grabbed her sweatshirt off the bed and at the last second she remembered to grab the diary, too. Jake's not going to believe me without some kind of proof, she thought, as she tore down the stairs.

Penny and GG turned when they heard Abby's thundering footsteps on the hardwood stairs. Abby wiped her eyes with the back of her sleeve, sniffling as she went past, tears escaping no matter how hard she tried to control them.

"Abby, what's wrong?" GG got up from the couch and came towards Abby with her arms out and a look of concern on her face.

"Please, just leave me alone," Abby said, not wanting to look at her grandmother.

"Where on earth are you going?" GG sounded very upset now, and made a move to stand in Abby's way. "Are you sure you should be driving?" Abby could hear the worry in her voice, but she needed to go now. There was no time to try to explain any of this.

Treading Water

"I'll be fine, GG, don't worry," she said as she grabbed the keys off the hook and ran out the door. She fumbled with the keys in the ignition, her tears blurring her vision. She took a deep breath to calm herself down. She needed to get a grip. She *had* to talk to Jake. Now. Tonight. He was the only one who would understand how she was feeling. She reversed and the car fishtailed on the wet grass as she drove away. She pulled onto the main road, her hands still shaking from the reality of what she had discovered. But this would upset him too. They would have to figure it out together.

Questions swam through her mind as she drove. Why wouldn't her parents have told her? Could her mother have kept this a secret from Glen as well? Was that even possible? And why hadn't Rick said anything? They had crossed paths often enough, working on this project, and he acted as though everything were normal. What if she hadn't read the diary? Would she have ever known? And now that she knew, what was going to happen? Would she open a can of worms that would send everything spiralling out of control? She tried to push everything away and focus on driving, but it was like pushing water with your hands, and her thoughts kept seeping back.

The fog had rolled in like a curtain. It hung heavy and cloying, the moisture tangible on her skin. Jake had told her that he and his dad were staying in cottages just beyond Queensland in the village of Hubbards. She hadn't actually been there, but there weren't too many cottages or hotels along this stretch of highway, so she hoped it wouldn't be too hard to find. She had driven this road so many times over the past few weeks on her way to the church. The cottages couldn't be that much further. The drive seemed endless tonight and it was getting harder to see, as the fog rolled across the road in waves. Abby slowed even more and could barely make out the church as she passed it on her right. She squinted, trying to focus on the road ahead, thankful that there were no other cars on the road. Before long she spotted a row of cottages and a sign that read Surfside Inn and Cottages barely visible through the mist. Five cottages lined up on either side of the main office, each one identical, white with black shutters, and a porch, the numbers feebly lit through the mist. She pulled up in front of Number 2, jumped out of the car and ran up to the door. Jake opened the door before she had a chance to knock. He stepped out to give her a hug and put his hand gently on her back to lead her inside.

"Are you okay?" Jake asked.

"Is your dad here?" Abby glanced around furtively. She hadn't seen his car when she pulled in, but she needed to be sure.

"No, he's at a meeting in Halifax ... Why? What's going on?"

Abby pushed past him, her hair a mess and her eyes frantic. "Oh God, Jake. I don't even know where to start."

She paced back and forth, chewing on her fingernail, her mind trying to put her thoughts in order. Her words spilled out in a torrent, the anxiousness of the drive being released all at once. "Did your dad ever mention me? Or my mom?"

Jake frowned. "What are you talking about? Why would he, other than if we were discussing the Project H? Come here and sit down. I'll get you a pop. Just start at the beginning."

Abby sat down slowly on the edge of the bed and took a deep breath. Her hands trembled as she took the Pepsi from Jake. She took a sip and continued.

"You remember that photo we found at the cottage, the one with your dad and my dad on either side of my mom? I wanted to find out what that was all about and I figured there must be something about it in her diary. Tonight I was up in my room reading, and I found it. My mom got pregnant with me when she was 16. And Rick, your dad, is my father."

"Holy shit." Jake sat down abruptly beside her. "*My* dad?"

"Do you realize what this means? We're related, for God's sake! It means we can't see each other any more!" Abby broke down in sobs. Jake pulled her into his arms and they hugged tightly on the edge of the bed. It just felt so comforting that for a moment she thought that maybe things would turn out all right.

"It just doesn't make sense. Don't worry, Abby. We'll figure it out."

Abby nodded and mumbled a reply into the front of his T-shirt. When she pulled her face away to look at him, there were dark spots all over the front of his shirt from her tears. Jake couldn't help but smile. "There has to be more to it. Let's not jump to conclusions." Jake sounded so convincing, Abby hoped he was right. But if it was true, it would absolutely change *everything*. It was too overwhelming to contemplate. They held each other for a long while, each absorbed in their own thoughts, trying to make sense of everything.

"So what should we do? Should I confront my mother? Should you talk to your father? Maybe I should call my dad — oh God, I mean Glen? Should I ask GG? Maybe they won't even tell me the truth if I ask them. Maybe they don't want us to know," Abby sobbed. "I'm so confused. I have no idea what to do."

"It'll be okay, Abby, I promise. We'll figure out the best way to find out how everything fits. Maybe it's not what it looks like at all." Jake gently squeezed her shoulder.

"But what else could it be? Look, it says it right there in her diary." She opened the diary to the entry at the end and passed it over to Jake. She watched as he silently absorbed what she had already discovered.

"Why would she not have told me? Don't I have a right to know?"

"It doesn't make any sense to me either," Jake said, passing the diary back to her.

They sat together for a long while, until Abby had calmed down. They discussed the possibilities and finally decided that they should go directly to the source. Jake would talk to Rick and Abby would confront Maggie, and then they would get together to compare stories. They would decide what everything meant after that.

Abby suddenly pulled back. "I'm so sorry, but I

really have to get going. GG is going to be so mad at me. I took the car without even asking and if I don't get home before midnight, my mother is going to have a fit. I'm sure you haven't forgotten the bonfire incident," she said, rolling her eyes. She stood up and pulled her sweatshirt on over her head, and pushed the diary into the front pocket. Jake gave her another hug before Abby stepped outside.

"Try not to worry. I'll call you tomorrow for sure, okay?" Jake said. "And just take it easy driving home."

"I'll be okay," Abby said through the open car window, and gave a little wave as she pulled out.

Abby's thoughts started churning again as she started the drive home through the pea-soup fog. Jake. She could almost envision his face in the mist, smiling and looking at her like no guy ever had before. She was finally excited to have met a great guy that she really connected with, and it was getting ruined — *again*! She thought back to the night of the bonfire. They'd been having such a good time up until her mother showed up. It had been so romantic, holding hands, sitting in the glow of the fire. And when they had gone for a walk he had given her the sweetest kiss ...

Her thoughts were interrupted when she briefly lost sight of the road in front of her. Her heart fluttered in her chest as she tried desperately to see the centre line. She had never driven in fog like this before. She flipped on the high beams to see better, but that only made it worse, the light stopping bluntly in front of the car as though hitting a wall. When she flipped them back to normal, the road had disappeared in front of her. She jerked the wheel desperately, searching for the pavement, panic rising in her throat.

The car jolted roughly over the embankment. It crashed heavily into the trees and came to rest on some bushes. Her thoughts of Jake kissing her morphed into a vision of Rick kissing her mother, as she lost consciousness. The only sound was the horn blaring hauntingly into the mist.

Chapter 41

Maggie padded across the gravel, trying to be careful of her footing in the dark. All this sneaking around with Rick was taking its toll, and now she had let Abby down in the process. She still couldn't believe that Rick would be naive enough to let Abby and Jake get together when he knew that they were related. She prayed that Abby hadn't done anything that either of them would regret. Rick had been very insistent about coming back to the house with her tonight, arguing that it was as much his fault as it was hers. She had flatly refused, saying this was something that *she* needed to deal with. Alone. With her daughter. She shook her head in disgust, remembering how the evening had played out. How could she have been so stupid as to think that he still loved her? How could she have thought that she might actually still love him? She had been willing to risk everything to find out, only to have him dump her one more time. Never again. She had told him that she never wanted to see him again, and yes ... thanks for the memories. She felt that she had finally gotten him out of her system, once and for all. She felt relieved.

She resolved to stop using her past as an excuse for putting her life on hold. That's exactly what she had been doing. She had been treading water for 16 years, just waiting for something to happen, waiting to be rescued. No more.

Maggie attempted to open the screen door quietly. It squawked like a tired parrot and she hoped that it wouldn't rouse her mother. She knew the inside door was unlocked so she just needed to give it a gentle shove. She couldn't remember the last time her mom had locked her front door. It was a convention Down East that nobody locked their doors. There was an element of trust here that you just didn't find anywhere else. It had certainly been convenient all those times she had come home late as a teenager. If she managed to navigate the door *and* the stairs without any creaks, she would be in bed, home free. She attempted to do the same now. She didn't want to have to explain where she had been to her mother, and wondered what her mother's reaction would be if she knew. Better not think about that just now.

She opened the door and was surprised to see the lights still on in the front room. Her mom was very diligent at shutting everything off before turning in for the night, leaving only the upstairs hall light on as a nightlight for those finding their way up the stairs. The minute she stepped inside, her mother scurried over to Maggie like a little mouse, wringing her hands, her eyes wild. "Maggie, thank God you're home! Abby's not home. She left in a rush. She was very upset. I have no idea where she is." The words spilled out in a cascade of worry.

"Oh, my God. And you just let her go?" Maggie held her hands to her head as though it might burst if she didn't.

"I didn't really have a choice, she ran out of here so fast. Oh, Maggie." Gil looked as upset as Maggie felt. Her mother's panic wasn't helping. The evening had been upsetting enough without coming home to this. She forced herself to think. "Mom." Maggie grabbed both her mother's arms, forcing her to look at her. "Where do you think she might have gone? Do you think she might be at Sarah's?" Maggie asked.

"I did call over to Sarah's but there was no answer. I didn't know what else to do. I just called the police."

"Actually, I think I might know where she is." Penny's sleepy voice came from the stairs. "Abby was upstairs tonight. When I came up to use the bathroom, I overheard her talking on the phone in GG's room. I'm pretty sure she was talking to Jake."

Jake? A million thoughts came rushing through Maggie's head but she pushed them all away. Focus. She needed to focus. "Good for you, Penny. Thanks." Maggie racked her brain. Rick had told her he and Jake were staying at some beachside cottages close to the church but she couldn't remember anything more than that. How could she possibly find Abby when she had no idea where she was?

"Penny, do you happen to know the name of the cottages where they were staying?" Maggie walked over to the railing and spoke softly to her, as much to calm herself as to not upset Penny.

Penny brightened. "Oh, sure. It's Surfside Inn and Cottages. We were joking about how a name like that kind of says it all. And that it would be so easy to remember. It can't be too far from Queensland because Jake's dad usually drops him off at the church on the way into Halifax. Maybe that's where Abby went." Penny appeared happy to have been able to help in some way. She came down the stairs and walked into GG's outstretched arms. They both looked at Maggie, clearly waiting for her to make the next decision.

"Good for you, Penny. Thank goodness you pay attention. I'm going out to find Abby." It was a statement that no one questioned. Maggie pulled the keys out of her purse and went back outside without any further comment.

The fog had rolled in full-force. Maggie was always amazed at how quickly it could move in and how all-consuming it could be. Every now and again the road would disappear before her eyes. All that was visible were the dark shapes of the trees along the side of the road, and every so often the centre line would disappear, barely a car length ahead of her. You could only truly appreciate how thick the fog could get when you were driving in it. Maritimers often said you could cut it with a knife. Every time she drove in the fog she was seized with a rush of panic. It reminded her too much of an incident that had happened one night when she was a child. She and her father had gone to fix a broken tap for a friend. He didn't think it would take very long so he had asked Maggie to come along for the ride. When it came time to leave, it was already starting to get dark and the fog had rolled in. Her father had a sixth sense for driving in the fog, even though Maggie didn't like not being able to see where they were going. They had almost reached their turnoff when another car came barrelling toward them on the wrong side of the road and her father had had to swing the wheel in the opposite direction to avoid being hit.

They had gone off the road and into a small ditch, her father hitting his head on the steering wheel. He kept asking her if she was okay, but he was the one with blood running down his forehead. He had told her he was fine, and they had managed to get the car back on the road. He had hugged her afterwards, the bright white bandage in sharp contrast to his tanned face. Maggie thought she would never forget the sight of the blood running down her daddy's face. Every time she drove in the fog she was reminded of that night.

Her hands gripped the steering wheel and she tried to calm herself by talking out loud, focusing instead on Abby. I'll be there soon, Abby. Just wait for me. I'll be there soon, Abby. Just wait for me, she kept chanting to herself, trying to keep any other horrible thoughts from entering her head.

Maggie knew this road like the back of her hand, but there were so many bends and turns it all looked foreign and unfamiliar in this weather. It seemed to go on forever tonight, every turn looking the same as the last. Her eyes were trained on the road directly in front of the car, trying to anticipate the next turn, when she saw the flashing lights of emergency vehicles up ahead. Her heart jumped into her throat. Oh, God. Please. No. She drew her breath in sharply as she noticed tire tracks that suddenly ended at the road's edge, as though the car had suddenly run out of road. She pulled quickly over to the shoulder and ran across the damp road. The steady drone of a car horn, muffled but distinct, blared ominously out of the mist. She willed herself to look and there below, lying across a crop of bushes, was her mother's forest-green Bonneville, one headlight smashed, the other a singular beacon reaching into the sky. Maggie started screaming.

Chapter 42

The sight of the car lying in the bushes flashed across Maggie's mind over and over as she drove frantically into the city. The fire trucks had still been on the scene securing the safety of the vehicle, but the ambulance had already gone by the time Maggie arrived. Ironically, Rick had come across the accident first, shortly after dropping Maggie off. They had embraced in mutual shock as they tried to absorb what had happened. Maggie had recovered quickly and had pulled herself away. She needed to get to the hospital. Rick said that he would go on to get Jake, and meet her there. She had barely remembered to stop at a pay phone to call Gil, her hands shaking as she dropped the coins into the slot. Gil said that she would call Jack to bring her and Penny to the hospital. As she was about to hang up the phone, Gil had said, "Abby needs you to be strong, Maggie. Now go and be with her."

Maggie had gained strength from her encouraging words and she pulled into an empty parking space. Maggie rushed through the front doors, looking around frantically for any signs of Abby. She asked the nurse at the desk for an update, explaining that her daughter had been brought in by ambulance. She was immediately led down a nearby hallway to a small waiting area where the nurse explained that Abby had been taken directly into surgery. The doctor would be out to speak with her once Abby was out of the operating room. Maggie wanted to ask more questions, but the nurse wasn't offering any more information.

She sat down heavily in one of the worn-out chairs and put her head in her hands. How could things have gone so horribly wrong? She had foolishly thought that by coming out East with the girls, she could somehow protect Abby from herself. And now here she was in the hospital, waiting for news of her daughter's injuries. She had failed miserably. If Abby had known about Rick, perhaps none of this would have happened. And the slight possibility that Abby might be pregnant was enough to put Maggie over the edge. Her thoughts were making her frantic. She paced the room alone, waiting for any word on Abby, and suddenly realized that she needed to call Glen.

Maggie found a phone at the end of the corridor. She tried to collect her thoughts. How was she going to explain all this to Glen? She clutched the receiver, her heart hammering in her chest. She was so upset she could hardly punch the numbers.

"Please check the number and dial again — this is a long-distance call." Damn. She slammed the receiver down and tried again. Tears coursed down her cheeks. Glen was her rock. How could she have ever doubted that? It made her physically ill to think she had been out with Rick when all of this had happened. I deserve this, she thought, but Abby doesn't. Was this to be her penalty, her price to pay for being with Rick when she should have been at home with Abby? She couldn't bear it if Abby were taken from her. She would do anything to make up for what she had done wrong. She heard the phone ringing at the other end and started chanting: Pick up, pick up, pick up, as she tapped her foot. It was two hours earlier in Ontario, and she prayed Glen wasn't out in the garage listening to his blues at full volume, or he'd never hear the phone.

"Hello?"

"Oh, Glen." Maggie cleared her throat in an effort to hide the tremble in her voice.

"Mags? Is something wrong?"

The sound of his deep voice was like drinking a warm smooth whisky and gave her the confidence she needed to continue.

"Glen, it's Abby. She's had an accident ... I'm at the hospital ... at the Izaak Walton Killam Hospital ... in Halifax." She took another deep breath. "You need to come as soon as you can." Their conversation was interrupted by a beep, followed by the intercom announcing "Dr. Emerson, emergency, paging Dr. Emerson, emergency." It was stressful hearing the doctors being paged, wondering if perhaps they were being called to help Abby.

"Abby?"

Maggie could hear Glen's voice break. She hated herself for doing this to him. It must be heart-wrenching to get a call like this out of nowhere. Glen still had some catching up to do. It would be a difficult flight for him, but she would explain everything when he got here. Meanwhile she would step up to the plate and take care of things until he arrived. Until then, she needed to be strong for Abby.

"What's happened? Is she okay?"

"She's been in a car accident. We're not even

exactly sure what happened yet. She was out with Gil's car ... the fog ... it was so thick. The nurse said she's pretty beaten-up. She's still in surgery." Maggie choked back her tears, not wanting to upset Glen any more than she already had. She felt so guilty for doing this to him.

"I'll be on the first flight I can get. Hang in there, baby. I love you," Glen said.

"Oh Glen, I love you too," Maggie replied, and this time she knew it deep down, with a truth as strong as the love she felt for her daughters. Maggie hung up the phone. As she reached for her purse, she saw her flask inside it. She took it out and dropped it in the garbage pail beside the phone. It had never helped anything. Not really. She fell into the sickly brown chair, put her face into her hands, and whispered to herself, "Oh, Abby, I'm so sorry ... I have so much to tell you. Please God, just let her be okay."

Chapter 43

It had been a long night. What a motley-looking crew they were, sprawled in various stages of distress in the hospital waiting room. Maggie lifted her head and immediately felt a crick in her neck. Sleeping curled up in an overstuffed armchair wasn't exactly comfortable, but at least she had nodded off for a while. The waiting was interminable. She would camp out here at the hospital for as long as necessary. Mr. Jack and Gil had stuck it out with her, Penny dozing between them.

Rick had gone to get Jake and they too had come to the hospital. They were each curled up awkwardly at either end of the couch. Jake was beside himself, as though this were somehow his fault. Jake had refused to go anywhere until he knew that Abby was going to be all right, and so Rick had bunked out with him. Maggie could see Rick half asleep out of the corner of her eye, but decided she wasn't in the mood for conversation at this point. She played out the events of the previous evening over and over again in her mind, but somehow nothing changed. What she wouldn't do to be able to rewind everything. Just then the waiting room door opened, interrupting her thoughts. She opened her eyes expecting to see the doctor, and Glen walked in.

"Glen! You're here!" Maggie leapt out of her chair and ran into his arms. Rick stood up as Glen entered, and Maggie prepared herself for the worst. He stood with his hands in his pockets, looking back and forth between Maggie and Glen, trying to gauge Glen's reaction. Maggie felt Glen's body tense as he caught sight of Rick over her shoulder. His eyes flared as he tried to make sense of the person before him. He pulled himself away from Maggie and took a step in Rick's direction, his hands balled into fists.

"What the hell are you doing here?" Glen said.

Rick took a step back, but before he could speak Maggie positioned herself between the two men, putting both hands on Glen's chest. She should have known this was going to get ugly. She should have at least warned Glen, but she hadn't really had the chance. Sparks were flying from his eyes. Despite his control, Maggie could feel the anger simmering below the surface. She gently turned his face toward her so that he was looking directly at her.

"Let me explain." Maggie skilfully turned Glen away from Rick's line of sight and he allowed her to lead him to the nearest chair. She took a deep breath and continued. "I should have told you on the phone, but I didn't want to upset you any more than you already were. Rick is in Halifax working on an environmental project. I think Abby may have told you in one of her phone calls that she was involved with Save the Harbour? Turns out it's the same project that Rick is managing. I'll tell you more about it later, but that's why he's here. He's just worried about Abby too." Maggie's words came out in a torrent to keep Glen's attention. She was amazed at how calm she sounded despite the obvious tension building in the room. She saw Rick moving towards Glen and braced herself for what was to come. Rick put his arm around Jake and held out his hand to Glen.

"Hey, buddy. I know you didn't expect to see me here. I just wanted to stay ... until we heard something ... or at least until you got here ... We're worried about Abby too. This here's my son, Jake. Jake, this is Glen — uh, Abby's dad."

Jake stuck out his hand awkwardly and Glen gave it a firm shake. "How're you doing, Jake? I'm pleased to meet you. I'm not sure you really belong here, Rick, but never mind for now. I've got more important things to worry about." He turned back to Maggie.

"Where's Abby? How is she? What have the doctors told you?" Glen was suddenly in father mode again, the worry filling his red-rimmed eyes.

"We haven't seen her yet. The nurse was just here and said Dr. Emerson would be along any minute to bring us up to date." Maggie's stomach did another flip just thinking about Abby but she knew she needed to be strong. No more tears and indecision. She was Abby's mother and would do whatever was needed to save her daughter. In some twisted kind of way it was her fault that they were all gathered here in this pathetic little room.

"Just tell me what happened," Glen said.

"Abby took Gil's car to go out, like she often does, only it was nighttime and the fog was really thick. She must have had trouble seeing, because the car went off the road." Maggie left out the part about Abby being upset, and about going to see Jake. There would be time enough to explain the details later. Maggie had yet to figure out what had upset Abby so much. She dared not think about it.

Glen sat bleary-eyed on the edge of the old leather chair, attesting to the name of the late flight he had managed to catch — the red-eye. Maggie hadn't seen Glen looking this rough in a long time. She glanced over at him, feeling her heart do a flip when he looked up at her at the same moment. She adored this man, and never had it been clearer in her mind than at this moment, with Rick on the sidelines to prove it. Glen hadn't even taken the time to change. He wore his ratty flannel shirt over his Eagles T-shirt. Every few minutes he would glance at the door, waiting for the doctor to show up.

Gil sat on the only loveseat in the room, Mr. Jack beside her with his arm around her shoulder. Gil looked tired, her face pale and drawn, squeezing a Kleenex that was beyond useful anymore. Gil had been completely distraught over Abby's accident, feeling somehow responsible, but when Rick and Jake walked into the hospital, Maggie thought Gil might give him a piece of her mind. Her mother was no slouch when it came to dealing with uncomfortable situations, and Maggie felt badly for having subjected her to this. But she had stayed calm, and rather than yelling at Rick, as Maggie suspected she might, Gil had listened to Maggie's explanation, and then collapsed onto the couch like someone had let the air out of a balloon. Penny lay with her head on her grandmother's lap, opening her eyes every so often to make sure she didn't miss anything, and Mr. Jack ran his hand up and down Gil's arm. Rick hovered near the doorway, trying not to intrude on their space, and Jake looked equally uncomfortable and worried.

Maggie sat on the arm of Glen's chair with her arm around his shoulder. She felt as though she were still in the fog of the night before. She kept thinking What if: what if she hadn't been out with Rick, what if it hadn't been foggy, what if she had told Abby about Rick, if, if, if. She needed to stop torturing herself, but this waiting was driving her insane. She wanted to run down the hall and push past everyone in her path to find her daughter. Just then the doctor walked into the lounge, glancing around the room to find the parents. Maggie hurried over, her hands clasped in prayer in front of her face, anticipating what he was going to say. Glen came over to join her.

"Dr. Emerson, this is my husband Glen, Abby's father," Maggie said.

"How is she? Can we see her now?" Glen said.

"Abby is awake now," Dr. Emerson said in an even take-charge voice, "but I must warn you she's in pretty bad shape. She's taken quite a beating. Our biggest concern is her kidneys. They've been severely damaged." He relayed this information so calmly it was all Maggie could do to keep from hurrying him on. She bit her knuckle to keep from crying.

Glen spoke for both of them. "So, what does that mean? Is she going to be okay?"

"Actually, she is going to need a new kidney. It is possible to function with just one kidney, but both kidneys have taken quite a beating. I'm not sure we'll be able to save them. As family members, you should give some consideration to being potential kidney donors, in case we need to act quickly. The chances of a good match are greater within the same family. I suggest that once you come to some decisions, we start some preliminary tests so that we are ready when Abby needs us. The nurse will let you know when you can see her." Dr. Emerson turned with a flash of his white coat, as there was nothing more to be said.

Maggie's stomach started doing flips. This was no time to be keeping secrets. She ran to catch up to the doctor at the doorway and placed her hand gently on his arm. "Doctor, can we speak with you for a moment ... in private?"

Dr. Emerson stepped into the hallway, with Maggie and Glen right behind him. Maggie's cheeks flushed, not really sure where to begin.

"You need to know that Glen isn't Abby's biological father. Abby doesn't know, and as far as she is concerned, Glen is her father. He raised her — we raised her — together. Her biological father is here, though. We're just worried, with all that has happened ... we just want to make sure that you have all the information you need to make Abby well again."

Dr. Emerson nodded and assured them that this information would be relayed back to the nurses' team. He reiterated that the sooner they started blood work, the better, and walked efficiently back down the hallway.

Maggie ran her fingers through her hair as she ran through all the possible options in her mind. Maggie would have volunteered her kidney in a second, but given her diabetes she knew they wouldn't consider her. They would never ask that of Gil, and Penny, well, they hoped it wouldn't come to that. She hated herself for what she needed to say next. She looked at Glen and hesitated. "I guess you'll go for tests too, just in case you could also be a donor?" She paused. "But isn't Rick the most logical choice under the circumstances?" She looked hopefully into his eyes, secretly praying that one of them would be able to help Abby.

"I can help her."

It was Jake. They hadn't heard him come into the hallway and now he stood before Maggie and Glen looking very serious, and much older than his 15 years. "Don't worry, I know everything. Abby told me, right before the accident." He looked straight into their eyes, waiting for their response. Maggie and Glen shot each other a look, suddenly realizing that he might be the best match of all.

Chapter 44

Maggie waited patiently for Glen to come back from having his tests done, this spot being a good vantage point to see him coming back down the hall. She was curled up uncomfortably in a beaten-up brown armchair near the pay phone, the pasty walls reflecting her mood. This chair must be the twin to the one in the waiting room. Were there no comfortable chairs in this hospital? No one had come by to use the phone, and if they did, she would pretend she was sleeping. Let them find another phone. She needed to talk to Glen, alone. She didn't think she could stand another minute in the waiting room, with everyone looking at one another for answers. God was really testing her patience with all this waiting: first waiting for Glen to arrive, then for news from the doctor, now for tests results, and of course, for Abby. She desperately needed to see Abby. She needed to see with her own eyes that she was going to be okay. She didn't even dare think about the alternative.

She needed time to talk to Glen about what had happened, and more importantly, to explain about Rick. She couldn't imagine how Glen must have felt when he walked into the hospital with concern for his daughter, only to find Rick there ahead of him. He had handled it in his usual controlled manner, but she could see from the way his jaw had tightened that he was seething inside. And he must have been equally stunned to meet Rick's son. Who else could keep their calm in such a bizarre situation? She was always amazed at how well he handled things. And that was exactly what she loved about him.

Glen had always been there for her. When Maggie was pregnant, Glen had never liked the way Rick treated Maggie nor understood why Maggie made excuses for Rick. Rick had always been big on promises, and even bigger at breaking them. And when the baby came, Rick had disappeared into thin air. He hadn't even come to the hospital. But Glen had been there.

Maggie looked up to see Glen walking slowly down the hall, his feelings written all over his face now that he thought no one was watching. She felt an overwhelming rush of love for him at that moment, and walked down the hall to meet him. His face lit up when he saw her, and he drew her gently into his arms, holding her tight.

"I sure hope one of us can help Abby," he said, "and right now I don't care which one of us that might be. I just want to get her out of here in one piece." Glen squeezed her hard.

"I know. Me, too. Want to go and grab a coffee?" Maggie suggested as she slipped her hand in his. He barely nodded and they made their way to the cafeteria. Maggie was relieved to see that it was fairly empty, so they could have the opportunity to talk uninterrupted. For a moment neither one of them spoke, the air between them thick with emotion. Maggie finally got up the nerve to speak.

"Glen, I ... I need to talk to you ... I don't even know where to start ... You know I saw this trip as an opportunity. I have been so frustrated at work that sometimes I feel like a hamster on a treadmill that keeps on running but never gets anywhere. I've been waiting for a break for years now, and I just don't know if it's ever going to happen. I thought getting away for a few weeks might be a good opportunity to step back and evaluate all of that. I haven't been happy with myself for a long time and I feel like I've been taking it out on you. I thought having some space would give us both a chance to get some perspective." She paused briefly to take a sip of her coffee and allow Glen some time to absorb what she was saying.

"And then it was just wonderful being here. It felt like the weight of so many things had been lifted off my shoulders. Oh, Glen, I miss it so much. I always wondered if things would have been different if we had stayed in Nova Scotia. I feel like I'm a different person when I am here. Like anything is possible. I honestly thought I was doing the right thing by coming out here this summer with the girls. After reading Abby's journal, it was hard to know what to do, but I obviously failed miserably at that too." A tear rolled quietly down her cheek and Glen reached over to wipe it away with his thumb.

Maggie was surprised that she was able to reiterate all of this information to Glen without hesitation. She had nothing to hide, and now that she had come to some decisions of her own, she felt confident in what she had to say. "And then, right in the middle of everything, Rick showed up. I had no idea that he was even in town. He is an environmental

Treading Water

consultant and he's here from Ottawa working on a project called Save the Harbour. His son Jake is here with him for the summer, helping out on the project. As a matter of fact, both Abby and Penny have been working on the project as well, along with Mr. Jack."

"Abby has been working with Rick the whole time she's been here?" Glen asked. He pushed his chair noisily back from the table, not being able to contain his anger any longer.

"Glen, wait. Let me finish. Please sit down. It's not what you think." She took his hand and looked up into his face. She could see him trying to control himself.

"Yeah, and how do you know what I'm thinking?" he snapped.

Maggie had never seen him like this, but he had every right to be upset. The fact that he hadn't slept in more than 24 hours wasn't helping. He had walked into a minefield that had all but exploded in his face. At that very moment Maggie realized that she would do whatever it took to make him understand. She was not going to risk losing Glen, too.

"You have a right to be angry, but please, just let me finish," Maggie pleaded.

The urgency in her voice must have reached home. Glen slowly sat back down. "Okay, go ahead. I'm listening." He grimaced as he took a sip of his coffee. "You know, this coffee is really terrible." They both laughed, breaking some of the tension, and Maggie knew things were going to be okay between them. He sat back in his chair and waited for Maggie to continue.

"Abby and Penny were working on the Save the

Harbour project and I had no idea that Rick was in charge. In fact, the girls had no idea who he was. While they were working they were making new friends, and Abby and Jake started getting friendly. I didn't think anything of it, because at that point I had no idea who Jake was. I wasn't sure what to do about Rick because I never expected to see him, but I had a lot of unanswered questions. So anyway, during my conversation with him, it came out that he has been working with Abby off and on all summer — and that he knew all along it was Abby. I was furious. And then he told me that Jake was his *son*! I finally put all the pieces of the puzzle together, but by the time I did, it was already too late. I didn't even know Abby had figured it out until Jake told us. That was obviously what upset her last night. I feel like all of this is my fault. Oh, Glen, if I had only told Abby about Rick, maybe I could have avoided all of this happening." Maggie burst into tears and all of the stress of the past few days came pouring out. She looked into Glen's eyes, holding her breath for his reaction. They had always been a good team, and she knew this time wouldn't be any different.

Glen put his hands on top of Maggie's and squeezed. "This is not your fault, Maggie. We will explain everything to Abby together. I just hope we're not too late."

Chapter 45

Glen and Maggie returned to the lounge and as they stepped inside, everyone looked up expectantly.

"Sorry folks, no news yet," Glen said.

There really was nothing more to say and he and Maggie squeezed into a spot at the end of the couch in the corner. The air in the lounge was stale and stuffy. They had taken all of the chairs in the cramped room and so it had become their own private lounge. Gil was still wringing her hands, with Jack's comforting arm draped around her shoulders. It was odd to see her mother, normally so capable and efficient, looking so worried. Maggie realized that Abby's accident had taken its toll on all of them. Rick was back from testing and paced nervously near the door, as though he might make a run for it at any second. It was probably taking everything in him to stay in this awkward situation. He was likely doing it as much for Jake as for himself. Jake was sitting on the settee, talking with Penny. He really is a good kid, Maggie thought. Gil had found a notepad in her purse and he and Penny were involved in a rousing game of hangman. He must be terribly worried about Abby too, and yet here he was distracting her younger sister.

Everyone continued to drink their stale coffee. The waiting seemed endless. Maggie leaned into Glen, and had just shut her eyes when Dr. Emerson entered the room. His starched lab coat was blinding compared to the dinginess of the room, and Maggie thought he looked like a ray of hope. He held his clipboard close to his chest, summoning Maggie and Glen with his index finger to discuss the results. He flipped once again through the forms, and motioned for Rick to join them as well. When they were collected expectantly in the hallway, he cleared his throat and imparted his news.

"I have the results of the blood work and it appears that we have a match." There was a unified sigh of relief as they all glanced at Rick. "The initial tests show that Glen is a good match, but we'll have to perform further tests to be certain that he could be a donor. Neither Rick nor Jake are possible candidates."

"What did you say?" Maggie furrowed her brow as she tried to make sense of what she was hearing. She grabbed the doctor's sleeve and looked questioningly at the doctor. "How can that be?" she whispered. "There must be some mistake. Rick is Abby's — her biological father."

"No, Mrs. Boutilier. As part of organ donation testing we also perform other routine blood tests, and according to these results, Glen is Abby's biological father."

Maggie shook her head in disbelief. Glen clutched Maggie's arms, holding her tight as he tried to absorb the news. Maggie thought she would crumble to the floor if he let her go. Rick stood off to the side, looking as though the wind had been kicked out of him. His face was pale and Maggie thought he might keel over any minute. She couldn't deal with him now.

"It's okay, Maggie. It's all good," Glen said. "We can help Abby — I can help Abby — and that's all that matters, right?"

"Yes, of course. Oh Glen, I'm so happy that you'll be able to help her." Maggie looked into Glen's eyes and he smiled back at her. "How is this even possible? All this time and we had it all wrong?"

"Maggie, I hate to say this, but deep down I always wondered ... about Abby. She's the spitting image of you with her strawberry blonde hair and freckles, but sometimes I see things in Abby that remind me of *me*. Do you remember when we first started dating? Before you even knew Rick? We'd slept together before you put the brakes on our relationship, and before I knew it, Rick was in the picture instead of me. When Abby was born prematurely, I wondered if it was more than just a coincidence. That maybe the dates were right all along."

Suddenly Maggie looked up at Glen, her eyes bright, a look of happiness behind the tears. "Why didn't you ever say anything before?"

"I didn't want to upset you. I wasn't really sure, and it just didn't seem right bringing up the past, when we had done so much to put it all behind us."

"It's such a relief to know the truth, and to know that you've been Abby's father all along. I can't believe that we had this hanging over our heads all these years. I feel like I've been waiting for something to happen since we left Nova Scotia, and now it's time to make some waves, and get on with life." Glen held her tight. There was no need to respond.

Chapter 46

Abby had been brought to her room and the doctor had given them the go-ahead to see her. Maggie looked expectantly at Glen. She felt she needed a chance to apologize, to let Abby know how she was feeling, just the two of them.

"Can you just give me a minute alone with her before you come in? Do you mind?" Maggie asked.

"Sure, I'm not going anywhere," Glen said, giving her hand a little squeeze. Maggie was glad he understood. It was time she took some responsibility. She took a deep breath and pushed open the door.

Abby looked up at her mom as she entered. Her head was bandaged, and bruising was starting to appear around her eyes. Her tears had left faint tracks on her face. She looked so young lying there. It took Maggie back to the first summer they had come back to Nova Scotia after moving to Ontario. Abby was just five. Glen had wanted to come too, but he had just started his business and just couldn't find the time to get away. They had stayed with Gil and had spent every moment together: on the beach, rocking on the porch swing, singing, and telling stories. Maggie had felt so close to her then, but as Abby got older, it had gotten tougher and tougher to maintain that closeness. As a teenager she had started to pull away and do her own thing. That's what teenagers are supposed to do. But Maggie had been so worried about protecting Abby from her own mistakes that she had been pushing her away all along. And look where that had

Treading Water

gotten them.

Maggie looked at her daughter. She was so proud of her. Despite all her hovering and obsessing, Abby had managed to turn into a lovely young woman anyway. Thank God Glen had been there to balance her out.

"Hey, baby. How are you doing?" Maggie's voice quivered a little. It was tough seeing your child hooked up to endless wires and tubes, but the relief she felt when Abby spoke was overwhelming.

"I've had better days." She tried to smile, but her attempt at humour was cut off by a twinge of pain. Maggie could see she was uncomfortable so she carefully rearranged the pillow and Abby let out a sigh. Maggie pulled the chair up to the edge of the bed and beamed at her daughter.

"Mom, can I ask you something?" Abby asked.

"Of course. What is it?" Maggie said.

"What was the *real* reason why you came out here this summer?" Abby asked.

"Promise you won't get mad at me?" Maggie asked, raising one eyebrow.

"I'll try," Abby crossed her fingers under the bedcovers.

"When I found your journal it was open to the page with your list of goals for when you turned 16. I was worried that GG would give you the freedom you were looking for, so I thought I'd better come too, so I could watch out for you myself. A fine job I did, too. I needed to be sure you wouldn't do anything stupid. I was worried that you might get pregnant, like I did at your age. And that's something that I've been meaning to talk to you about your whole life. I'll have lots of time to tell you the whole story while you are recuperating." She smiled a weak smile. "I guess it's about time. But according to Jake, you already know."

"Yeah, I was pretty upset. Why didn't you ever tell me before?"

"I meant to, honest I did, but it just never seemed like the right time. And I wasn't sure how you would react. I was worried you might love your dad less," Maggie said.

"Why on earth would you think that?" Abby asked.

"I don't know. I just wanted to protect you from everything." Maggie reached over and gently started rubbing Abby's arm, being careful to avoid the tubes. She stopped. "But wait. Then how *did* you find out?" Maggie asked.

"Well, I found *your* diary too." Abby grimaced as she mustered a smile.

"You found my diary? Where?" Maggie asked.

"Under the floorboards in your old bedroom. I accidentally kicked loose a floorboard and there it was, lying underneath. I found the photos too, out at the cottage. What a great place, mom." Abby smiled at her mom.

Maggie was stunned by what she was hearing. She had completely forgotten that she had hidden her diary. Another piece of her past that she had tried to forget. And what was this about Abby having been to the cottage? How did she even know where it was?

This conversation wasn't going at all the way she had planned.

Abby tried to giggle. "Pretty ironic, eh, Mom?"

"Oh Abby, I'm so sorry all of this had to happen — and for nothing." Maggie put her arms gently around her daughter and gave her a hug. "I was so worried that you would follow in my footsteps that I couldn't step back long enough to see the real you."

"You're not kidding." Abby gave her mother a look that made Maggie laugh.

Glen poked his head around the door. "Hey, can I come in now?"

"Dad! You're here! Mom and I were just playing True Confessions." Abby grinned at her mother as though they were sharing a secret joke. Maggie had never felt this close to Abby. She hoped things would continue now that they'd had a chance to talk. It was a great feeling.

Glen laughed. "I'll just bet you were! I see you haven't lost your sense of humour." He leaned in to give her a peck on her forehead. "Have you told her the rest?" He looked to Maggie for confirmation.

"The rest of what?" Abby asked.

Glen sat down at the end of the bed. "I'm sure the doctors have told you that you are going to need a new kidney. We all had tests done to determine if any of us could be a potential kidney donor. It turns out that I'm the best match. But you want to know the best part? The tests also showed that I am your biological father. Not Rick, like we thought."

Abby didn't say anything at first, and then smiled

the biggest smile she could manage. "Wow. That's the best news ever. There just couldn't be any other dad but you."

Now it was Glen's turn to well up with tears, but before he could respond, the door opened and Jake stuck his head in.

"What's a guy gotta do to get a hug around here?"

Chapter 47

Maggie and Abby walked barefoot along the beach, Jep zigzagging beside them with the ebb and flow of the tide, and Maggie stopping periodically to snap a photo of the stunning sunset. Abby padded slowly along at the water's edge, splashing her toes in the water as the waves teased her feet and ran away again. Maggie focused the lens on her daughter's face. After the kidney operation, Abby had spent a lot of time reading on the front porch next to her dad, who was also slowed down by his operation, or playing Scrabble with Penny, and the sun had coaxed her childhood freckles back to life. Now the setting sun cast a warm glow across her cheeks, making her look healthy and happy, happier than Maggie had seen her in a long time. The accident had certainly taken its toll on all of them, but the young heal quickly, and Abby's recovery had been nothing short of miraculous. But now, even four short weeks later, Abby looked different. Her demeanour had changed. The beach had done more for her in one month than any amount of bedrest could have done. When Maggie looked through the lens she saw a girl who had become confident and content. Yes, that was definitely the word for it — content. And if she was totally honest with herself, she'd have to say she felt content too. What was that quote she had read? "For whatever we lose, like a you or a me, it's always ourselves we find in the sea." And she truly believed that. Maggie caught Abby smiling at her through her lowered lashes.

"What?" Maggie said.

Abby giggled. "I just keep thinking how ironic it was that we found each other's diaries."

"You didn't think that when you first found out yours was missing," Maggie reminded her.

"That's true. But see what happens when you don't read the whole story?" Abby said.

"I never intended to read it, but when I saw your list I just needed to make sure that you didn't do anything stupid. Any mother would have done the same thing," Maggie said. "And I'm actually glad, in some bizarre way, that you found my diary."

"You are?" Abby said. She stood at the water's edge letting the waves roll over her feet, and then listening to the suction as the water tried to pull her toes back out with it.

"I certainly never expected that my 16-year-old daughter would ever read my diary, but now you know everything," Maggie said.

"Why didn't you just tell me?" Abby asked.

"I had every intention of telling you, but it never seemed to be the right time. When you were young it just wasn't important, and then when you got older," Maggie paused. "No mother would want to admit to her teenage daughter that she got pregnant at age 16. And worse, that she slept with two guys, and that her daughter's father wasn't her real father at all. We did what was best for you. It was important that we move on. Besides, what good would it have done to tell you that your father wasn't your biological father?" Maggie stopped walking and took both of Abby's hands.

"Abby, I'm not proud of what I did, but I have you because of it, and never for a moment have I regretted that."

Abby smiled and Maggie gave her daughter a hug. They continued walking as the seagulls swooped and squawked overhead.

"I'm really glad things worked out this way, Mom," Abby said. "I mean of course I wish the accident had never happened, but if it hadn't, you would still have thought that Rick was my real dad and that would have messed everything up. I guess everything happens for a reason."

"That's for sure. Who made you so smart?" Maggie asked.

Abby just smiled and picked up a piece of driftwood, waved it teasingly at Jep, and threw it into the waves. Always ready for a challenge, Jep dove into the waves head-on to retrieve his prize. They both shielded their eyes to watch him rise and fall with the incoming waves, and finally return to deposit the stick at their feet for another turn.

"Crazy dog!"

Abby quickly threw it again and Jep was off again like a shot. Abby attempted to tuck her hair behind her ears, but the wind quickly teased it out again. Her cheeks glowed pink from the ocean breeze and Maggie knelt in the sand to catch a different angle of Abby. Suddenly Maggie screamed and jumped up in shock. The incoming tide caught her totally off guard, soaking her jeans, the camera narrowly avoiding the splash.

"Mom, you should know better!" Abby laughed.

"Never mind, it'll dry soon enough. It could have just as easily been you getting wet, young lady," Maggie teased.

"Whatever do you mean, dear mother?" Abby asked, feigning ignorance and grinning the whole time. Abby knew exactly what Maggie was talking about, and just wanted to hear the story again.

"I remember one evening when you were only five or six. We were here on vacation and we were out for one of our usual sunset walks along the beach. You were wearing one of GG's lovely handmade dresses, spinning until the skirt swirled around you. We didn't consider putting on swimsuits because it had gotten considerably cooler after supper, and no one was planning to go swimming. Of course the waves gradually lured you towards them and with one good splash you were totally soaked. You looked down at your wet dress and said something like, "Oh, well, I might as well go swimming," and jumped into the next wave. You were so matter-of-fact about it that Dad and I laughed until our sides hurt."

Jep chose that particular moment to return and spray them with sand and surf as he did a full-body shake. They held up their hands to shield themselves and laughed at the uselessness of it.

"Those photos at the cottage were really good, Mom. I never knew that you liked taking pictures. Why did you stop?" Abby asked.

"That's a good question. After we moved, I needed a job that would help pay the bills, and photography just got pushed to the back burner. I just never got back to it," Maggie said.

"But you're so good. I'm so glad you have decided to pull out the camera again," Abby said. "So you can take pictures of your lovely daughter!" and she pirouetted in circles, totally splashing herself as well.

"Me, too. I forgot how much I enjoy it. I guess something good came from running into Rick again. He made me realize some of the things I had given up, and that it wasn't too late to pursue what I love. While I kept you company in the hospital, I was working on notes for a proposal to my boss. He has agreed to give me an opportunity to contribute to the paper by writing a travelogue, including photos, of course. I'm really excited about it. I've been getting my feet wet, so to speak." Maggie laughed at her own joke.

Jep continued running circles around them, splashing in and out of the water. Abby stood still, making designs in the sand with her toe. When she looked up she had tears in her eyes. Maggie pulled her in close and hugged her gently. Abby wiped away the tears with the back of her hand.

"What is it?" Maggie asked.

"I'm just so happy that we have decided to move back. We're more like a real family when we are here," Abby said. "I think this is where we're supposed to be."

"I think you're right. I just can't believe that it took nearly losing you for us to realize what's really important; what makes us happy. After all these years of wishing I was here in Nova Scotia, doing a job that was making me irritable, it's finally time to go after what I really want. Even your dad is excited about coming back. Who knows? Maybe I can talk him into doing a little travelling with me, too." Maggie smiled. "And Abby, I'm so proud of the girl you have turned out to be. It has been a real joy to watch you putting your heart and soul into this harbour project."

"Thanks, Mom." Abby beamed at Maggie.

They continued walking arm in arm as the sun sank lower in the sky. The water was aflame with colour, reds and oranges so bright they had to squint to look out over the water. Maggie continued snapping photos, occasionally running ahead for the perfect shot. And as she looked through the lens, she could see the shadow of their combined footsteps in the sand, side by side, along the water's edge.

Treading Water

Acknowledgements

A special thank you to Paige Leslie for creating the cover design, Susan Fish of Storywell for her support and editing skills, and Ray Charbonneau of Y42K Book Production Services for publishing the book.

Made in the USA
Charleston, SC
10 August 2013